David Shepherd was
Lancaster, in 1942. H
School in Derbyshi
Durham. After Univer
Linlithgow, West Lothian and a student at the Episcopal
Theological College in Edinburgh. From 1968-1979, he
was Chaplain of St Paul's Cathedral, Dundee and
Anglican Chaplain in the University of Dundee from
1973-1979. Since 1979, he has been Rector of St Mary
Magdalene's Church, Dundee.

Seven detective novels have now been published:

Who Killed Sophie Jack?
Murder Within Tent
Slaughter at the Polls
A Christmas Cracker
A Mishap in Majorca
A Prospect of Rye
Murder on the Mallaig Express

Copies are available from:

Meadowside Publications
14 Albany Terrace
Dundee DD3 6HR
Telephone 01382 223510

Further details can be obtained from our website:
http://www.crime-fiction.com

MURDER

ON THE

MALLAIG EXPRESS

A DETECTIVE NOVEL

BY

DAVID SHEPHERD

MEADOWSIDE PUBLICATIONS
DUNDEE
2004

Meadowside Publications
14 Albany Terrace, Dundee DD3 6HR

Printed by
Prontaprint
Dundee, Scotland

The Characters portrayed in this novel are all imaginary and bear no intended resemblance to any person alive or dead.

ISBN 0 9520632 6 3

Meadowside Crime
is a © imprint of
Meadowside Publications,
Dundee.

CONTENTS

The story is set in Mallaig
on the west coast of Scotland
in August, 1989.

1. *Anyone for tennis?*

Detective-Inspector Raynes stood on platform fifteen of Euston station, waiting for his train to arrive. It was the night sleeper which would take him to Mallaig, on the west coast of Scotland, where he had been invited to join a weekend house party.

The house party had been arranged by Molly Palmer, a rich and charming divorcee, who advertised in the quality Sunday newspapers, inviting like-minded people to join her in some remote country hotel. There, good food and good company could be enjoyed, whilst everyone tried to solve a murder mystery devised by Molly herself. The plots were often a little fanciful and the clues sometimes confusing, but Molly never failed to pull them in.

Each summer, between May and September, she organized six such weekends in different parts of the country. They were certainly not cheap – £950 was the figure mentioned in the advertisements – but that did not seem to put people off. Normally, there were eight guests – four males and four females – whom Molly vetted carefully to achieve the right balance. No male under twenty-five was ever considered – and no female over sixty. Married couples were strictly debarred since they might share secrets or gang up against the rest of the party. No one had yet been killed at any of her weekend events, but quite a number of romances had been launched. It seemed that the very act of investigating some gruesome murder lowered people's inhibitions; and the intermingling of complete strangers generated unexpected passions.

To all her house parties Molly liked to invite some senior police officer, a forensic surgeon, a lecturer in criminology or – if all else failed – a writer of detective fiction. They would act as umpire or referee. That way, any criticism or complaint could be deflected away from her. The umpire would also be expected to entertain the guests with tales of some interesting murder they had been involved with – together with pictures or slides illustrating the tragic event. Molly had found that this went down very nicely after dinner when her guests were supping coffee in the lounge.

Molly always tried to find the best and most accomplished speakers. Her victims would be flattered and cajoled with letters and phone calls. They would be offered an all-expenses-paid weekend, with perhaps a casual affair thrown in for good measure! Detective-Inspector Raynes had been to one or two of her previous house parties so he could be relied upon to enter into the spirit of the weekend, adding a few extra clues to confuse her guests – and her! He always had lots of interesting cases to relate and would provide very frank and full replies to questions raised. Raynes said that what he enjoyed most about the weekends was the food. He would do anything for a decent meal!

So here he was, waiting for the train that would take him north to the Ellachie House Hotel in Mallaig. A specially chartered train had been laid on for those going up to the West Highlands to shoot grouse, stalk deer or even, perhaps, catch the odd salmon. The Glorious Twelfth was on a Saturday this year and the night sleeper would leave Euston on Thursday at 9.30pm. Molly had managed to secure nine berths on the train. (She herself always arrived at the hotel two or three days in advance to make sure everything was ready.)

Slowly, the platform began to fill with a variety of distinguished passengers – lords and ladies, rich businessmen, foreign princes, a couple of government ministers, rich Americans, assorted mistresses – and even the odd dog. Gun cases, fishing rods and golf clubs were much in evidence. Raynes noted that many of the women were extremely pretty – and wearing expensive jewellery.

That set him thinking.

It might be quite a profitable operation to hijack the train and rob all these well-heeled passengers. His mind, naturally attuned to all things criminal, considered how the heist might be achieved.

A few miles south of Crianlarich. That would be a good place! In the middle of deserted countryside – far from any police station. The telephone wires would have to be cut. A couple of red lights put on the track. The driver would be overpowered as he left his cab. He would be ordered to drive on to the next road bridge, where the rest of the gang would be waiting. The guard and the sleeping car attendants would have to be tied up. (There might be some problems there.) But once they were neutralized, the passengers could be woken up one by one and relieved of all their valuables – rings, jewels, wallets and credit cards.

It would take six men about an hour and a half, he reckoned, to comb the train. Then, into a couple of waiting cars or a van – and away into the night. By the time the alarm was raised, the robbers could be anywhere in Scotland.

Yes, it was an interesting possibility. He just hoped the idea had not occurred to anyone else. He had no desire to be woken in the middle of the night facing some thug with a pistol. Fortunately, the night sleeper to Mallaig did not have the cachet of the Orient Express.

It would require a very specialized knowledge on the part of the robbers, and very good planning – something the criminal fraternity were notoriously lazy about.

But one could never be sure.

Before the Inspector got on to the train, he made a mental note to hide the better part of his money in his left sock – just in case!

2. *Snookered*

Raynes survived the night.

He was woken by the sleeping car attendant who brought him an early morning cup of tea and a small packet of biscuits.

The Inspector had hoped that he might enjoy a full English breakfast before he reached his destination; but those days had long since passed. There was no restaurant car on the train.

Feeling decidedly hungry, Raynes stepped down on to the small station platform at Mallaig.

Molly Palmer was on the platform, waiting to collect her guests. She had a large white card with "MURDER

WEEKEND" written in blood-red letters. Even though other drivers and couriers were sporting cards of their own and calling out the names of their estates, there was no danger of any of Molly's guests getting lost.

She ticked off eight names – including the Inspector's – and then looked up.

"Mr Potter? Mr Bernard Potter? Has anyone seen Mr Potter?"

No one had the slightest idea what Mr Potter looked like.

He remained an enigma for another five minutes and then emerged from the crowd – a tall, distinguished-looking man with a smoke-blue tweed jacket and a tartan tie.

Raynes looked him over. Mr Potter had a broad forehead, receding brown hair and a honey-gold beard. A university lecturer? Or a civil servant?

Mr Potter apologized for keeping everyone waiting.

Molly's guests were ushered into a courtesy coach provided by the hotel. No one said anything. But the journey was quite short. A mere half mile and they were sweeping up the driveway to Mallaig's premier hotel.

"You will be glad to hear," said Molly, "that the hotel has prepared a splendid breakfast for you. I'm sure you're all extremely hungry. The staff will take your luggage to your rooms.

"When you have had a chance to freshen up, you will find everything laid out for you in the dining room – just off the main reception area. There will be coffee and a formal introduction in the Highland lounge at 11.30am."

Raynes was pleasantly surprised. He had expected something more primitive; stags' antlers on every wall; tartan curtains and carpets; pictures of Bonnie Prince Charlie and Flora Macdonald on their flight from Culloden; porridge and bannocks for breakfast. But the hotel was owned by some international conglomerate which had a standard line in hotel decoration. The catering was also cosmopolitan – as Raynes discovered when he came down to breakfast.

He ordered grapefruit, muesli with fresh strawberries and cream, two fried eggs, bacon, sausage and mushrooms, followed by toast and Oxford marmalade. Black coffee – as strong as possible. He sat back and began to feel much better.

Mr Potter was placed at his table. He too seemed to be enjoying a hearty breakfast which started with kippers.

Raynes looked at them with slight dismay.

"Are you a Scot, Mr Potter?"

Mr Potter smiled.

"Not at all. Born and brought up in Tunbridge Wells. But I had a grandmother who came from Dumfries . . ."

"I just wondered. The kippers . . ."

"They're a local delicacy. That's why the West Highland Railway built the line to Mallaig. To make sure the herrings reached the market as quickly as possible." Mr Potter looked at him with a certain superiority. "You don't know about these things?"

"I'm from down south. Grasshallows."

"And what d'you do in Grasshallows, Mr . . .?"

"Raynes. Richard Raynes. I'm a police inspector."

"Really?"

Mr Potter did not seem very impressed.

"And what d'you do?"

"I'm in the Home Office. Drugs enforcement. Do you have much of a problem in . . .?"

"Grasshallows. No, not really. Now and again, the students have parties. People take overdoses. But it's mostly a private affair. I don't think we've dealt with any dealers . . ."

Mr Potter looked at the Inspector fiercely.

"The problem's much more serious than you think. Drugs are rife. They're being imported into the country day and night. Tons of them. You need to keep a closer watch. You'll find there's a massive drug market operating just under the surface of every city. If you know the signs, it's easy to spot it . . ."

Raynes was not expecting to have a lecture at breakfast-time. He finished off his muesli and strawberries.

"Have you any family, Mr Potter?"

"Yes!"

The reply was cold and blunt.

The Inspector began to feel a marked antipathy towards Mr

Potter. But the latter recognized that he had been unnecessarily brusque.

"I'm sorry. You touched a raw nerve. My wife left me a few months ago. Nervous breakdown. She's receiving treatment."

He finished his final kipper.

"Are you married?"

"No. Divorced."

"D'you find you get on better with your work? I do."

"Well, there are certainly fewer distractions. But I have several female friends."

"So do I. Molly and I have been seeing a lot of each other just lately. She's been restoring my faith in womankind."

Raynes smiled politely.

But it was another nail in Mr Potter's coffin. Raynes had come to Mallaig with happy memories of his last murder weekend when he and Molly had spent a night together. He had been hoping to pick up where he left off; but Mr Potter had pipped him to the post.

"She greatly enjoys these murder weekends."

"Can't say I'm really interested in playing stupid games. But she twisted my arm. Said I would enjoy it. D'you often go to such things?"

"I'm the referee," explained Raynes. "Invited to make sure there's fair play. No cheating. Yes, I quite enjoy them. Especially the food."

He looked at his plate.

"I think we're going to be fed quite well here. The lunch menu looks excellent."

"Well, that's some comfort, I suppose," said Mr Potter. "But the sooner I'm back in London, the happier I shall be."

"I'm sure Molly'll lift your spirits," said Raynes encouragingly.

"I doubt it."

Raynes could not resist a certain sense of *schadenfreude* at the prospect of Molly's somewhat joyless weekend.

3. *Game on!*

At half past eleven, Molly's guests assembled in the Highland lounge. They seemed a very mixed bunch. Two of the women looked young and exciting; the other two well-preserved but fast approaching middle age. Two of the men appeared very business-like – they were still wearing their suits; but the third was clad in an old sweater and crumpled jeans. His face had an unhealthy yellow look and his eyes were cold and shifty. Without doubt, Mr Potter was the most distinguished of the four men – still wearing his smoke-blue tweed jacket.

Everyone was helping themselves to coffee when Raynes arrived. At this stage, there was little conversation; no one had been introduced and in the best British tradition, people were unwilling to appear too pushy or over-friendly.

One of the older women was finishing off the crossword in the morning paper; one of the younger ones was painting her nails. Raynes poured himself a cup of strong black coffee with three heaped teaspoonfuls of sugar and selected a plain chocolate biscuit. He then settled himself in a large, comfortable armchair on the right hand side of the room whence he could, unobtrusively, observe the other guests.

Molly swept into the room and greeted everyone with one of her warm, welcoming smiles.

"Good morning, everybody! Welcome to Mallaig. To our magical mystery weekend. I'm glad you all managed to arrive safely. I hope you've all had a splendid breakfast. Feeling refreshed and cheerful? Ready to have some splendid fun?"

Her charm melted the hardest of hearts. Even that of the Inspector who had heard it all before.

"Now," she continued, "although we're all going to be acting out our own individual parts – and although I want everyone to enter into the life and spirit of the characters they've been given – you might like to know who your neighbours are."

She looked round the room.

"Bernard Potter. A civil servant from Tunbridge Wells."

The tall man graciously inclined his head.
"Lady Emily Andrews. A research student from Oxford."
A bit old for a student, thought Raynes.
"Stanley Dixon. An accountant from Cheshire."
One of the suits.
"Kenneth Savage. A company director from Malvern."
The other suit.
"Gloria Markham-Jones, from Hastings. How shall I describe you, Gloria?"
"A lady of leisure, Molly?"
Someone with plenty of time to do crosswords.
"Suzanne Tempest. A model . . ." Molly looked anxiously to see whether she had got the right word. Suzanne nodded. " . . . a model from West London."
Mr Dixon looked at her with interest.
"Simon Larkin. A Canon of Truro Cathedral."
The man in the crumpled jeans smiled apologetically.
"An ex-Canon, I'm afraid. I've been put out to grass."
No one showed the slightest interest.
"And Dorothy West, a doctor's wife from Woodbridge in Suffolk."
"I am a pharmacist by profession."
Mrs West's eyes twinkled behind a pair of rimless glasses.
Molly looked at her notes.
"So you are."
She turned to the Inspector.
"And finally we have Richard Raynes who is a detective from Grasshallows. He is going to be our referee. He's done this twice before for me and always been scrupulously fair."
Her eyes flashed a look of gratitude towards the Inspector.
"Now, none of the rest of you have ever been to one of my murder weekends, so let me give you a few details about what is going to happen. Each day, we shall have a different scenario. Today, it will be 'Dead Woman's Folly'; on Saturday, 'Chicago, 1929'; and on Sunday, 'Desert Island Deaths'.
"We shall start each day at 11.00am, identifying the body, finding out the cause of death and generally putting ourselves into the picture. We shall establish our own identities as well as

that of the corpse." She smiled. "After lunch, we shall try to discover the motives for the murder; there will be plenty of time for discussion and questioning. You will probably find it helpful to make a note of certain facts as they are revealed.

"You will each be given a folder containing your own private details which are unknown to everyone else. Some of those details you will be obliged to disclose – but others you must keep secret.

"After a break for afternoon tea, the pace will get quicker. You will be given your final briefing notes which will tell you whether you are the murderer. You will know – but no one else. It will then be up to you to lie as convincingly as you can. To accuse everyone else. A splendid free-for-all.

"Finally, at about five o'clock, we will all say whom we think the guilty party is – and why. The Inspector will then tell us the truth and will present a bottle of champagne or vintage claret to the winner. If more than one of you guesses correctly, then it will be a question of free drinks in the bar."

She smiled.

"After dinner, if you can bear any more, the Inspector will entertain us by telling us about some of his more spectacular investigations of real-life murders – and answer any questions you may want to ask.

"However," she smiled apologetically, "I must ask you not to take the games too seriously. The weekend is intended to be as relaxing as possible. I want you to have a lot of fun – together. There is no rush to reach a solution. There will be ample time for general conversation. For food and drink. Think of the weekend as a series of crossword puzzles which we are here to solve together."

Gloria frowned.

She preferred to tackle such things alone.

"If you want to dress up for your character – to pretend you are that person, it will make everything that much more enjoyable. I have brought with me a collection of props which you might like to use . . ."

Oh dear, thought Raynes, not the feather boas again!

"If you want to put on an appropriate accent, feel free to do so. But please remember – at six o'clock – to return to being your normal self." She laughed nervously. "We don't want to find ourselves dining with a raving psychopath. Spare us!"

Everyone laughed.

Molly had broken the ice.

Now they knew the form, they were ready to start.

Molly dipped into her leather brief case and pulled out eight small cardboard folders with the name of each character written boldly on the front cover.

"Inside these files, you will find a brief outline of the character you are to play. Please spend the next ten minutes reading through the first page of notes. You will see that we are in Nasse House, a large country house in Devon where Sir Stanley Dixon and his elegant wife, Lady Gloria, are hosting a Garden Fete in their substantial grounds. The event has been running for about an hour and a half when the manager of the White Elephant stall . . ." she looked at Raynes " . . . rushes into the house to tell me what he has found." She smiled confidently as she handed out the cardboard folders.

"Ten minutes from now, the game begins."

4. *Just not cricket!*

Raynes looked at his watch. The ten minutes were almost up.

It was his job to rush into Nasse House and declare that a body had been found in the summerhouse. Faithful to his role, he left the Highland Lounge and went down the steps into the garden. He walked over to the rather ornate Victorian building where Molly had positioned her victim.

It was only a model, but it looked quite realistic – slumped over a small circular table with an oriental dagger thrust deep into its back and a large quantity of tomato ketchup oozing out of the wound.

He checked the "body" to see if all the props were in place – the little clues by which the identity would be established. Satisfied that everything was as it should be, he ran back to the hotel lounge and burst through the door.

"Mrs Oliver! There's a woman lying dead in the summerhouse! You'd better phone the police!"

This was the cue for a succession of suspects to head for the garden whilst Molly was supposedly phoning the police.

The first one to arrive at the summerhouse was Kenny Savage who seemed bemused.

"Is this the right place?" he asked.

Raynes nodded.

"I'm expecting to find a body."

"Step inside," said Raynes. "What part are you playing?"

"I'm the doctor."

"Well, in that case, you'll have to determine the cause of death."

Kenny stood staring at the motionless figure wrapped in a purple cloak, emblazoned with stars, moons and other cabalistic symbols.

"Well, it's bloody obvious, isn't it? The poor woman's been stabbed."

"With a dagger," added Raynes.

"Fancy bit of work," said Kenny. "Must have cost a bob or two."

"Probably," said Raynes, who imagined that Molly had picked it up in some junk shop in South London.

Mr Savage looked round the summerhouse rather vaguely – not sure what he should do next.

Raynes gently steered him in the right direction.

"What's her name?"

Mr Savage picked up a piece of card lying on the table.

"Gipsy Rose Lee." He looked at Raynes. "I thought she was a stripper."

"That was her sister."

Kenny looked coldly at the Inspector.

"You're taking the mickey."

"It's a game!" said Raynes.

"Well, I'm not used to dead bodies."

"How long has she been dead?"

Raynes pointed to a wrist watch lying on the floor.

"Ten past three."

Mr Savage was about to pick it up.

"Don't touch it! The police will want to examine it."

Kenny straightened up – red-faced. This was too much like the real thing.

Raynes looked thoughtfully at the doctor.

"And where were you half an hour ago?"

"I was with you in the lounge. Inspector . . . Oh, I see what you mean . . ." He took his notes out of his pocket.

"Hm. I was on the bottle stall. Will that do?"

"For the moment."

Kenny showed no desire to prolong his visit to the summerhouse – and so missed several other clues.

* * * *

Stanley Dixon, who followed close upon his heels, seemed to have entered into the spirit of the game more fully.

"What a dreadful business, Inspector! An afternoon when so many people have come to Nasse House to enjoy themselves. I never thought such a terrible thing would happen."

"You know her?"

"Mrs Lee? Yes. Local artist. Didn't think much of her paintings. Far too modern for me."

Raynes pointed to the card.

"Yes. Her Christian name is Rose. We used to tease her that she had gipsy blood."

"So what's she doing here?"

"I should have thought it was perfectly obvious, Inspector. She was our fortune-teller."

He pointed to the crystal ball which had fallen off the table and rolled into a corner. "The trouble with these sort of people is that they can predict everyone else's future — but not their own."

"Did she tell your fortune?"

Sir Stanley had the grace to look a trifle embarrassed.

"As a matter of fact, she did."

"And what was it?"

"She said my wife and I would be going for a long holiday

in the near future."

Raynes raised his eyebrows.

"Parkhurst?"

Sir Stanley laughed nervously.

"No. As a matter of fact, we're planning to go on a cruise to the Caribbean. She was right there."

He looked down. Sadness filled his face.

"So sad to think she won't paint any more pictures."

"I thought you said you didn't like them?"

"I didn't. But it's tragic to see a creative spirit extinguished." A tear rolled down his cheek.

A good actor, thought Raynes.

* * * *

Lady Emily was even more dramatic. Clasping her hands together, she wailed: "Poor Rose! Poor Rose!"

"False!" said Raynes.

"Pardon?"

"That's not what it says in your notes."

"How d'you know what it says in my notes?"

"Because I've done this game before. You're supposed to hate her."

"Well, she was a loose woman . . ."

"Very argumentative."

"Yes. She could be abrasive."

"Which is why you put her on her own at the Fete. Doing her fortune-telling in the summerhouse would avoid any problems with other people."

"She was very good at it. Even in real life, she would read your cards, your palms and your tea leaves . . ."

"Don't stand on it!"

Raynes had noticed that Lady Emily was about to put her foot on the wrist watch.

"Oh, sorry!"

"Destroying vital evidence . . ."

"I suppose it is important." She looked down. "Ten past three."

"And what were you doing at ten past three?"
"Me? I was going round the stalls, trying to encourage folk to spend. One loses count of time."
"Had you been to have your fortune read?"
"Certainly not! I don't believe in such things."
Raynes immediately registered a lie.
He moved the corpse's head a fraction to expose the Tarot cards lying underneath.
"The Lovers? It wasn't you?"
Lady Emily blushed.
"Well, I've had a few in my time," she said modestly. "But down here, you have to be careful. People watch you all the time."
Raynes smiled.
"So you would think that someone would have noticed who was going into the summerhouse – and who was coming out?"
"I suppose so."
"But not the lady who was organizing the Fete? Not the lady who was encouraging the punters to spend their money? She didn't see anything?"
Raynes took quiet pleasure needling Lady Emily.
"I was at the Tombola stall. That's one of our big earners. We always aim to raise £500."
"And how much of a float do you give to your stall-holders?"
"Ten pounds in silver."
Raynes looked pointedly at the table. Lady Emily followed his gaze.
"Yes," she said. "her money's gone . . ."
" . . . and her handbag," said Raynes. "I think that's significant, don't you?"

* * * *

Mrs West, the doctor's wife, arrived with a twinkle in her eye.
"Do we have to keep meeting like this, Inspector?"
Raynes responded gallantly.

"I can think of better places to meet."
"So can I."
She looked round the murder scene.
"Too much ketchup!"
"That's what they all say."
"I think murders should be a little more . . . subtle, don't you?"
Raynes agreed with her – before returning to the case in hand.
"So where d'you fit into the plot?"
"I'm just a casual visitor – down from London. I saw the poster on the noticeboard outside the church and I thought it might be fun."
"And is it fun?"
"I'm sure it will be. One meets a better class of policeman."
"You're referring to Mr Potter, of course?"
"Of course."
Mrs West made a face.
"And what d'you think has been happening here?"
Mrs West examined all the clues carefully and even discovered the torn page of a calendar pinned to the wall, which had escaped Raynes' attention.
She pointed to the fifteenth day of the month which had been circled in red ink – or red paint.
"The Ides of March?"
"Her birthday?"
"I think it must be a clue."
"Julius Caesar was killed in March . . ."
". . . by his friends . . ."
". . . stabbed in the back."
"Makes you wonder who her friends were."
"I think it might be more helpful if you concentrated on her enemies . . . she must have had one or two . . ."
"Village life is so brutal."
"The dagger looks cosmopolitan."
Mrs West looked at the blade more closely.
"Empire made," she said.
"Someone who lives abroad?" suggested Raynes.

Mrs West smiled sweetly at the Inspector.

"I know you won't believe this; but I used to have a dagger just like that . . ."

Her eyes filled with tears.

"Was it stolen?"

"No," she said. "When my husband died . . . the police took it away."

"The police?"

"Yes. He died a sudden . . . and a tragic death."

Raynes was not sure whether she was play-acting or describing an event in real life. But he had no opportunity to ask.

There was a discreet cough.

Canon Larkin was waiting to inspect the body.

Mrs West apologized for holding him up.

* * * *

"One of your flock, vicar?"

"Indeed, yes. A very talented woman."

"You liked her paintings?"

"Er . . . no. I couldn't say that. Her taste was somewhat bizarre; but she could turn her hand to anything. She did me a beautiful picture of my two cats."

"Cats?"

Raynes struggled to remember if there was anything about cats in his notes. As far as he could remember, Mrs Lee was supposed to have done a painting of the church.

"Purcell and Schumann." Canon Larkin smiled.

"And was it a good likeness?" asked Raynes.

"Most lifelike. Even my cats thought so."

The Inspector returned to the body.

"This must be very distressing for you."

"Very. It's sad to think that one of our own small community has felt moved to lift a vicious hand against another."

"Perhaps he'll come to you and make his confession?"

"I doubt it. As you well know, Inspector, the people who do the really serious crimes never get caught. They keep their mouths shut. It's the small fry who blab. They come to confession and reel off all their petty sins. God knows who they're trying to impress! It always leaves me completely cold."

"Yes," thought Raynes. "He looks like a cold fish."

But – back to the game.

"Would you like to look round the murder scene and see if there's anything you recognize?"

Canon Larkin looked closely at the crystal ball.

"The last time I saw that . . . it was in Lady Emily's front room."

"Really?" said Raynes. "Perhaps she lent it to her for the afternoon?"

"Perhaps."

Raynes lifted the victim's head.

"Tarot cards."

"The Devil's picture book," said Canon Larkin. "That's what the Puritans called them."

"The Lovers?" said Raynes thoughtfully. "Who could that be? You and Mrs Lee?"

"Certainly not!" The vicar sounded quite shocked. Then he smiled a rather sinister smile. "If you're looking for lovers, Inspector, you'd be better asking Sir Stanley . . ."

"Or his wife!"

Gloria was standing on the bottom step of the summerhouse. Neither of them had heard her approach.

"I'm surprised to hear you discussing my husband's private life with a complete stranger!"

Canon Larkin seemed acutely embarrassed – and tongue-tied. He left the building as quickly as possible.

* * * *

"That got rid of him!" said Gloria, in a business-like manner. "Horrible, slimy creature! I can't think why Molly allowed him to come on the weekend. She has absolutely no taste."

"Perhaps he sounded more congenial on paper than he appears in the flesh?"

"Perhaps."

Raynes continued to speculate on Canon Larkin's condition.

"Cirrhosis, d'you think?"

"Probably AIDS. It doesn't look as if he's got long for this world. It would be much better if people like that were put down . . ."

Raynes raised his eyebrows.

"Well, you know what I mean . . ."

The Inspector knew exactly what she meant. But even if he agreed with her, he was too diplomatic to say so. Instead, he said: "Is there any truth in his accusations?"

"None whatsoever!"

Her reply did not carry conviction.

"Mrs Lee seems to have been a very attractive young woman."

Gloria was withering in her contempt.

"Mutton dressed as lamb! After all the operations she'd had, her body was like an Ordnance Survey map!"

"But she was a talented painter?"

"No one can deny her that."

"With a fascination for the occult?"

"She dabbled. In fact, I think she let it rule her life too much. Wouldn't start a picture unless the cards were right; wouldn't go up to London unless the day was propitious."

Raynes lifted up the victim's head.

"Yes. Those are her Tarot cards."

"The Lovers?"

"Lady Emily and Kenny Savage."

"You think so?"

"Lady Emily and anyone!" She laughed. "No," she said, "that's unfair. I think that even Lady Emily would think twice before grappling with the vicar."

"And you maintain that the cards do not relate to Mrs Lee and your husband?"

Gloria gave the Inspector a long, hard look.

"Theirs was a business relationship. That was as far as it went."

The next visitor was Suzanne Tempest. She was wearing a scarlet wrap-around skirt with gold sandals and brightly painted toenails. She glided up to the Inspector – the aroma of Guerlain positively overpowering.

Raynes felt slightly light-headed.

"And who are you supposed to be?"

"The reporter."

"You could have fooled me!"

"And me!"

Raynes noted that Suzanne had very large, expressive, grey eyes.

"And which newspaper has the honour of employing you?"

Suzanne looked heavenwards.

"Let me get this right . . . *The Torquay and District Advertizer*. Founded in September 1890."

"And you were covering the Garden Fete?"

"Someone has to do it. They normally give the boring jobs to the cub reporters. They think we've got nothing better to do on Saturday afternoons."

"So you had obtained all the information you needed?"

"Yes. I was just about to go when some boring peasant rushed in to tell Mrs Oliver that there'd been a murder . . ."

The ghost of a smile played over her lips.

"So I got out my notebook and started quizzing the locals."

"Who were equally boring?"

"How did you guess?"

Suzanne looked round the summerhouse.

"I've also been kept waiting an awfully long time. I was so fed up, I went and had a shower and a change."

"And you feel all the better for it?"

"I do. But I expect everyone is miles ahead of me by now."

"I shouldn't think so. The real hard work begins after lunch."

Raynes pointed out the various clues and explained what they meant.

The Tarot cards left her unmoved.

"The Magician or the Falling Tower would have been more appropriate," she said.

"Are you into that sort of thing?"

"I used to concoct the astrology column. Taurus is moving into Virgo and a dinky little Sagittarian is expected nine months hence!"

Raynes looked at her thoughtfully.

"So it is quite possible that you visited Mrs Lee earlier in the afternoon?"

"I couldn't resist having my palm read."

"And what did it reveal?"

"A large scoop. Lots of money. Promotion. A fashionable wedding. Two children. All the usual guff."

"Did she seem happy whilst you were here?"

"Now that you mention it – no. She'd had a letter from someone complaining about one of her pictures. I think she said they'd been asking for their money back. She was quite upset about it."

"Did you see the letter?"

"It was sticking out of her handbag."

"Which has now gone," said Raynes.

"So I see."

Suzanne looked at the empty space where the bag had been.

"Which would suggest," said Raynes, "that the handbag was taken by the murderer. Who came in after you?"

"Stanley . . ." She quickly corrected herself. "Sir Stanley. He likes to be given his title."

But Raynes knew she was lying.

* * * *

Bernard Potter lumbered into the summerhouse – and looked around him.

"Is this it?"

"I'm afraid so."

Mr Potter shook his head.

"To think people waste their time playing these stupid games!"

"And pay through the nose for it."

Mr Potter looked coldly at the Inspector. He was about to say: "I wouldn't dream of paying for this rubbish . . . Molly's paying," but he felt that if he said that, the Inspector would despise him. Instead, he said: "Hm . . . we all make mistakes."

He looked down at the motionless figure.

"So this is supposed to be Mrs Lee?"
Raynes nodded.
"And I'm supposed to guess who murdered her?"
The Inspector felt obliged to remind the civil servant of the realities of life at the sharp end of police work.
"Sometimes we have even less evidence than this to go on. Just a charred skull – or a lost shoe. But we still manage to make an arrest."
Mr Potter did not take kindly to the rebuke. He stared dumbly at the mannequin in its garish clothes with its black wig and the lavish smears of ketchup round the knife wound
"So what d'you deduce from this grisly scene?"
"You're supposed to be the policeman," said Raynes mildly. "You know these people. Examine the clues and see where they lead you."
Mr Potter still seemed unimpressed.
"A dagger?"
"Find out whose dagger it is. Did someone steal it – or borrow it? Has anyone seen the dagger during the past week?"
"The watch?"
"Note the time of death. Who was where at ten past three? Is it the victim's watch or did the murderer drop it in his haste to escape?"
Mr Potter considered the crystal ball.
"I presume that's part of the kit?"
"Could be," said Raynes. "Or it could be a red herring. One of the suspects said that they saw it in Lady Emily's front sitting room. But that's obviously a lie because she says she doesn't believe in such things."
"She's a liar!"
"I think you'll find everyone lies like mad round here. You will too when the powder trail leads to your own front door."
"But I'm the policeman."
"Everyone's a suspect – even Molly. She's playing her part."
"She's calling herself Mrs Oliver. It's very confusing."
Raynes looked at Mr Potter sadly. Why couldn't he let his hair down and enjoy himself like everyone else?
"Mrs Oliver is one of the characters in an Agatha Christie

novel. She was invited to a Garden Fete in Devon where something nasty was expected to happen . . ."

"The fortune-teller was murdered?"

Mr Potter clearly hoped there was some sound explanation and logical reasoning behind all this play-acting; but the Inspector had to disappoint him.

"No. The victim was a schoolgirl in the boat shed."

Bernard shook his head despairingly.

"I think I'm quite out of my depth."

Raynes smiled.

"I think you probably are."

5. *Bezique*

They were back inside the Highland Lounge.

"Canon Larkin, would you be kind enough to identify the corpse?"

"Certainly. It is Mrs Rose Lee, lately of Honeysuckle Cottage, Nasse, in the County of Devon."

"You are quite sure about this?"

"Absolutely. I recognized her delicate ears."

Molly was a little surprised by Mr Larkin's capacity for invention. As far as she remembered, the mannequin had no ears.

"Occupation? Sir Stanley?"

"Artist. A very accomplished artist of the modern school. She exhibited frequently at the Royal Academy."

"And I believe you assisted her in selling her works to the general public?"

"I did."

"So your relationship was one hundred per cent professional?"

Sir Stanley hesitated a fraction before replying. "It was."

Lady Emily looked surprised.

"You're an art dealer?"

Stanley nodded.

"You told me you were an estate agent."

"Same thing. Selling other people's property."

Gloria intervened.

"I don't see why my husband had to tell you anything. All you village people do is gossip!"

Mrs West smiled. As she had always said, village life was mean and brutal – full of petty squabbles and vicious spite – the perfect breeding ground for murder. One saw so much of it in Suffolk.

Molly turned to Kenny.

"Now, Dr Savage, perhaps you could tell us the cause of death?"

"Too much tomato ketchup!" said Gloria, quick as a flash.

Everyone laughed.

"Well," said Kenny, "it seems quite straightforward. The lady had been stabbed right between the shoulder blades. She must have been struck from behind and collapsed on to the table. I remember seeing an Arab do that once. Chap lost his temper. Bloke had his back to him. Wham! Straight in. Bull's-eye. Instantaneous death, I should say."

"An unnatural death, Inspector Potter?"

"Very much so. The victim was taken unawares."

"And the time of the murder?"

"We are led to believe that the incident took place at ten past three."

"But you don't believe that?"

"The hands on the watch could have been adjusted by the murderer to provide him with a convenient alibi."

"Good thinking. In fact, the battery had also been removed."

Kenny looked accusingly at Raynes.

"I wasn't even allowed to touch the watch."

"Fingerprints," said Mr Potter. "Much better to leave that to the forensic department."

"I believe you already have the results?"

Bernard consulted his notes.

"No fingerprints on either the watch or the dagger."

Molly looked at him thoughtfully.

"Can we be sure that the watch was hers?"

Lady Emily was happy to contribute her tuppenceworth.

"Of course it's hers. She's been wearing it for years."

Molly sighed sadly.

"I hate to contradict you, Lady Emily, but the watch was yours. You lent it to her for the afternoon."

"Perhaps that's why you tried to step on it – or kick it out of the way," said Raynes. "Trying to destroy vital evidence."

"And who removed the battery?" asked Mr Potter.

"She probably couldn't afford one!" said Gloria.

Lady Emily looked hurt.

"Everyone's got it in for me this morning," she said.

Everybody laughed.

"There's worse than you around," said Molly.

"I'm glad to hear it!"

Molly turned to Suzanne.

"Did our local reporter pick up anything?"

"Not literally." Suzanne laughed. "But I noticed a few things that were missing . . ."

"The float. Ten pounds . . ."

"Yes, there was that. But I was more anxious about the handbag. When I went in earlier in the afternoon to have a 'reading', the handbag was sitting on that wooden bench which runs round the inner wall of the summerhouse. The float money was in a little plastic box beside it. But in her handbag, there was a letter. I think she'd just received it – and it had upset her . . ."

"Did she show it to you?"

"No, she didn't. But it was poking out of her bag. She said that someone had been complaining about one of her pictures. I think they'd even asked for their money back."

"I don't blame them," said Gloria. "She painted the most awful rubbish. I remember a particularly dreadful picture – a sort of tangerine orange and yellow chessboard, slightly blurred, with a single red leaf in the bottom right hand corner. It actually hurt your eyes to look at it. What did she sell it for?"

"Four thousand pounds," said Stanley.

"It's quite unbelievable! I don't know how anyone could live with it. If they want their money back, they have my sympathy."

"They're not getting back my commission!"

"Of course not, darling."

Canon Larkin cleared his throat.

"I don't seek to defend her – but when she was painting ordinary scenes – such as a picture of the church – or of my cats – she did it beautifully."

Lady Emily chuckled.

"But did you see the one of the Witches' Sabbath? All those men and women dancing around naked. You wouldn't have approved of that."

"I was aware of her interest in witchcraft and I deplored it. There's no doubt that if people indulge in such things, they get hurt."

"Are you suggesting that might have been the cause of her death? Divine punishment?"

Canon Larkin stroked his chin.

"You remember the picture of Dorian Gray? Oscar Wilde?"

This literary allusion was too much for Dorothy West.

"I think it's far more likely to have been one of her lovers!"

Everyone looked at Stanley Dixon.

"Don't look at me!" he said.

Molly came to his rescue.

"This is not the time to start making accusations. We're here to establish the facts. To identify the corpse. To agree about the cause of death. To take note of all the clues. I'm sure we've all got our private theories, but there's still plenty of water to flow under the bridge before teatime."

She turned to Lady Emily.

"What about the crystal ball?"

"What about it?"

"It was lying on the floor."

Raynes looked at Lady Emily.

"Canon Larkin believes that he saw it in your front room. Does it belong to you?"

"Of course not!"

Mr Potter looked up.

"Your fingerprints were on it."

Lady Emily twisted and turned, wondering how she could get out of this one.

"She came to give me a reading."

"You told me you didn't believe in such things." Kenny Savage sounded quite upset.

"Well, I don't really . . . but things were getting quite difficult . . . I didn't know what to do. Rose – Mrs Lee – offered to help. But then she got a call to see some people – and rather than take it with her, she left it in my house. It was there for about a fortnight."

Lady Emily cheered up. Put that way, it sounded quite plausible.

"Another pack of lies!"

Lady Emily gave Mr Dixon what could only be described as a dirty look.

Molly turned to Gloria.

"D'you think she would have seen the murderer in her crystal ball?"

Gloria was dismissive.

"You know I don't believe in such things."

Raynes intervened again.

"And yet you recognized the Tarot cards! You confirmed that they belonged to Rose. How could you be so sure if you hadn't been to her for a reading?"

For one deliciously indecisive moment, Gloria stared at the Inspector. Eventually she said: "My husband told me about them. She said we were going on a cruise. He was full of it."

Raynes smiled. To himself, he said: "Gotcha!"

Molly said: "There seems to be some uncertainty as to who had their cards read by Mrs Lee at the Garden Fete. Could we find out who actually claims to have been in the summerhouse this afternoon?"

"I was there," said Suzanne.

"So was I," said Mrs West. "It was the most entertaining part of the afternoon. It also gave me a chance to sit down. My feet were killing me."

"Mr Larkin?"

"Certainly not!"

"Dr Savage?"

"Not on your nellie!"

"Stanley?"

"My wife has already landed me in it."
"Lady Emily?"
"Not this afternoon."
"Inspector Potter?"
"A moment of weakness."
"And what did she predict for you?"
Bernard looked at Lady Emily.
"I wouldn't dream of telling you. It'd be round the village in no time!"
Molly smiled.
"I'm sure we shall discover later." She looked at her notes. "I see no one's said anything about the calendar."
"I didn't know there was one . . ."
"I didn't see one . . ."
"It was on the wall – with a red circle around the 15th March."
"The Ides of March," said Gloria thoughtfully. "How appropriate."
"Was the date circled in paint or Biro?"
"It could've been lipstick."
Mr Potter leant forward.
"You're quite right. Our tests have revealed it to be lipstick."
"It must be a special date for somebody."
Kenny Savage suddenly came to life.
"Fifteenth of March? It's my birthday!"
Everyone laughed at his obvious surprise.
"I wouldn't advertize that, if I were you," said Molly. "They'll all be after you."
Mercifully, at that very moment, the gong rang out in the hall to announce that lunch was now being served.
Molly laughed.
"Saved by the bell! Well, I think that's enough evidence for one morning. We have one or two surprises for you this afternoon, but now it's time for all of us to head to the bar and have a quick drink before lunch. It's all on the house, so if you want double whiskies or double gins, you have only to ask."
Symbolically, she zipped up her briefcase with all its secrets. Raynes got up out of his armchair and stretched his legs. He

walked over to Molly and waited till Gloria had finished complaining about the lack of real blood at the murder scene.

"I think it lacked fourteen letters beginning with 'v'."

"Verisimilitude," said Raynes.

"How clever you are!" said Gloria.

"I do the *Telegraph* crossword every day."

"That's nothing to boast about," said Gloria. "Everyone knows *The Times* is much harder."

Raynes turned to Molly.

"You didn't mention that the Dixons bought Nasse House from Lady Emily – hence all the aggro . . ."

"No, I'm saving it till later."

"You might also have told us that Inspector Potter was having an affair with Rose."

Molly's eyes twinkled.

"I don't approve of necrophilia!"

Raynes looked pointedly at Bernard Potter.

"You could have fooled me!"

6. *Ninepins*

"Thirsty work being a detective!" said Kenny.

"Very much so," said Raynes. "I survive on a diet of black coffee, claret and gin."

"I prefer beer myself."

He was already deep into a pint of McEwan's 80/- ale.

"Good stuff, Inspector."

Raynes sipped at his ice-cold gin and tonic.

"What d'you make of all these people, Mr Savage?"

"Very combustible, Inspector. Very combustible, I would say. Light the blue touch paper and stand clear."

"Mr Dixon seems very taken with Suzanne."

"Yes," he said, "that seems pretty obvious – but he might be biting off more than he can chew. I think she's the sort of woman that uses men. Sucks 'em dry and throws 'em away. I've met a few like that in my time."

Kenny downed the rest of his pint and ordered a

replacement. Whilst he was waiting, he gave the Inspector a sly smile.

"To be honest, the one I've got my eye on is Lady Emily. She's young and she's got class."

"She's a research student in Oxford."

"Oh, I don't believe in all that guff. She's just marking time – just marking time. When I get her over to my place – my estate in Worcestershire, she won't be bothering her head about research. No way."

Raynes thought he should utter one word of caution.

"According to my notes, she may have a bit of a drink problem."

Mr Savage laughed heartily.

"Well, that makes two of us! I was intending to make this a teetotal weekend – drying out after the last binge – but if the drinks are on the house, then who am I to refuse?" He turned to the barman. "You can pull me a third one and bring it through to the dining room." He turned to the Inspector. "D'you want another?"

"No," said Raynes. "I'll stick."

* * * *

At lunch, Raynes found himself sitting next to Mrs West.

"I tell you honestly, Inspector; I don't like my character; not one bit."

Raynes thought that, come the afternoon session, she would like it even less.

"I don't believe in all this card-reading and trying to find what's in store for us. I believe in taking fate as it comes. I should hate to know that I was going to die in a car crash in three months time."

Mrs West unrolled her crisp, white napkin.

"Did you get any warning before your husband died?"

"None whatsoever. He seemed perfectly well. A lovely home. A good job. A very able and loving wife. What more could he want?"

Raynes was reminded that Mrs West was a very eligible widow.

"What did he die of?"
Mrs West looked down at her bowl of steaming hot, home-made game soup as if uncertain how to reply.
"Suicide," she said quietly.
"And why was that?"
"The pressure of work. It got to him. It was all very sudden."
She picked up her spoon.
"This looks delicious."
"No oriental daggers then?"
Mrs West managed to smile.
"No. My husband couldn't have endured making a mess. Blowing his brains out or slashing his wrists. He simply gave himself a quick injection and that was it."
There was a silence whilst both of them consumed their soup.
"But your lot made it worse than it need have been."
Raynes looked blank.
"The police. They went into everything. Looked at all his drug books, his bank balance, emptied all his drawers and cupboards. They left no stone unturned."
"Investigations can be very unpleasant."
"I know they have to be thorough— but it's not much fun being on the receiving end, especially when you're in deep trauma yourself. It can be deeply offensive."
"Are you managing to build yourself a new life?" asked Raynes, trying to steer the conversation away from the police.
"I'm a pharmacist. I work in the chemist's in Woodbridge. I try to do lots of interesting things. That's why I'm here. What do you do when you're not working, Inspector?"
Raynes could think of any number of things he got up to when he wasn't working – but he wouldn't dream of revealing them to Dorothy West.
"I like going out for meals. I have one or two close friends. I spend evenings with them. I recently bought a new house so I've had to do quite a lot of gardening."
"Is there a Mrs Raynes?"
"No. I'm divorced."
"Was it your fault or hers?"

"Oh, mine. I spend very long hours at work. When you get a really juicy murder, you tend to forget about ordinary things. You just work round the clock. I'm not surprised she left me."

"Surely you don't have all that much crime in Grasshallows? It seems a very quiet, respectable sort of place."

"Well," said Raynes, "I've only been there fourteen months, but in that time we've had five quite interesting murders. Quality, not quantity. And I've been involved in two others outside Grasshallows."

"Are you going to tell us about the royal kidnapping? You were involved in that, weren't you?"

Raynes consumed the last of his soup and reflected that Mrs West was very well informed about his background. He had intended to find out a lot more about her, but she had very neatly turned the tables on him.

"Yes, I was." He smiled. "I see that you did your homework before you came."

"I asked a few friends if they'd heard of you."

"And they had?"

"They spoke very highly of you."

"Well," said Raynes modestly. "I do enjoy solving crimes."

He looked round the dining room where Molly's guests all seemed to be chatting and laughing – the ice well and truly broken.

"Do you expect any murders round here?"

"Oh, just one or two," said Mrs West. "I think Suzanne would make a very suitable victim. Beautiful, tragic, star-crossed . . ." She lowered her voice. "Mr Dixon could be blackmailed. I'm sure he has lots of money. I think Mr Savage could be persuaded to beat Mr Potter over the head with a blunt instrument; and Lady Emily would need very little persuasion to steal Molly's pearls . . ."

Raynes tucked into his saddle of roast venison.

"I've been watching them all morning. They're a very interesting cross-section of people. Some of them quite lonely and vulnerable. They could easily get hurt."

Raynes had come to much the same conclusion himself. He sliced another delicious piece of venison and ate a couple of roast potatoes before he asked his next question.

"And does Mrs West have any victim in sight?"

Mrs West's eyes twinkled.

"Inspector, I thought you'd already guessed. I was thinking of you!"

Raynes laughed.

"I asked for that one." He looked at her with a mischievous smile. "So what are you going to choose for the murder weapon? Not the oriental dagger?"

Mrs West responded with equal frivolity.

"Well, I've been thinking about that. Seeing as there's no Mrs Raynes to worry about, I thought my best weapon would be a black, see-through negligée and a bottle of expensive perfume. Would Paris be worth a little murder?"

Raynes tried to be a little more serious.

"I've told you. I don't have a very good reputation where women are concerned."

Mrs West looked back at him with clear grey eyes.

"I think you'll do for the weekend," she said. "Remember, it's only a game."

* * * *

Canon Larkin was sitting at the other side of the large circular dining table, watching the Inspector's growing rapport with Mrs West. He said to Lady Emily: "They seem to be getting on very well together."

"That's what a murder weekend's all about. Developing relationships. Exploring relationships. Destroying relationships All in quick succession. One mask after another so that you never know what is actually real. A sort of bizarre world where time is suspended – where anything goes. Today, I am a penniless aristocrat thirsting for revenge. Tomorrow, I may be a flapper seducing Al Capone. On Sunday, I could be an heiress studded in diamonds . . ."

"And on Tuesday you're back to being a research student in Oxford."

Lady Emily laughed.

"At least I never get bored."

Canon Larkin had chosen the fresh salmon. He poked anxiously amongst the pink flesh looking for bones.

"And what are you studying at Oxford?" he asked.

"Business management," said Lady Emily. "But I don't take it all that seriously. It's the social life I enjoy."

"I was at Oxford once," Canon Larkin observed sadly. "Since then, it's all been downhill."

"But you're a Canon. You must have achieved something."

The clergyman shook his head.

"Oh, no. It's one of those honours they bestow on you – just to get rid of you. They give you a pension and throw in an honorary canonry. It doesn't mean anything. It's just a sop to your pride."

"Why did you retire? You don't look old."

"Ill health, they called it. But if the truth be told, it was just too much booze. When you're a lonely bachelor, stuck in a cathedral close, it's either choirboys or the bottle. I preferred the bottle. It damaged my liver. Proved a deep embarrassment to my fellow clergy. They never got over my singing 'Happy Birthday' to the Bishop during Solemn High Mass on the Feast of the Assumption. The choir looked quite shocked. The Bishop went purple with anger. 'Get that man out. He's drunk!' But I clung on to the altar rails and they had quite a fight before they finally dragged me out. It must have been awfully funny to watch, but I didn't know what I was doing. They sent me to a clinic where I got dried out. Most effectively. But they didn't want me back. They asked me to go quietly – so I went."

"And what are you doing now?"

Canon Larkin smiled ever so sweetly.

"I'm looking after my two cats — Purcell and Schumann – and I'm writing my autobiography."

"Your revenge?"

"You're a perceptive young woman. Yes, it's my revenge. I think it'll be a best seller. I won't be able to mention people's actual names but I'll make sure everyone knows whom I'm writing about. Whilst I was in the drying-out clinic, I made a list of every vice and every peccadillo I knew about my fellow clergy – their spite, their back-stabbing, their greed, their wives – oh, their wives! You should have met some of them! Their children on drugs. I made a list. And, believe me, compared to some of them, I was a saint! So I thought I'd write a book about them. I'm calling it *Sacred and Profane*."

"Will any publisher take it?"

"Well, if they don't, I'll print it myself – privately – and go round all the libraries popping copies into the shelves. It's the exposure I'm after – not profit."

"A lot of people are going to be very angry."

"Terribly angry! In fact, it might be worth their while to pay me not to publish it. I fear it may bring a swift end to many promising careers."

Lady Emily felt it necessary to offer a word of caution.

"Don't you think someone might try to silence you? I mean, if they knew what you were doing, they might try to bump you off."

Canon Larkin smiled – a chilling smile.

"First of all, they wouldn't dare. They're cowards – every one of them. Secondly, knowing the clergy, they'd probably bungle it. Shoot themselves by mistake. Drink their own poisoned brandy. Get arrested for carrying an offensive weapon."

"I think you should take precautions."

"I'll probably go abroad. I've been thinking of moving to the Dordogne. Such a beautiful part of France . . ."

"The wine?"

"Alas!" Canon Larkin pointed to the glass of mineral water. "No more wine. No more whisky. If I am to live, I have to stick to water."

"How old are you?" asked Lady Emily.

"Forty-six."

"It must be terrible never to be able to touch alcohol ever again. I just love it."

She swigged down her second glass of Muscadet and asked the waiter to bring her a Cointreau with ice to go with the sweet.

"And how old are you?" asked Canon Larkin.

"Twenty-eight," said Lady Emily.

She caught his doubting look.

"Well, thirty-three, actually. But I'm told I look young for my age."

Canon Larkin took another sip of mineral water.

"I wish I was thirty-three again."

* * * *

"Do you think it was wise allowing someone like Suzanne to come along?"

"Oh, I think so," said Molly cynically. "She keeps all the men happy. They flock round her like bees round a honeypot. Everyone hoping they're in with a chance. Most of them will be disappointed."

She looked at Bernard.

"You mustn't let your own troubles warp your judgement."

"It's not that. I just think she's a disruptive influence."

"Of course she is. That's what helps the whole weekend to go with a swing. People get annoyed. Passions are raised. Everyone gets worked up – but you channel it all into the game. To start with, it's real life – then it becomes play-acting. Most people are still half-and-half. But you can see them lowering their inhibitions. At least, some of them are . . ."

She looked round the tables.

"Mrs West is going to end up in bed with Hercule Poirot. I thought she would. And if he isn't careful, Stanley Dixon is going to end up with our sex-bomb from Oxford."

She chuckled scornfully.

"Of course he'd have been better matched with Suzanne. He has all the things she needs."

"Money?" said Mr Potter.

"Yes, money. But unfortunately she longs to be dominated by brutes so she'll probably fall for Kenny Savage. Stanley will then get very jealous. There might be a punch-up – or even worse."

Bernard stopped eating his pavlova and looked at her.

"Do you enjoy all this?"

"Of course I enjoy it. I'm a born matchmaker. I love to see people enjoying themselves. Sometimes I get invited to their weddings. They may not last very long but they're fun to begin with. It's fascinating watching quiet little people come out of their shells; sad people learning to laugh; bullies getting their come-uppance. Besides, it makes me £16,000 a year tax free and gives me a chance to pig in without anyone calling me a slut."

"Is that why you invited me?"

"I felt sorry for you. What with Rebecca going off and leaving you – and then discovering what she was doing behind your back."

"As long as no one talks, I shall be all right."

"People always talk. The thing is – have you got rid of the stuff?"

"I hope so. But it was hidden all over the place – little plastic bags in the most peculiar places. I flushed most of it down the lavatory but there's probably one or two bags I haven't discovered. Short of taking the house to pieces . . ."

"Why on earth did she do it? She didn't need the money."

"A sense of adventure. The excitement of doing something illegal. Perhaps she enjoyed the company . . . all those people coming to the house."

Molly put a hand on Bernard's arm.

"Subconsciously, she was attacking you. Damaging your career if she was found out. Women can do a lot of damage when they feel sexually frustrated."

"Her – frustrated?" said Mr Potter angrily. "What about me?"

Molly smiled.

"Well, you've always been able to have a little bit on the side. What about that secretary you told me about? She was all right, wasn't she?"

"I had to get rid of her in the end." He sighed sadly. "But I could have done with her now."

Molly smiled again.

"Well, you've got me for the weekend. That should cheer you up." She squeezed his hand. "You didn't bring any of the stuff with you?"

"Good heavens, no!"

"What a pity," said Molly. "I'm rather partial to cocaine."

At the window table, the other four were slogging it out – much as Molly had predicted.

"Have another glass of wine, Sue."

"No, Kenny; if I drink any more, I shall be absolutely useless this afternoon. I believe this is the difficult bit."

"Well, it all seems very complicated to me. I don't suppose another pint would make much difference."

"You've already had three." Stanley Dixon had been counting.

"Four," said Kenny proudly. "I'm the sort of bloke who can hold his liquor. It's good stuff, that McEwan's draught. Have you tried it?"

"No. I'm more of a wine and spirits man."

Gloria was anxious to avoid any conflict between the two men. She had decided that the best way to humiliate Kenny was to expose his ignorant and boorish character.

"Are you enjoying the game, Mr Savage?"

"Blessed if I can understand it, love – do call me Kenny – everyone does. That Inspector chap really confused me. Told me I'd be driving a Rolls-Royce. I was looking forward to that."

Kenny beckoned to the waiter. "Another pint, lad. Same again."

He pushed aside his coffee cup. "I used to have a couple of Rollers. Damn fine cars. Bought them at the motor show." He looked thoughtfully at Suzanne. "Do you go to many motor shows, love?"

The question took Suzanne by surprise.

"No. Why?"

"When I used to go to the motor shows – you know, at the Exhibition Centre in Birmingham – they always had these models draping themselves over the bonnets of the expensive cars. Couple of blondes or a brunette. Quite good-looking, some of them. Helped to sell the cars to the punters. Never mind the style; look at the birds! Worth their weight in gold, some of them."

Suzanne smiled.

"I'm not that sort of model, Kenny. I do pictures for fashion magazines – for catalogues – things like that. I'm normally fully-clothed."

"Well, that's a pity and no mistake. What I say, love, is 'if you've got it, flaunt it!' Never did me any harm. Used to throw pound notes around like confetti in the olden days. Learnt my lesson the hard way."

"What lesson was that?" Gloria asked.

"Money can't buy you friends," said Kenny. "I thought all these people were on my side but when I had a spot of trouble, they melted away like snow in summer. Fortunately, I had quite a bit stashed away abroad – which they didn't know about. That pulled me through. But I'm a wiser man today."

The pint of beer arrived. Kenny handed the waiter a generous tip.

Mr Dixon watched him putting away half the glass and asked provocatively: "Have you ever thought about life insurance?"

The question was a red rag to a bull.

"At my age?" said Kenny. "I'm only forty-eight. What do I need that for? And who's going to collect the lolly? That's what I want to know."

"Don't you have a wife?" asked Gloria.

"No. She went with the business," said Kenny. He wiped the beer off his lips. "Or more accurately . . ." He belched. "Sorry. Drank that lot a bit too quickly . . . She went off with the accountant. Complete tosser, if you'll excuse the language. She thought she was on to a good thing but I had a word with his superiors – the Chartered Society of Accountants – or something like that. I gave them chapter and verse – and he was booted out, good and proper. That took the smile off her face. Mind you, he's probably crawled his way back into some other cosy number. Those sort of people always do."

He looked at Stanley suspiciously.

"Why did you ask me about life insurance? Don't tell me you're into all that?"

"I used to be."

"Made your pile in double quick time, eh?" Kenny downed the rest of his beer. "Well, I'm sorry. I don't wish to be offensive but I've no time, no time whatsoever, for parasites –

yes, parasites – living on other people's hard-earned savings.

"Now, I'm not saying anything against you, Stanley – nothing personal. I'm sure you're as good a bloke as the next. But I just can't stand people sucking other folks dry." He folded up his napkin. "I'm happy to give. Don't get me wrong. I've given thousands to the Conservative Party – not because they asked me – but because I believe they're good for my business. But these life insurance guys, they're not interested in the likes of me. They're busy feathering their own nests. Collecting their ten per cent commission. And I tell you this, Stan, if I ever catch another of those blokes pulling a fast one on me, I'll break his bloody neck. I'm not a violent man – but if a bloke crosses me, I wouldn't hesitate."

Kenny realized that he had got a bit carried away. Said too much. Perhaps looked a bit of a fool. But he had only said what he believed. Nothing wrong with that.

Gloria was looking at her watch.

"I think it's almost time for the next session."

She and Mr Dixon got up from the table.

"Thanks for the advice, Ken."

As they went away, Suzanne smiled.

"You put him in his place."

"I didn't mean to," said Kenny apologetically. "But he just asked for it. Life insurance, indeed!" He looked at Suzanne's soft flowing curves. "See here, Sue," he said, "I don't like asking favours from young ladies like you; but if you have any really nice photos – with you modelling swim-suits or something like that – something really special – would you send me a signed copy – just as a memento? Something to put over my shaving mirror – to cheer me up in the mornings?"

Suzanne smiled even more broadly.

"If you ask nicely, Kenny," she said. "If you ask really nicely, I'll give you the full monty!"

7. *Chinese whispers*

Whilst everyone was having lunch, the body of Rose Lee was removed and all traces of tomato ketchup disposed of. But the cards were still there, together with the watch, the calendar and the crystal ball. The "corpse" would doubtless reappear in a different guise the following day.

After lunch, Molly's guests gathered around the summerhouse to collect their second set of notes, revealing in more detail their part in the plot.

It was a warm afternoon. (No one would ever claim it was swelteringly hot in Mallaig.) But the sun was out. Bees were buzzing in and out of the pink and yellow flowers. There was a gentle breeze.

And Mr Potter was still moaning.

Raynes heard him say, "Do we really have to go through with all this?"

And Molly's sharp reply: "People have paid for this! A lot of money. They enjoy it – and so do I. Don't be such a drag!"

Raynes smiled to himself.

It would have been better to have left Mr Potter at home.

* * * *

Suzanne was standing beside the sundial chatting to Lady Emily.

"Have you always lived in the village?"

"All my life. I was born and bred here."

"In one of those lovely little cottages beside the river?"

"No. In Nasse House."

"You lived here?"

"All my family did. But when my father died, I had to pay the most horrendous death duties. You've no idea! The only way I could pay them was by selling the estate."

"That must have been a terrible wrench."

"It was." Lady Emily allowed a tear to roll down her cheek. "But I still pretend it's mine. The owner's often away and I come up here quite often."

"Do you like Sir Stanley?"

"Not at all! I think he's the most frightful, jumped-up, ignorant, self-made man. But, of course, he's got money and that pays the bills. It also provides jobs for people in the village. But that doesn't mean we like him."

Stanley Dixon was standing only a few yards away, trying to work his charm on Dorothy West. He heard every word she said. Sadly, he turned his head and looked at her.

Lady Emily smiled broadly.

"Good afternoon. Sir Stanley!"

* * * *

The owner of Nasse House turned back to Mrs West.

"I'm sorry about that. Still thinks she's Lady of the Manor. What were you saying?"

"I was saying that my husband once bought a painting from you."

"Really?"

"I didn't recognize you when I first saw you at the Fete; but my notes tell me we've met before."

"D'you remember the painting?"

"Yes. It was a Renoir."

Mr Dixon looked as if he was skating on thin ice – as indeed he was.

"Which one?"

"*La vie en rose*, I think it was."

Mr Dixon felt a compelling desire to move away as quickly as possible. He had another appointment . . . It was time to take the dog for a walk . . . Inspector Raynes wished to see him . . . But if he ran away too quickly, it might appear suspicious. So instead, he waxed poetic.

"Always enhances a room, a Renoir. The rich colour, the texture, the sheer joie-de-vivre in every brush stroke. Have you still got it?"

"No, we sold it."

"I hope you got a good price for it?"

"No," said Mrs West, her eyes ice-cold behind her rimless glasses. "It was a fake. We got peanuts."

Mr Dixon tried to appear surprised.

"A fake? You should have let me know."

"We tried; but you'd moved on. We were told you had gone abroad."

"I may have done. Much of my work is done in the States."

"D'you sell fakes over there?"

"I can assure you, my dear, this comes as a great surprise. We are a highly reputable company. I can't think what could have happened. Nothing like this has ever happened before . . ."

Mrs West smiled a chilly smile.

"Are you sure? The man at Sotheby's said he'd seen at least three copies of the painting. All by the same artist." Mrs West looked towards the summerhouse. "I wonder who it could be."

* * * *

Inspector Potter took Kenny to one side.

"Come on, admit it! You've been supplying her with drugs for years."

Dr Savage was pained at the allegation.

"I have to maintain the confidentiality of my patients," he said.

"Not when they're dead! The time has come for you to admit that you knowingly supplied her with hallucinogenic drugs which were used at her . . . 'private parties'. There's no use denying it. I've been down to the local chemist and looked at his records. I've seen what you've been prescribing."

Kenny put his thumbs behind his red braces.

"I had no alternative."

"Of course you had. You could always have said no."

Kenny shook his head.

"She had me by the short and curlies. Said that if I refused her, she'd report me to the General Medical Council for professional misconduct."

"Blackmail?"

"Very much so. But once I'd given way, all she had to do was tighten the screw."

"You must have resented it?"

"I did. But what could I do? I wasn't going to get myself struck off because of her."

"It could have provoked you to murder."

Kenny looked at Inspector Potter.

"It could. And maybe it did. But you'll have a damn hard job proving it."

* * * *

Lady Emily had no doubts as to who was responsible for Rose's death.

"You're just jealous!" she said to Gloria. "You couldn't stand her. You knew that if your husband got the slightest chance, he'd have given you the heave and married the goose that laid his golden eggs. All that crap about being 'only business partners' . . . Everyone knows they've been lovers for years."

Gloria was bemused by her attack.

"I think you're reading too much into a couple of cards."

Lady Emily's eyes gleamed with malice.

"She saw it in the crystal ball. She knew you had it in for her; but she never expected to be attacked in such a public place."

Gloria shook her head sadly.

"I was nowhere near the summerhouse. I was on the work stall. There are at least five people who will vouch for the fact that I was there the entire afternoon."

"But it was your knife that killed her."

"It most certainly wasn't!"

"I saw it in your sitting room!"

Raynes, who was acting as the proverbial fly on the wall, smiled. Molly's guests had entered fully into the spirit of the game. The origin of the dagger was proving a most effective red herring.

"If anyone's jealous," said Gloria, "it's you. You can't stand us being in this house. You'll do anything to get us out. If anyone killed Rose, it was you – eliminating a dangerous rival! Now, you hope, by accusing me, you can get rid of me and get your claws into my husband. You'll lie . . . you'll cheat . . . you'll kill to get what you want. As a matter of fact, I saw you scurrying away from the summerhouse with Rose's handbag."

"You couldn't see that from the work stall."

"You'd be surprised what I could see," said Gloria, "and I didn't need a crystal ball to do it."

* * * *

"I notice that you didn't deny the possibility of divine judgement."

Mrs West had cornered Canon Larkin beside the ornamental pool. She wondered whether he was contemplating suicide. He had spent several minutes staring at his reflection in the water.

He looked up.

"It would be foolish to deny the possibility. She pushed her paganism to dangerous lengths. It was more than a game to her."

"It sounds terribly exciting – everyone dancing around naked and having drunken orgies in the moonlight."

"I suppose – to an outsider – such things sound quite tempting. But it has a corrosive effect on the people involved. Their characters change. Marriages are destroyed. Superstition induces fear." He looked sadly at the gentle ripples on the water. "A child went missing . . . October 31st last year . . . Never been seen again."

"Hallowe'en?"

"Yes. Most people think it's completely harmless. Witches on broomsticks. Tricks and treats. Pumpkin lanterns and all that. But behind the mumbo-jumbo, there are serious people worshipping Satan and offering human sacrifice."

"You think Mrs Lee was involved in that?"

Canon Larkin shrugged his shoulders.

"No one knows for certain. Everything was hushed up. The police didn't do anything." Canon Larkin looked round cautiously to make sure no one was listening. "Of course that didn't surprise me. She has some very influential people in her group – lawyers, doctors, landowners, even the police . . ."

"Inspector Potter?"

"I'm afraid so. His wife left him. She was disgusted with his behaviour. I hoped that would bring him to his senses – but it didn't. He still proceeded to dabble in the occult. I believe he tried to conduct some of his investigations through his contacts in the spirit world."

Mrs West looked surprised.

"D'you think they'll help him solve this case?"

"Judging by his success so far, I should think they're working for the opposition! It's my personal opinion that Rose's death may have been a last desperate attempt to escape from her clutches."

* * * *

Dr Savage asked the question which should have been asked long before: "Who will benefit from her death? Who gets the lolly?"

He put the question to the owner of Nasse House who probably knew more about Rose's finances than anyone else. But Stanley was not all that sure.

"I think it'll be a close-run thing between the Pagan Society and the Inland Revenue. She often talked about writing a will, but I don't think she ever got down to doing it."

"How much had she got stashed away?"

"Over half a million."

Kenny whistled in amazement.

So much for poor artists living in garrets!

"And no relatives? No next of kin?"

"None that I know of."

Kenny looked thoughtful. His briefing notes told a different story. Rather hesitantly, he said, "Didn't she have a daughter?"

Stanley seemed genuinely surprised.

"She never said anything to me about it."

"I'm sure she did. She'd been given away. Adopted."

Stanley shook his head.

"It's news to me."

Kenny imparted more privileged information.

"That was why she came down to Devon. To be nearer to her."
"She knew where she was?"
"I believe so. But I don't think the girl knew she was her mother."
"That would put a different complexion on it."
"A rich heiress?"
Stanley smiled. "Almost worth a murder . . ."
Kenny grinned. " . . . or a second marriage!"

* * * *

Stanley went straight to his wife.
"You've no idea what that peasant has just told me! He says that Rose had a daughter! She had her adopted but she's living down here in Devon."
Gloria looked thunderstruck.
"That's blown it.! She'll get her hands on all her money."
"I don't think she knows anything about it – not yet anyway."
"She will. If Dr Savage knows, the story'll soon get around. He's not going to stand by and watch us walking away with all her money."
"The will is fairly explicit."
"It's forged – and you know who did it."
Stanley sighed deeply. "What are we going to do?"
"Turn the tables. Quickly. Before she points a finger at us."
"But we don't know who she is . . ."
Gloria looked at her husband sadly. "I should have thought it was obvious."
Stanley's eyes lit up. "Suzanne?"
"Who else?"

* * * *

There was a brief pause for afternoon tea.
The clink of china cups on saucers. Spoons dropped on the lawn. Voices saying: "I'll have two lumps . . . Thank you."
"No milk for me . . ."
"Salmon and cucumber sandwiches? I'll have another.

They're so good . . ."

Dorothy West sought out Kenny Savage.

"I was interested to hear your birthday was on March 15th."

Kenny laughed.

"I was told to keep mum about it. Might incriminate me."

"It's an important day for me too."

"Is it your birthday?"

Kenny bit greedily into a large cream cake.

"No. It's the day my husband died."

"Oh, I am sorry, love. Was it recently?"

Mrs West nodded.

"This year. He died of a broken heart."

"In love with someone else, was he?"

"No. He discovered that all his pictures were fakes . . ."

Kenny had assumed that Mrs West was talking about her real-life husband. He suddenly realized she was still playing the game.

" . . . He'd spent thousands of pounds building up his collection. He was so proud of it. And he used the pictures as collateral for his business. When things got tight, he tried to sell one. It was then he discovered the awful truth. They were all fakes. He was so distressed, he shot himself . . ."

"Get away!"

Kenny was so shocked that he put his cake to his nose rather than his mouth. He wiped off the cream with his napkin and, in the process, upset his tea into his saucer.

"I hope you sued them."

"We tried to but they were a very slippery bunch. However, I found out who painted the pictures."

Kenny looked at the summerhouse.

"Her?"

"I wrote to her; but, of course, she never replied."

Kenny got the point.

"So you didn't turn up at this Fete by accident? Didn't just happen to be passing by?"

Mrs West shook her head.

"No. I intended to confront her. Catch her unawares. But, by the time I went in to see her, she was dead!"

"Well, I never!" said Kenny. "And what time was that?"
"Half past three."

* * * *

Molly discovered Suzanne crying – or, at least, pretending to cry – in a distant corner of the hotel garden. She was sitting on an elaborate ironwork bench beside a tall, dark hedge. Molly instantly adopted her role as Ariadne Oliver.

"My poor dear!" she said. "What on earth has happened?"

Suzanne looked up – her eyes full of tears.

"She was my mother."

"Who?"

"The woman who's been killed."

Molly put an arm round her shoulders.

"That must have been a terrible shock for you."

"I never even knew she was my mother."

"Who told you?"

"Lady Gloria. She was really nasty about it. She said that I'd deliberately killed her in order to get her money." Suzanne put a handkerchief to her eyes. "I didn't even know she had money."

Molly put on her most comforting voice. "I wouldn't listen to her. She's just jealous."

"Jealous?"

"Because Stanley showed more interest in Rose than he did in her. The only reason Gloria kept quiet was because of all the commission he made out of selling your mother's paintings. Now that she's dead, she can say what she wants."

"I think she's horrible."

* * * *

Sir Stanley was dispensing the same poison.

"I think I should tell you, Inspector, that our local reporter, Miss Suzanne Tempest, was seen in the summer house at 3.00 this afternoon. You may not know who she is, but I am reliably informed that she is Mrs Lee's daughter. She was adopted by a family in Torquay many years ago and that was why Mrs Lee came down to Devon – to be near her. I am told that she was adopted on March 15th – hence the circle round that date in the calendar. My wife and I are convinced that she killed her mother so that she could lay claim to her estate. Now what are you going to do about it? Are you going to arrest her?"

Mr Potter looked at Mr Dixon with amused contempt.

"Well, for a starter," he said, "I was in the summerhouse at 3.00pm and there was no sign of Miss Tempest. I think you had better check your facts before you make such wild allegations."

* * * *

As the afternoon went on, Bernard Potter found the game becoming increasingly unpleasant.

Dorothy West was the next one to lay into him.

"I wrote to you . . . but you didn't reply."

"You made serious allegations against Sir Stanley Dixon."

"I accused him of fraud – of knowingly selling fake paintings. He's been doing it for several years. I think it's high time he was charged and brought to justice."

"You gave no evidence."

"I told you what the man at Sotheby's said."

"The matter is under investigation."

Mrs West sneered.

"I very much doubt it. You wouldn't do anything to upset your high-priestess – or whatever she's called. Canon Larkin tells me you were completely besotted with her. Even when your wife left you, you still didn't realize the hold she had over you."

Mr Potter reacted angrily.

"I don't think Canon Larkin should be discussing the private lives of members of his congregation with complete strangers!"

"Don't you think he has a right to be concerned about these disgusting pagan rituals being performed in his parish? What about that child who was sacrificed last October? Is he supposed to ignore such things?"

"There's no truth in that! None whatsoever!"

Although Inspector Potter appeared to be angry, his notes

suggested that there might be some truth in the allegation.

"I think the time has come for the general public to make their feelings known."

"Is that why you came down here? To take the law into your own hands?"

"Certainly not. I came here to confront Mrs Lee. To get her to admit that she painted those pictures. That Stanley Dixon sold them knowingly on her behalf." Mrs West opened her handbag.

"You see? I brought a tape recorder with me. I got a full confession. She didn't know our conversation was being recorded. Once this gets into the hands of senior officials at Scotland Yard, Stanley Dixon will go down for several years!"

There was a glint of triumph in her eyes.

"You'd better give me that tape."

Mrs West laughed.

"And let you destroy it? Don't be so stupid. Once this gets into the hands of the authorities, you'll be for the high jump as well!"

* * * *

"She knew she was going to be murdered . . ."

Lady Emily looked over her shoulder to make sure no one could hear her.

" . . . and she knew it was a woman who was going to do it."

"Really?"

Canon Larkin was surprised to be receiving such confidences from Lady Emily. Was she trying to infiltrate yet another red herring into the proceedings? Or was her conscience troubling her?

"That's why she came to my house with her crystal ball. She wanted to know if I could see what she was seeing."

"And did you?"

"No. All I could see was a red mist. But she saw it quite clearly. It was . . ." she whispered in Canon Larkin's ear, " . . . Stanley's wife."

"Lady Gloria?"

"Sh! She saw her coming up behind her and attacking her. She saw it quite clearly."

"But Gloria didn't go into the summerhouse."

"That's what she says. But I saw her going over to the house – at about half past three!"

Canon Larkin shrugged his shoulders.

"Well, I didn't see her at all. I was too busy on the bric-a-brac."

It was as good excuse as any.

Lady Emily leaned closer.

"Are you sure you didn't sell her that dagger?"

"The murder weapon?"

"I saw it on your counter. On the right hand side – beside the cutlery and plates."

"I don't remember selling it."

"You might have used it yourself!" said Lady Emily provocatively.

Canon Larkin shook his head.

"You've just said that she knew it was a woman!"

Lady Emily looked coy.

"She could have been wrong, you know!"

* * * *

Much to Kenny's delight, Suzanne finally turned to him for advice.

"Dr Savage, you seem to know more about this than anyone."

Kenny was modest. "It's not me, love," he said. "It's these notes." He waved his briefing folder in the air. "Without them, I'd be as dim as the proverbial glow-worm's armpit." He stooped to pick up several sheets of paper which had fallen on the lawn. He put them back in his folder and smiled a false smile at Inspector Raynes who was passing nearby. "Anyway, Sue, what can I do to help you?"

"It's about my mother. I didn't know she was my mother. Not till this afternoon."

Kenny reflected that there were quite a few things he hadn't known until that afternoon, including how much more respect you were accorded if you were a doctor rather than a haulage contractor.

"Did she tell you when you went to get your cards read?"

"No, she didn't say a word. It was Gloria who told me – very brutally. She accused me of killing my mother in order to get her money!"

"You'd never met her before?"

"No. She was a complete stranger."

Kenny wondered how much he should say.

"I was a witness to her will . . ." he said slowly. "I think she was frightened of dying suddenly and unprepared. She said, 'I leave all my estate to my daughter, Suzanne'."

"She knew who I was?"

"She knew your name and address, but she may not have known your face. I think she felt terribly guilty about giving you away."

"It was a rotten thing to do."

"Well, I dare say there was some good reason at the time." He looked at Suzanne in a speculative manner, wishing this was real life rather than play-acting. "Anyway, she's left you quite a bit of money."

"Has she?"

Kenny nodded.

"How much?"

"About half a million smackers!"

"Half a million? Gosh!"

"Not that you'll see all that much of it. I reckon dear old Stanley and his missus have been planning to pinch it. As you know, they're heading off for a Caribbean cruise. The money'll probably go with them."

"The beasts!" She looked at Kenny. "What d'you think I should do?"

Kenny laughed.

All sorts of erotic visions passed through his mind.

"Well," he said, "there's a question! I could think of a number of lovely things you could do!" He pulled himself together. "You could spread a few rumours of your own. You could say that you saw Stanley cutting out that calendar . . . Lady Emily getting rid of a pair of blood-stained gloves . . . Canon Larkin losing his pistol . . . No, you'd better not say that!"

Suzanne gave Kenny a grateful smile – and moved on.

Poor girl! She would never know – and he hadn't the heart to tell her – that not only was Rose Lee her mother, but Stanley Dixon was her father! Her genes were hopelessly flawed – but (Kenny's eyes raked over every inch of her luscious body) her figure was divine!

8. *Hoopla*

Molly looked round the Highland lounge to see if everyone was there. She did a quick count. Yes, everyone had survived – even Bernard – though he seemed to be sulking.

She looked at her watch.

"Now we've had four hours on Mrs Rose Lee," she said. "Quite long enough to comprehend the picture, to consider the complexities of the case and to draw a final conclusion."

She handed out the final briefing envelopes.

"One of you is the murderer. You will have to lie like mad to convince us of your innocence." She looked sharply at Lady Emily. "Don't let anyone see the contents of your envelope! When you have read them, hand them back to the Inspector."

Raynes went round collecting the envelopes. He looked at their faces, hoping to see signs of instant guilt. But everyone looked bemused. Perhaps they had all done it? No, that would be ridiculous!

"Dr Savage?"

"Why pick on me?"

"I believe Mrs Lee had put you in a very difficult position. Demanding that you supply her with drugs – but with the ever-present threat that, if you stopped, she would report you to the General Medical Council. Many murders have been committed by those who tried to silence their blackmailers. I should have thought that was an excellent motive for murder."

Kenny assumed an air of injured innocence.

"Ah, no. Quite the contrary. You see, as a doctor, I have to abide by the Hypocritic oath . . ."

"Peasant!" murmured Gloria.

" . . . to preserve life – not to destroy it. As you say, Mrs Lee placed me in an impossible position. I cannot deny that her death was a great relief to me; but at no point did I consider murder. I never went anywhere near the summerhouse. I was extremely busy on the bottle stall all afternoon."

Kenny did not sound entirely convincing.

Molly looked at Dorothy West.

"I don't think that's entirely true. Didn't you carry a letter down to the summerhouse?"

"Ah, well. That was a lot earlier. About two o'clock."

"And did you call back later to recover the letter?"

"No."

Molly turned to Dorothy West.

"I believe you were the person who wrote the letter?"

"Yes, I was. I was deeply distressed about the fake paintings – which resulted in my husband's tragic death."

She seemed to choke a little on the words.

"As you know, I tried to contact the dealer who had sold the pictures – but he was a very slippery customer." She looked at Mr Dixon reproachfully.

"I had written to the local police inspector but received no reply. So I decided the only thing I could do was to confront Rose herself. I had been told she was the actual painter but I didn't know what she looked like or where I could find her. So I asked this kind man on the bottle stall if he knew Mrs Lee and whether he could deliver a letter to her. Once I saw where he had gone, I knew where to find her."

"And did you speak to her?"

"I did. I told her what damage her deceit had done; but she said that she had never realized that Mr Dixon would pass them off as originals. He had told her that one or two rich Americans had asked for copies. So she had done them – and not been paid much for her efforts."

Stanley Dixon bristled with anger.

"That's a lie! She got twenty thousand for each of them."
Dorothy West shook her head sadly.
"And my husband paid £450,000."
Molly asked, "Did Rose show any remorse?"
Mrs West looked thoughtful.
"Yes, I think she did."
"But she didn't offer you any money – any compensation?"
"No. She said she'd have to speak to Mr Dixon."
Molly looked at Stanley.
"Did she?"
"As a matter of fact, she did. She asked me to call in at the summerhouse to discuss the letter. And whilst I was there, she gave me a reading."
"You weren't very busy?"
"No. I was weighing the pig."
He looked at Lady Emily.
"No need to get personal!"
Everyone laughed.
"Did she give you the letter?" Molly asked.
"No, she hung on to it."
"And what did you decide to do?"
"Nothing."
"Not a penny?"
Stanley shook his head.
"You realize," said Molly, "that this refusal may have driven Mrs West to kill Rose? She would have felt so helpless – so angry."
Stanley shrugged his shoulders.
Dorothy West intervened.
"But what had I to gain from killing Mrs Lee? Certainly no money. Whilst she was alive, I could have sued both of them for passing off counterfeit goods. Now she is dead, I am unlikely to get anything."
"Very true," said Stanley.
Molly turned back to Dorothy:
"Is that your defence?"
"If I need one."
"Everyone needs one," said Molly firmly. "Especially . . .

Lady Emily." She looked at the plump beauty lolling in a deep armchair. "I believe you have shown a great deal of hostility towards this woman?"

"Not at all," said Lady Emily dismissively. "She and I have become the greatest of friends."

"That's not how most people see it."

"People see what they want to see. But I tell you – Rose shared her secrets with me."

"What secrets?" sneered Sir Stanley.

"Her secret fears – of being killed by that infatuated fool!" She pointed dramatically at Inspector Potter. "He was hopelessly in love with her. He had threatened her; 'If you don't marry me, I will kill you!' She was so frightened that she asked me to come and spend the night with her at Honeysuckle Cottage. I went prepared! I took my father's old pistol with me. If he had set foot inside the door, he'd have been blasted to kingdom come."

Inspector Potter managed to keep his voice calm.

"D'you have a licence for that pistol?"

"Of course not."

"It's a tissue of lies," said Sir Stanley. "Everyone knows that she went round the village calling Rose 'the gilded tart'. It was one of her ways of getting at me. She made her life hell."

"So," said Molly, "if *you* had been murdered, the prime suspect would be Lady Emily?"

"Most certainly."

"But why would she want to kill Rose?"

Molly looked at Gloria.

"I imagine your motives are more obvious?"

"I don't see why. I've put up with the situation for almost twenty years. I knew what my husband felt for her. He was only interested in her as a money-making machine. He didn't care about her as a person. Who would? With a body like that?"

Molly felt that this was unnecessarily cruel.

"Surely," she said, "you must have experienced a lot of humiliation, knowing that she was the source of all your wealth?"

Gloria shrugged her shoulders.

"As I've said before: 'why kill the goose that lays the golden eggs'?"

"Perhaps she'd stopped laying?" suggested Kenny. "Too drugged up? The sort of things she was taking often destroy people's creativity."

"A good point," said Molly.

She turned to Mr Potter.

"You must have been aware of this?"

"Well, I knew she was obtaining drugs, but it was only recently that I discovered that she was getting them on prescription and that he was providing them in large quantities."

He looked accusingly at Dr Savage.

Molly asked, "Is there any truth in Lady Emily's accusations that you threatened to kill Rose?"

Bernard was impressive in his denunciation.

"None whatsoever. I may have been a weak man. Possibly a fool. I admit that my marriage had broken down and that I spent a great deal of time with Rose. She was fun . . . she was bohemian . . ."

"A cheap grind," said Gloria.

" . . . I found her lifestyle attractive. I enjoyed all the rituals, the secrecy, the sex. I felt quite liberated. But I was fond of Rose as a person. I tried to protect her. Once I saw that second letter from Mrs West, I knew she was in danger. I warned her that she was vulnerable; but she wouldn't take me seriously. If she had listened to me, this murder would never have happened."

Molly turned to the reporter.

"Suzanne?"

"Well, I don't really come into all this. If I hadn't been sent by my local newspaper, I wouldn't have been there. I knew nothing about Mrs Lee. I didn't know she was my mother. And I was certainly not aware that she had left me a lot of money. Even had I known any of these things, I would still have had no desire to kill her. I'm a very peace-loving person."

Molly decided that she couldn't let her get away with such a bland denial.

"I don't think that you've told anyone that you used to work – perhaps still do work – for a private detective agency and that you used them to track down your real parents?"

"There was nothing about that in my notes."

"I think you'll find there was. Nor have you told us that Stanley Dixon was your father!"

"Good God! How awful!"

Suzanne's reaction was so spontaneous – and so crushing – that it was difficult to believe she was holding anything back.

"Didn't Kenny tell you?"

"No."

Molly continued. "I think you have also failed to tell us that you are deep in debt; that you are currently owing the credit card companies £70,000. Rose's money would have been very handy, wouldn't it?"

"I still wouldn't have killed her."

Molly looked at her notes.

"And finally, Canon Larkin?"

The cleric put his fingers together – arched, as if in prayer – and looked heavenwards for inspiration.

"I know that in most detective stories, the murderer is often the person who is least suspected – someone who has no obvious motive; but in real life, the villain of the piece is very often family, friend or lover. I believe that in seventy per cent of murders, this is the case. Now, I am no relation of Mrs Lee; I am certainly not her lover and I cannot be classed as a close friend. She has done me no personal harm. My opposition to her concerns her disgraceful private life, which has completely divided the village.

"Like Dr Savage, I find in her death a great sense of relief – a burden lifted. I feel that there has been an element of judgement – of cleansing. We shall now have a chance of restoring Christian morality in the village."

"Hear, hear!" said Lady Emily, looking daggers at Mr Potter.

Canon Larkin cast a pitying smile in her direction.

"You mustn't think I believe any of this crap; but that is what a vicar is supposed to say! My duty is to preach against evil – not to murder the ungodly."

"But you had access to the murder weapon. It was on your stall. You say that you didn't sell it to anyone. I put it to you that you used it yourself."

Mr Larkin did not look particularly perturbed.

"If I am going to be found guilty of killing Mrs Lee, it would at least be in a good cause – and leave the world a cleaner place."

"Well," said Molly, "that is the case for the defence. One of you is a murderer and I must say you have disguised your guilt extremely well. If I had not had the benefit of knowing who the murderer was, I should never have guessed."

Molly drew out a plain pad of paper from her briefcase.

"Now we come to our final decision. Who is guilty? And who is not? *J'accuse . . .*"

There was a buzz of excitement. Everyone was ready for the final dénouement. Even Mr Potter seemed to have cheered up. His purgatory was almost over.

Molly looked around the room.

"I think we'll keep to the same order. Dr Savage?"

Kenny felt quite confident about going first. He had long since made up his mind.

"Well, Madam Chairman, I'm sorry to point the finger at such a distinguished local figure, but my money's on Stan. All the way through this shameful business, he's shown himself to be a liar and a cheat. He's sold fake pictures at grossly inflated prices; he's drawn up dodgy wills; he's deceived his long-suffering wife; he's even sold life insurance policies! I'd say he was capable of anything – even murder."

Mr Dixon did not look very pleased.

"That's the last time I give you a box of Pouilly-Fuissé for your bottle stall!"

"Dorothy?"

"Oh, I think Mr Potter is the villain of the piece. Things were getting too hot for him. His entire professional future was at risk. He had to get out of it somehow. He hoped others would take the blame."

"Thank you," said Molly. "Sir Stanley?"

"Ever since I came to Nasse House, Lady Emily has been my

sworn enemy. She has made no secret of it. At every opportunity she has attacked me with gossip and innuendo, but I believe . . ." Mr Dixon paused. "I believe she is basically harmless!"

All the wind went out of Lady Emily's sails.

"Oh!" she said.

Mr Dixon smiled.

"I feel," he said, "that we should not lose sight of the clear financial motives behind this killing. I had nothing to gain by killing Rose but I had a lot to lose. Whereas, to a scheming little money-grubber, it was the chance of a lifetime. I accuse Suzanne Tempest."

"Your own daughter?"

"Says who?"

Molly was pleasantly surprised at the way things were going.

"Lady Emily, can we expect you to be equally gracious?"

"Good heavens, no!" said the former owner of Nasse House. "Stanley Dixon is an out-and-out shit, but I don't think he did the dirty on Rose. I think it was either Gloria or that randy little policeman."

"You can't have both."

"Well . . . Potter!"

"Gloria?"

"I'm not so sure about Mrs West. I'm sorry about this, Dorothy, but it seems to me that all this trouble began with you writing a letter to Inspector Potter. Then you turned up at the Fete – with another letter. Accusations – terrible accusations – have been made against my dear husband who would never hurt a fly. I think you brought all this trouble upon us. I can't think why, but I hold you responsible."

"Bernard?"

"I share Dr Savage's opinion – and for the same reasons. It has to be Stanley Dixon."

"Suzanne?"

Suzanne twisted the gold bangle on her wrist.

"Well, I suppose any one of us could have done it. Everyone had a motive. I think that Kenny did her a lot of harm, giving her all those drugs. And I think that Canon Larkin hated her;

but I don't think he would have killed her. Bernard wanted to protect her . . . Stanley to exploit her . . ."

"Go on!"

"It's very difficult, isn't it . . .?" A long pause. Then: "Gloria – because she's so spiteful and nasty. I know we've been told she was on the work stall all afternoon. But she did it – somehow."

"And Canon Larkin?"

"Well, of all my parishioners, the one who causes the most trouble . . . the one who always lies . . . the one who can never forgive . . . the one who is full of bile and suppressed anger . . ." He turned to the woman on his right. "Lady Emily it is!"

Lady Emily almost squawked in anger.

"Just you wait! I'll poison your cats!"

"That would simply prove my point."

Molly consulted her notes.

"That makes two for Bernard and two for Stanley. One for Gloria, Dorothy, Suzanne and Lady Emily. Canon Larkin and Dr Savage seem to have escaped suspicion."

She turned to Inspector Raynes. "Perhaps you would tell us who is right?"

Raynes stood up. He felt better standing up.

"Let us – once again – consider the situation. Mrs Lee feared that she was about to be murdered. She said that she had seen this terrible event in her crystal ball. She hoped that perhaps she had been mistaken and so she came to Lady Emily to see if she could see anything. But all she could see was a red mist."

"Probably drunk!" said Gloria.

Lady Emily blushed angrily.

Raynes looked reprovingly at Gloria.

"It was you whom Rose saw in her ball."

"It's a load of rubbish."

"Lady Emily took Rose's fears seriously. She wondered what she could do to protect her. Because she had little confidence in Inspector Potter, she invited an old friend down from London – Mrs Oliver." Raynes smiled at Molly.

"This lady has always enjoyed detective work, so she put her on the work stall during the Garden Fete so that she could keep an eye on Gloria during the afternoon. Mrs Oliver reported that Gloria did not leave the stall till 3.35pm when she said she must go to the toilet. As she was making her way back to the house, she saw Lady Emily hurrying away from the summerhouse, carrying Rose's handbag. Lady Emily has told us that, when she left the summerhouse, Rose was dead.

"Now it seems that Inspector Potter had received some information about fake pictures being sold by Stanley Dixon. Bernard would have been aware that Rose had painted those pictures. The allegations suggested fraud on a massive scale. Most unprofessionally, he warned Mrs Lee – and I would expect that she then spoke to Mr Dixon. Am I right?"

Stanley nodded.

"I imagine that, at this point, you and Gloria decided that it was high time to go on a long ocean cruise." Raynes smiled briefly. "But you knew that one word from Rose would bring the police chasing after you. Perhaps the goose which laid the golden eggs had outlived her usefulness? Perhaps the time had come to silence Rose so that there was no way she could testify against you?

"You had already forged a will, suggesting that Rose had left you all her earthly goods. It therefore came as a rather nasty shock when Dr Savage mentioned that Rose had a daughter. Perhaps she had left everything to her?

"We now come to the day of the actual Fete. Rose was installed in the summerhouse in her colourful costume. And Kenny was given a letter by a complete stranger who asked him to take it to Mrs Lee. At 2.00pm – or shortly after – Dr Savage visited the lady in the summerhouse – although he has spent most of the afternoon denying it.

"Rose was naturally devastated by the letter, which accused her of fraud. She was even more upset when Dorothy West arrived – supposedly to have her fortune told – but in fact to confront her with the evil her paintings had caused. What could Rose do? Of course she blamed Stanley, little knowing that her words were being secretly recorded.

"As soon as Mrs West had departed, Rose's chief aim would have been to warn Sir Stanley. Probably she asked Lady Emily to contact him immediately. I would also imagine that she told Lady Emily the contents of the letter. Did she?"

"She did."

"Mr Dixon came hotfoot to the summerhouse – not, as he has said, to have his cards read – but to discover how much damage had been done. He must have seen that this was the ideal moment to kill Rose and lay the blame on this unknown woman who had caused her so much distress.

"Stanley then spoke to Bernard . . .?"

Mr Potter nodded.

" . . . and he too made his way to the summerhouse to comfort his beloved. We are told that he was there between 3.00 and 3.15pm. He must have been very conscious of the dangers he faced. Mrs West had spoken to him and reminded him that he had done nothing about her allegations. She also refused to hand over the tape. She said that she would put it into the hands of senior officials at Scotland Yard. His own career was in jeopardy.

"Now we have been led to believe that the murder was committed at ten past three – just at the time Bernard was with Rose. Did he kill her?"

Lady Emily nodded enthusiastically.

Raynes was cautious.

"We must be careful not to jump to conclusions. Other potential assassins were waiting in the wings. An ornamental dagger had vanished from the bric-a-brac stall. Dr Savage may well have decided that this was a good moment to get rid of his blackmailer. Perhaps he too had read Mrs West's letter."

"The envelope was open."

"I thought so," said Raynes. "But then again. Canon Larkin might have decided to get rid of the resident satanist whose pagan rites were polluting his parish. The murder weapon was to hand. Nothing could stop him. Or again – Suzanne – having been told that Rose was her mother and a tidy bit of money was coming her way – might have seen this as the ideal opportunity to solve all her financial problems.

"Any number of people could have decided that this was the moment to strike . . ."

The atmosphere in the Highland lounge was getting more tense.

"And so we come back to Lady Emily, who is no longer at the Tombola stall. The fact that she was seen carrying Rose's handbag means that she visited the summerhouse some time after 3.15pm. It seems clear to me that Lady Emily set the hands of the watch to ten past three – and then she removed the battery from the watch – her watch – in order to incriminate Mr Potter.

"She also went through the Tarot cards and placed 'The Lovers' on the table to suggest that Sir Stanley was having an affair with Rose. Her plan was to confuse the police and draw attention away from herself."

"What a dirty trick!" said Gloria.

Lady Emily said nothing.

"Mrs West told Dr Savage that when she returned to the summerhouse at half past three, Mrs Lee was already dead. This raises one or two questions. 'Did Stanley return to the summerhouse after Bernard had left?'"

Stanley shook his head.

"Interesting! So we come to my second question: 'Did Mrs West pay her second visit before or after Lady Emily?'"

No one moved.

"Well, let me put it another way." Raynes looked at Dorothy West. "Was Rose's handbag still there when you called?"

"No."

Everyone looked at Lady Emily.

Raynes allowed them a few moments to think the matter over. Then he returned to Dorothy West:

"You're a liar! The bag was still there – and your letter was in the handbag. You came back to collect that letter so that there would be no evidence that you had ever been in the summerhouse – or even at the Fete. You could have walked quietly away.

"This was a revenge killing. You held Rose responsible for your husband's death. She knew that the murderer would be a woman. It was not Gloria – but you.

"You told me this morning that you had once had a dagger

like the one which killed Rose. That was perfectly true. You stole it from the bric-a-brac counter. Popped it into your handbag when no one was looking."

Mrs West's face went red. But she said nothing.

"On your first visit, you went down to the summerhouse – not to confront Rose – but to spy out the land. She gave you a reading. You had a chance to rest your feet. As you said, you found the situation very entertaining. But, even if you had a tape in your handbag, there was no tape-recording.

"On your second visit, you probably asked Rose if there was any significance in the date – March 15th. A special date to you – and, of course, to Kenny. Mrs Lee looked deep into her crystal ball. She may have seen something – who knows? You probably asked her if you could come round and have a look. As you stood behind her, you stabbed her in the back.

"Then you put the calendar up on the wall. You circled the date with Rose's lipstick. A curious thing to do; but as Dorothy Sayers once said: 'Murder must advertise'." He paused. "Then you left the summerhouse. No one saw you. The perfect crime! But if you care to empty your handbag, I think we shall find both the letter and Rose's lipstick – which will prove conclusively that you were there."

Very reluctantly, Mrs West opened her bag. There were the two tell-tale items.

Raynes smiled.

"When did you put them there?"

"Whilst you were having afternoon tea on the lawn."

Mrs West tried to look shocked.

"Is nothing sacred?"

Molly said, "You're surrounded by very ruthless people."

Stanley Dixon came over and shook Raynes' hand.

"Well done, Inspector. I'm glad you got me off the hook."

Raynes laughed.

"You didn't really deserve it!"

Molly reached into her bag.

"A bottle of champagne for the winner!"

Gloria received her prize with obvious pleasure.

"I shall enjoy this."

Molly turned to Lady Emily. "And where is Mrs Lee's handbag?"

"It's here."

Lady Emily reached down into the depths of the armchair.

"So you did steal it!" said Gloria.

"Don't you accuse me of being a thief!" said Lady Emily angrily.

Molly intervened quickly.

"Girls! Girls!" she said. "The game is over."

"Not for me it isn't."

Lady Emily unzipped the handbag – and much to everyone's surprise, pulled out her father's old pistol.

"I'm sick of all your sneers! I've put up with them for long enough!"

She aimed the pistol at Gloria and pulled the trigger. There was a loud explosion – and a smell of cordite.

Gloria registered that she had not been hit. Lady Emily had fired a blank. She was still alive.

Lady Emily grinned happily, wiped the pistol clean of fingerprints and handed it back to Molly.

Everyone breathed a deep sigh of relief. For a moment they had thought it was for real; but it had only been play-acting. With the release of emotion came a well-deserved round of applause.

Molly turned to Gloria.

"I'm sorry to have frightened you; but we thought it would make the ending more exciting."

"Exciting?" said Gloria. "That woman's a bloody psychopath!"

9. *Hide and seek*

After dinner, Molly's party retired to the library for coffee and liqueurs. The library was a small, cosy room in the oldest part of the hotel. Two walls of the room were filled from floor to ceiling with books. A third wall contained two windows looking down on to the garden. The final wall was panelled in oak, surrounding a large stone fireplace. Raynes decided that this would form the perfect backdrop to his speech. But, first, he would have a small whisky.

Four or five other guests from the hotel had asked if they could listen to the Inspector and Molly welcomed them in.

With every chair filled and two to each window-seat, it was as good an audience as Raynes could hope for. There was a warm, relaxed atmosphere in the room – a feeling of deep satisfaction after an excellent meal; a sense of cheerful familiarity built up during the day; and a stimulating glass of spirits in every hand.

Raynes was an accomplished after-dinner speaker and enjoyed nothing more than talking about his famous cases to a company of intelligent people. He had no doubt that they would enjoy it as much as he.

Molly waited till the flow of idle chatter had abated, then she called upon the Inspector to speak. He put his glass of whisky down on the mantelpiece and looked at the friendly faces surrounding him.

"One of the types of criminal behaviour which most attracts the public imagination is the serial killer. The individual who moves from one murder to the next for no apparent reason, leaving bodies scattered over several counties. You will all remember the cases of the Black Panther and the Yorkshire Ripper. Such a person causes acute fear in the community and people always blame the police for not catching them more quickly.

"Very often, we have no idea who it is who is doing these terrible deeds. And we have to build up a profile which may explain the motives: the geography, the sort of mentality which lies behind these killings. To start with, these things are not always apparent. But give the police a name, a photograph, a set of fingerprints, a DNA sample – and there is a chance of an arrest being made.

"But even when you have all these things, it may still prove difficult because of the erratic behaviour of the murderer himself.

"Tonight, I am going to talk to you about a case which happened eleven years ago. On that occasion, we had all the evidence we could wish for – a name, a photograph, fingerprints; we knew her complete background. But the lady herself remained invisible – except when she killed people. Even at those moments, she left very few clues. So it took us several months – and a lot of luck – to track her down.*

"I first became involved with Catherine Fellowes when she escaped from jail – from an open prison in Cheshire – near where I was working. As you may imagine, that was not the beginning of the story – not by a long chalk – but as she had killed two prison officers in the course of her escape, it was up to us to catch her – and the case landed on my desk.

"Mrs Fellowes was an adopted child. Her mother was a German girl employed as a kitchen worker in a minor British public school. She got pregnant and when the baby was born, it was adopted by a farmer and his wife who lived in Herefordshire.

"They had great hopes of Catherine but she constantly disappointed them. She was bright enough to get to university but not diligent enough to stay there. She failed her first year examinations and was thrown out. She headed for London and became personal assistant to a very disreputable businessman called Sam Orchardson.

"After working for him for a couple of years, she had a nervous breakdown. During her illness, she was befriended by a young social worker whom she later married and by whom she had a child.

* *Unpublished MS: "The Catherine Wheel"*

"The marriage was not a very happy one and, soon after the baby was born, Mrs Fellowes killed it. Her action was put down to post-natal depression – for which there was abundant evidence. But it was perhaps the first sign of what was to come.

"She was taken briefly into custody – but then released. I imagine it did not make her marriage any easier. Several months passed – and her husband vanished. Where he had gone, no one knew.

"The police suspected foul play – but where was the evidence? The local police examined the house, dug up most of the garden, looked for the slightest sign of new cement – but found nothing. Mrs Fellowes seemed to be innocent of any offence. Indeed, she showed a lot of anger that he should have deserted her in such a callous way.

"I have to tell you – she was a natural actress – a beautiful woman. She could wrap men round her little finger – and did.

"Time passed and Mrs Fellowes sold the house. It was a bungalow in Cambridge. She made for Dover with her car and all her money. Had they let her go abroad, it would have saved us a lot of trouble. But the police were still not entirely convinced of her innocence. She was arrested on suspicion of murder whilst further enquiries were made. And during that time, she was held at an open prison in Cheshire.

"She struck down the two prison officers with great brutality. One was strangled – the other clubbed with a brick. Then she vanished into thin air. We assumed that she would be found within a twenty mile radius of the prison and we flung a search cordon round the area. But the bird had long since flown.

"She had stolen a bicycle, ridden to Crewe station, and with money she had taken from the murdered officers, she took a succession of trains – from Crewe to Birmingham, Birmingham to Bristol, Bristol to Exeter and then a local train down to Barncombe – a little seaside resort in Devon, where Mr Orchardson, her former employer, had a boat. A large, old-fashioned cabin cruiser called the *Pterodactyl*.

"For us, the trail went cold. Quite obviously, she was miles away from Cheshire. She was living openly on the boat. Sunbathing. Nobody saw anything suspicious. Once again, there was a lull in proceedings. We talked to her parents. We approached every known contact. We set one or two traps for her if she did visit her parents. But it all seemed quite pointless.

"Until, one night, her parents' home was blown up. Completely blown up. It was a very solid Herefordshire farmhouse – not easily destroyed. We believe that she entered the house, turned on all the gas fires – but didn't light them. She then set the timer on the electric cooker to come on several hours later. The explosion was tremendous. Her parents' bodies were so mutilated that they could only be identified by their dental records. It was a horrendous murder. Later, I learnt – from Mrs Fellowes herself – that she had killed both her parents – pushed them down the staircase – broken their necks – before she turned on the gas.

"By now, we had six people dead and still no sign of the murderess – even though she had driven off in her parents' car. I don't need to tell you that my superiors were getting more frantic by the day – demanding instant results. Police in many other counties were becoming involved, but there was just no evidence to go on, no recent photograph – she had dyed her hair – and once more, she had gone to ground. We still don't know where.

"The only incident of any significance was the burning of a boat in Barncombe harbour. The boat owned by Sam Orchardson. Now her parents had mentioned a yacht owned by a Mr Jacobson and we had already instituted extensive enquiries to try and find the man and his boat. But they had given us the wrong name. And the wrong type of boat. When the cabin cruiser went up in flames, my younger colleague drew my attention to it. We contacted Mr Orchardson in London and warned him that Mrs Fellowes might be coming his way. He laughed at us.

"Naturally, we went down to Barncombe to look at his boat. But there was nothing to see! It had been a spectacular blaze which had given enormous pleasure to the inhabitants of Barncombe. A sort of midsummer bonfire party. However, all was not sweetness and light. Whilst we were there, we were told about a young policeman from Newcastle who had gone missing. He had been holiday-making on another small boat in the harbour. When we broke into his boat, we discovered a series of pencilled notes, sufficient to suggest that he had been watching Mrs Fellowes in a rather lustful way.

"I immediately came to the conclusion that he had approached our lady – and that she had killed him. It was pure supposition because, once again, we had no evidence. Mrs Fellowes later told me that he had come to her boat and sexually assaulted her. She had retaliated – and to cover her tracks, she had burnt the boat. So we now had a total of seven bodies.

"However, from the notes left by the young policeman, I noticed that Mrs Fellowes had been absent from the boat overnight – the night before the *Pterodactyl* went up in smoke. I wondered vaguely where she had been; but one of my colleagues had been reading the local paper and told me of an event which he thought would interest me. A retired colonel had died in his bath. There had been a report of a coroner's inquest.

"I checked to see what date the colonel had died. It was the night Mrs Fellowes had been absent from the boat. I could not resist putting two and two together. We examined the colonel's cottage and spoke to his charlady. Nothing!

"But when we examined the colonel's car – locked away in its garage – we found Mrs Fellowes' fingerprints. She had met him in the local casino, gone home with him and murdered him – drowning him in his bath. So we were now obliged to add an eighth corpse to our list.

"Looking back, I often wonder why my superiors didn't take me off the case and put someone more experienced in charge. Perhaps it was because I went on finding bodies! Perhaps because it would be easier to blame me if anything went wrong!

"Once again, we warned Mr Orchardson to be on his guard, but he was up in Scotland – not very far from where we are tonight – shooting grouse. He did not want to be disturbed. He felt quite safe. But Mrs Fellowes knew his passion for shooting grouse and where he was likely to be found in August. A couple of nights later, he too was dead.

"He was killed for an address. Mrs Fellowes claimed that he

was the only person who knew the address where this other man lived. It would have been much better if she had simply broken into his room and looked at his address book. But she insisted on Mr Orchardson telling her the details face-to-face. She also had sex with him before she dispatched him.

"He was extremely foolish, thinking he could handle a mass-murderer. He should have phoned the police the moment he saw her. But he probably thought he had plenty of time.

"So, whilst we were examining Mr Orchardson's body in a Scottish hotel, Mrs Fellowes was heading down to Yorkshire to perform her tenth and final killing.

"This was another businessman – a Mr Trevor Peters – whose private hobbies included witchcraft and black magic. It appears that, on occasions, Mr Peters, in his own perverted way, celebrated a black mass on the naked body of a young woman. At one such ceremony, Catherine Fellowes had been the sacrificial victim.

"In Mr Peters' eyes, it was all good, harmless fun – an excuse for an orgy with his friends – but it was this incident which had caused Mrs Fellowes to have her initial nervous breakdown, whilst she was working for Mr Orchardson.

"She believed that a spell – or a curse – had been placed upon her and that it could only be lifted by the murder of Mr Peters. She broke into his house early one morning, slit his throat with a sharp knife and then laid his dead body on the altar in his private chapel. She covered his body with heaps of vestments, service sheets, curtains and anything else she could find – then she poured petrol over the whole pyre – and burnt the lot.

"It took a few days before we saw the connection between this incident and the other murders. Needless to say, our friends in Yorkshire had a field day on the case. But they found photographs and notes in Mr Peters' diary which revealed conclusively his connection with Mrs Fellowes.

"We now had ten murders staring us in the face – but we still could not lay our hands on the murderer. It was most frustrating. We knew who she was; most of what she had done; but we had no idea where she was – or who she might kill next.

I decided to give the whole story to the press in the hope that someone might know where she was at that moment.

"It worked. Only about forty miles away from our incident room, a young dentist went out to buy his Sunday papers. Not being in a particular hurry, he skimmed through the main stories – and read my piece. He realized that Mrs Fellowes was the mystery woman who was living with him. He realized that he might be her next victim. He phoned us up, gave us his address, and within the hour, she was arrested.

"Some of you may remember the trial. It was a very difficult case to prove. So much depended upon her own statement. There was very little corroborative evidence. Her defence lawyer claimed that from the moment she had taken part in the black mass, she had been under a spell – and was in no way responsible for her subsequent behaviour. She was, if you like, 'possessed'. Now, in killing Mr Peters, she was free of the spell – she was now 'clean'. But in the process, she had committed ten murders. She could not be released.

"When I questioned Mrs Fellowes, she was very forthcoming. She told me everything. Filled in all the details. The only thing she couldn't tell me was what had happened to her husband. She claimed that it was as much a mystery to her as it was to us. I did not believe her.

"I felt she knew very clearly what she had done. It was an astonishing mixture of psychopathic mania and ice-cold self-control. It seemed that she had deliberately murdered anyone in her life who had ever hurt her. It had been calculated revenge – carried out with absolute precision. She had covered her tracks beautifully. But whether she was 'possessed' by Satan, I do not know. I think not.

"This case happened eleven years ago. Mrs Fellowes was jailed for life. She lost her case in court though she attracted a lot of public sympathy. She has been in a secure gaol for a number of years. Now, once again, she is in an open prison. I am told that she has been a model prisoner in every way. She has never hurt a fellow prisoner or assaulted any prison officer. Some time soon, Mrs Fellowes will be released on parole. What do you think will happen then?"

The Inspector sat down to a well-merited round of applause. The Catherine Fellowes case always went down well.

First of all, the gruesome succession of murders never failed to appeal to people's most jaded tastes. Everyone enjoyed a good, juicy murder. They would all like to be a Sherlock Holmes – or at least a Dr Watson. (Being Holmes was perhaps a little too energetic and, anyway, didn't he smoke opium?)

The fact that Raynes had actually caught the wretched woman – even after ten murders – was cause for the heartiest of congratulations. He was obviously not some common-or-garden policeman but a detective of the highest calibre.

Their appreciation of his skill was always pleasing; it contrasted so markedly with the cursory and offhand treatment he had received at the time.

But secondly, the very ambiguity of the case never failed to divide an audience and provoke a host of interesting questions. Some people would always support Catherine and claim she was innocent – usually the men! Others – normally the women – would condemn her. The more people discussed the case, the more complicated it appeared. Even after the passage of several years, people would still stop the Inspector and say: "There's a question I've always been meaning to ask you . . ." And without fail, it related to some aspect of the Fellowes case.

Molly waited till the clapping ceased.

"Are there any questions for the Inspector?"

Mr Savage was the first to raise his hand.

"If she was 'possessed', Mr Raynes, then it would seem that we have jailed an innocent woman?"

"No one could prove it one way or the other," said Raynes.

"But surely, in this country, people are innocent until they're proved guilty?"

"With her own hands, she had committed ten murders. She admitted that. That was enough for the jury."

"Inspector, you said that she never told you how she murdered her husband. How do you think she did it?"

A nice hypothetical question from Gloria.

"I would love to know. If I ever meet her again, I hope she'll tell me."

"Are you expecting to meet her again?"
"I think that perhaps when she comes out, she might just head my way."
"Aren't you frightened that she might attack you?"
Bernard Potter reflecting his own fears.
"A little. But forewarned is forearmed."
Lady Emily raised a languid wrist.
"Do you think it was men she hated? Most of her victims seem to have been men."
"Two of her victims were women – but they had very masculine characteristics. One was a prison officer. The other – her adoptive mother – was a heavy, dominant personality. Her father was much more passive and feminine."
Stanley Dixon wanted to ask about her adoption. Was that perhaps the origin of her mental instability? He had read in a book somewhere that the Germans had the highest rate of mental illness in Europe. Could this have been inherited from her German mother – or was it perhaps caused by her relationship with her adoptive mother?
Raynes smiled.
People were now beginning to get to grips with the case.
"I think," he said, "she was probably completely normal – mentally – when she went to work with Mr Orchardson. With him and his friends, she lived a very wild and immoral life. I believe she even acted as a human fox for some of his night-time hunting parties. She was quite often on drugs and amphetamines. I think the black mass might just have tipped her over the edge."
Raynes still had the whole case at his fingertips.
"Do you see it as an ethical case at all?" asked Canon Larkin. "Did she have any morals?"
"None at all. I think she was totally amoral. She thought about nothing except herself and her own survival. She used people and then discarded them. She killed to cover her tracks. As I said, she was more like a wild animal than a human being."
"And yet she had charm?" said Mrs West.
"She had great charm."
"And was she beautiful?" asked Suzanne.

"Very much so," said Raynes. "She was very tall. Over six foot. Long legs. A nice figure . . ."

"Trust you to notice that!" said Gloria.

"She had an oval face. Dancing sort of eyes. They seemed to laugh at you. Perhaps they were. She had long, dark hair – although she dyed it a variety of colours. I would have said that she would have made a very striking model – just like yourself!" he added, with a generous smile.

"What happened at the black mass?" asked Molly. "I think we're all dying to know . . ."

Raynes answered all their questions as best he could. They continued for over an hour. By that time, the Inspector was feeling in need of another – and stronger – whisky; and Molly realized that it was probably better to stop the session whilst everything was going well, rather than let the questions peter out.

She rose to her feet.

"Now I think we have given Detective-Inspector Raynes a good grilling. We shall still have plenty of time to question him over the weekend. I think we should call a halt tonight – and perhaps someone can go and get him a much-needed drink from the bar."

But people did not hurry away.

They still talked and argued about the case with each other. Even the other hotel guests, who were not part of the murder weekend, got involved in lively disputes and various people came up to Raynes to ask him if he supported this view or that.

Kenny Savage came up and said forcibly, "Well, whatever you say, Inspector, I still say she was innocent! She was a wronged woman. I shall be glad when she's released."

"Rubbish!" said Gloria. "She was a complete psychopath!"

Mr Potter came over, looking anxious.

"Don't you think the Home Office should look again at her sentence?"

Mrs West came up to the Inspector and pressed a note into his hand. When most of the throng had departed, Raynes took a long swig of malt whisky and opened the note.

If you have no better offer, I should be delighted to entertain you in Room 21.

By the end of the evening – although universally acclaimed by all the guests – Raynes had received no better offer.

He smiled to himself and returned thoughtfully to his room.

10. *Blind Man's Buff*

Inspector Raynes drank two glasses of tonic water whilst he decided whether he should take up Mrs West's kind invitation. It was inevitable that he would succumb to temptation. He always did. But it was equally inevitable that he should carefully consider why he should not succumb.

First of all, he would be stepping down from his pedestal as "the great detective" and showing himself to be an ordinary, lustful human being. Secondly, he would be mixing business with pleasure – something which was always dangerous.

Mrs West might prove possessive and demanding – which could be tiresome and even ruin his weekend. Thirdly, he was not sure that Mrs West excited him all that much. Given a chance, he would have much preferred Suzanne – or Molly herself.

Mrs West, whatever her charms, was perhaps too old for him. Fourthly, he had drunk too much to be able to perform as well as he should. She might mock him – or, even worse, despise him. Finally, there was a very good book he was reading; he had been looking forward to finishing it.

But, on the other hand, invitations to a lady's bedroom did not come every day – or every night. He was only human.

It would probably be quite good fun. He didn't really care what people thought about him. He would never be seeing any of them again. If he did not take up the offer now, it might never be repeated and, by tomorrow, he might be kicking himself for his timidity. As for the book . . . well, he could always read it another night.

There seemed, on balance, to be as many good reasons for accepting as for refusing; but Raynes was reluctant to forgo any opportunity for self-indulgence. He felt that it was always better to say "yes" rather than "no". And for most of his life, that philosophy had served him well. (When he had been wrong, the consequences had been truly disastrous!) But this was no time for self-doubt. He had a quick wash and shave, put on a clean shirt and headed for room 21.

To begin with, he was not completely sure where the room was. It was not in the main corridor. He went up and down looking for room 21. But eventually he found a small side passage running out from the main building to one of the Victorian turrets. He climbed a short flight of stairs and, looking to the right, he saw a thin strip of light from a door just slightly ajar. He tapped gently on the door.

"Come in," said a welcoming voice.

Mrs West was no longer wearing her rimless spectacles nor her rather garish evening dress. She was standing in the middle of the room wearing a long pink slip with white lace straps. Her feet were bare. She looked several years younger than she had downstairs – which removed yet another of the Inspector's inhibitions. In fact, he could see that she had an excellent figure.

She smiled.

"The door, Inspector!"

She walked over to her dressing table and picked up a bottle of champagne wrapped in a green towel. Two glasses were already standing in front of her lighted mirror.

"Don't you think we should toast this auspicious occasion?"

"Haven't we drunk enough already?"

"Who cares?"

She handed the bottle to the Inspector.

"You open it. These things always frighten me."

Raynes took the bottle over to the far side of the room, loosened the metal wires and gradually eased the cork to the right as he turned the bottle to the left. Despite his gentle ministrations, the cork exploded violently out of the bottle; there was a cool icy mist at the neck and some of the champagne ran over his fingers.

"Bravo!" said Mrs West, holding out her glass.

Raynes filled it – and then his own.

"By the way," she said, "my name's Dorothy. Most people

call me Dot. What do they call you when you're not being a policeman?"

"Richard, usually."

Dorothy raised her glass. "To us – cheers!"

They drank down the first glass and Raynes poured a second round.

Dorothy looked at him mischievously.

"What did you do to Mrs Fellowes when you met her?"

"Handcuffed her, charged her, put her in a locked van with two policemen and sent her back to prison."

"But didn't you question her?"

"At great length."

"Were you alone with her?"

"Not really. The interviewing room had two glass walls and there were two prison warders constantly watching us."

"In case she attacked you?"

Raynes nodded.

"Could she have murdered you?"

"It would have spoilt her story."

"But you couldn't be sure?"

"She was a very fast mover. I used to watch her hands. You can often tell what people are thinking by looking at their hands."

Mrs West raised her index finger.

"Precisely," said Raynes.

Dorothy looked at the Inspector with half-closed eyes.

"Wasn't there something you'd have liked to do to her?"

"I didn't have the opportunity – and it might not have been safe."

"Well," said Dorothy, "you have the opportunity now - and you're quite safe. I'm not Lady Macbeth – even though this was once a Highland castle." She put down her glass beside the mirror and picked up a silver-backed brush.

"Would you like to break the ice by brushing my hair?"

It was an unexpected suggestion but, as she said, it was a very convenient way of breaking the ice. It would have been ridiculous to start necking like a pair of adolescents.

"You see, I find it very sensuous."

She sat down on the padded stool in front of the dressing table and smiled.

Raynes gently brushed her hair, running his fingers softly around her neck and just touching her ears. He caressed her shoulders and looked down at the perfumed abyss beneath her slip.

Dorothy's eyes watched him.

"Don't hurry," she said. "It turns me on."

Raynes continued his brushing more confidently. He stroked her arms and her shoulders, occasionally running his tongue around her neck. Dorothy's eyes closed. He ran a finger down to her left breast and touched her nipple. It was pleasantly hard. He massaged it between his thumb and first finger, Dorothy murmured contentedly.

"I think," she said eventually, "that it would be even nicer if you took off your clothes so that I could see your manly chest." She paused. "Among other things."

Raynes agreed that it would certainly help things along.

He stripped off in a leisurely manner and resumed his brushing and stroking. He could feel her body pressing against him and her hips were beginning to wriggle provocatively on the padded stool. Raynes pulled the lacy straps of her slip over her shoulders and with both hands caressed her breasts.

They looked good. They felt splendid. Dorothy rubbed her back against him. But Raynes did not need arousing.

He was feeling incredibly randy.

Dorothy turned round on her stool to face him. Her hands and her lips worked over him.

"What is it they call it?"

Raynes told her.

"I think it sounds much better in Italian."

Raynes stroked her head and her neck as she ministered to him. The tension was becoming unbearable. Dorothy looked up.

"Would you like to do it to me?"

"Of course."

"On the bed."

It was only a couple of feet away but Raynes was frightened

he would burst. Fortunately it didn't matter that he did come - prematurely – because they went on to make love three more times during the night.

The heavy drinking of the evening before did not seem to have impaired his skill. Indeed, as the night went on, he felt stronger and more virile. Dorothy seemed to bend her body to his every desire. Just two things he noticed. Although there was a great deal of kissing and caressing between them, she would not give him her lips. It was strange that she held back – when she gave everything else.

And later, when she was coming back from the toilet, he noticed that she moved her wine glass away from his – as if it were infected in some way. He thought it was curious but, by that time, sleep was beginning to creep up on him and he put his arm contentedly round Dorothy's waist.

His bedmate picked up her bedside clock and set the alarm for 7.00am. As she snuggled down into the Inspector's arms, she wondered if she had forgotten any detail of what had been arranged.

11. *Postman's knock*

Raynes had just finished his breakfast and was crossing the main hall, when an unknown woman approached him.

"Are you Inspector Raynes?"

He nodded.

"Molly Palmer's private detective?"

Raynes tried not to appear offended by her deliberate sneer.

"I am acting as referee for her murder weekend, if that's what you mean?"

"You're not a personal friend?"

Raynes hesitated.

"No. Not really. Why do you ask?"

Fiona Stewart thrust a copy of *The Scotsman* at him.

"Have you read the paper this morning?"

"Just *The Telegraph*. Not the local rags."

Fiona noted the sharp bite of contempt in his voice.

He was the sort of man she liked to deal with.

"They've found a body!" she said.

"Where?" asked Raynes.

"Beside the railway track near Crianlarich. It was found there yesterday morning."

Raynes realized immediately what was in the offing. His mind went ice-cold. He could perceive all the ramifications of the case before she said another word.

"I think it's a friend of mine."

Raynes looked around him.

"Would you mind if we discussed this elsewhere?"

"Out in the garden?"

"A bit public."

"My room?"

Raynes nodded.

They went up the stairs in silence and along the corridor to the north-eastern corner of the hotel where Fiona had not just a bedroom, but an entire suite reserved for her use.

She shut the door.

Raynes could see that her hands were shaking. She was in more of an emotional state than he had realized.

"Sit down," he said, "and let me see the piece in the paper."

"It's on page five."

Raynes turned up the story.

POLICE FIND MYSTERY BODY

The naked body of a young woman was found beside the railway track near Crianlarich on Friday morning. At first, it was thought that the young woman had attempted suicide, but police now believe she may have been murdered. The possibility that she might have fallen from a passing train has been considered, but no one has been reported missing. Police enquiries are continuing.

Raynes looked up.

"And who d'you think it is?"

"Jill Graham, my assistant. She was travelling up from London on the special overnight train. She was supposed to have everything ready for me when I arrived. I flew up to Inverness yesterday morning and I was expecting her to meet me. But she didn't. And when I got to the hotel, she hadn't even checked in. No luggage. Nothing! Not even the typewriter. I went down to the station and found all the suitcases in the ticket office. But no Jill."

"Why are you so sure that this is her body?"

Fiona snorted.

"A woman's instinct. I know she was on that train to Mallaig. I bought her the sleeper ticket. She didn't arrive – but the luggage did. Someone must have bumped her off and pushed her out of the train in the middle of the night."

Raynes looked thoughtful.

After all, he had been on that same train.

"Well," he said, "it's very easy to find out. All you have to do is phone the police; tell them Jill is missing; and that you fear the worst. Once they get hold of her dental records, they'll know whether it's her or not. And if it is, you'll have to go and identify the body."

Most unusually, tears appeared in Fiona's eyes.

"I don't think you understand, Inspector."

Raynes looked at her with a calm, steady gaze.

"Of course I understand," he said. "Miss Graham was travelling in your name, carrying your luggage. To someone who didn't know her well, she might have been you. You are thinking that Jill was killed by mistake. The person who attacked her and threw her body out of the train thought it was you."

Fiona looked at the Inspector with more respect.

He had got to the heart of her anxiety right away.

"Yes . . ."

"And you are also thinking that the person who murdered Jill may perhaps even now be living in this hotel?"

Fiona nodded.

"And they may be tempted to strike again once they know you are still alive?"

"That's about the sum of it."

Raynes asked the obvious question.

"But why should anyone want to kill you?"
Fiona seemed to recover some of her nerve.
"You don't know who I am?"
Raynes shook his head.
"You don't read my articles in the papers?"
"I told you. I only read *The Telegraph*."
"Oh, they don't buy my stuff; but the tabloids do."
She smiled more confidently now they were on professional ground.
"My name's Fiona Stewart. I run a press agency. Just a small outfit. Investigative journalism . . ."
"Muck-raking?" said Raynes.
Fiona shrugged her shoulders.
"Some people call it that. We do our best to expose the seamy side of life. Drugs, child abuse, tax fiddles, embezzlement, fornication in high places – you know the sort of thing – 'who's sleeping with whom' – we bring it out into the open and sell it to the newspapers. Not just in Britain. We sell it to the States and Canada. Even to France and Germany. It's very profitable."
"I'm sure it is. But it must bring you some powerful enemies?"
"It does. But being a woman helps. If I was a man, I would have been beaten up long before now – but for some reason, they don't touch a woman. Perhaps they're frightened of what more we might reveal. We always keep a little back – just in case."
Raynes was interested to see who it was who dug out all the stories that he read in the tabloids. Of course, like most people, he read them avidly – but he wasn't going to admit that to Fiona. Instead, he asked: "And what was Jill's role in all this?"
"Well, she's been my personal assistant for the past two years. I corner our subjects and she takes notes . . ."
Miss Stewart looked at Raynes. "Well, she doesn't really take notes. She just makes the odd heading. She's wired up with a miniature tape-recorder so that everything the subject says is fully recorded. They can't deny they said it, because we've got it – straight from the horse's mouth. Jill tends to sit in the

background so they hardly notice her. Because they don't see a microphone, they assume they're safe. But they can't complain."

Fiona seemed happy telling him the tricks of her trade. He made a mental note to be very careful what he said to her. There were things in his past which would make extremely lurid copy. He didn't want to see himself plastered all over *The Sun*.

"So you don't think anyone would have wanted to kill Jill – as Jill?"

"No."

"But someone might have wanted to kill you?"

"It's always possible. But I've never considered it – not until now. When I saw that piece in the paper, I felt it here. "

She pointed to her central breastbone.

"You may well be right," said Raynes. "But there is one comforting thought. You came into the hotel last night; you ate in the dining room; you've slept all night in your bedroom – and no one has attacked you so far. If someone was really determined to get rid of you, they have obviously drawn back. The fact that they now know the wrong person has been killed may have given them pause for thought."

Fiona shook her head.

"I don't find that at all comforting. If they didn't know who we were – and if they thought I was Jill – they wouldn't have known who I was when I came into the hotel. But they'll find out sooner or later. They'll probably know by now. All they have to do is ask at reception." She took a deep breath. "I think I'd be safer back in London."

Raynes was inclined to agree with her. There was safety in numbers and she would be better able to protect herself in more familiar surroundings. She could at least go and stay with friends – if she had any!

He asked Miss Stewart to give him a description of Jill.

"About five foot six. Fresh face. Curly brown hair. Brown eyes. Quite ordinary really. But she was a lovely person. Most efficient. Best assistant I ever had."

Raynes put up his hand.

"Wait a minute," he said. "We can't be absolutely sure it is her body."

"I know it is."

"I'll phone through to the police in Glasgow and ask them."

"Would you?"

"Willingly."

Fiona Stewart looked much happier.

"But first," said Raynes, "tell me what you were both intending to do up here." He looked at the typewriter already set up for action. "Was it business or pleasure? It looks like business to me."

Fiona looked a little cagey.

"If I tell you, you must promise not to tell anyone."

"Of course not," Raynes lied happily. "Secrecy is part of our professional code. When people tell us things, they don't leak out."

He looked at Fiona expectantly.

"Is it something to do with Mrs Palmer?"

"Partly. But it's her escort we're really after. Bernard Potter. Do you know him?"

"He's one of those taking part in the murder weekend. I met him yesterday for the first time. I was rather hoping he might be the murderer – in the game, that is."

Fiona sniffed contemptuously.

"He's a wimp. At least as far as lifting his fists is concerned. But he's a bully by nature. He works for the Home Office. A very powerful civil servant. He's responsible for catching drug smugglers; but we've found he's into cocaine."

Raynes smiled.

"And into Molly as well?"

"Yes. You can almost see the headline now. *Drug-busting Civil Servant's Double Life!* By the time we've finished with him, he'll be out on his ear."

Raynes felt instant sorrow for the victim.

"Doesn't it ever worry you . . . what you do to people like Bernard? Shattering their careers . . .?"

Fiona shook her head.

"No. If they're hypocrites, they're fair game. They take high pay. They accept top jobs. A position of trust. They're paid to keep their noses clean. If they don't, they deserve to be thrown out. There's plenty more to fill their places."

"Do you think Mr Potter – or Mrs Palmer – are aware of your interest in them?"

"I doubt it. We've only just begun to draw the threads together. One of Bernard's exes gave us a lead. We're taking it from there. We were planning to close in on Sunday night. Perhaps get a photograph of Molly and him all over each other. We thought he'd probably try to talk himself out of it. Then we'd have got him."

He could hear the note of triumph in Fiona's voice. She clearly relished her work.

She looked at the Inspector.

"But you won't say anything?"

Raynes felt incredibly disloyal as he replied: "No, of course not. It seems that we have bigger problems to deal with. I take it that if it is Jill's body beside the railway line, you wouldn't be thinking of continuing your investigation?"

"No, we always work as a team."

"So do I," said Raynes. "But this is my long weekend. I have no jurisdiction in Scotland, but I can phone through and ask. Even if it's not Jill, we shall still have to report her as a missing person."

"I know it's her."

"Did she have any distinguishing features?"

"I don't think so."

"Any rings?"

"A small silver one. I think it belonged to her mother."

"Any scars? Appendix? Slashed wrists? Pierced ears? Did she smoke? Nicotine stains? Varicose veins? Corns? Ingrowing toenails?" Raynes ran through the whole gamut of human deformities. "Gold fillings in her teeth? Plucked eyebrows?"

Fiona did her best to remember everything she could about her assistant.

Raynes picked up the phone and dialled his own office in Grasshallows to obtain the Glasgow number. That way, no one in the hotel would be aware of who he was phoning. He got the information he required.

He then dialled the Glasgow number and after giving his

name, age, rank and number, he asked if he could be put through directly to the officer handling the case of the body found beside the railway track near Crianlarich.

He said he thought he could be of some help. He was given the number of the police station in Oban. He also discovered – to his immense satisfaction – that he actually knew the officer in charge of the case. They had sat next to each other at the last police conference he had attended. More importantly, the officer remembered him. It was a small world.

Raynes quickly delivered his description of Jill Graham. Did she fit the bill?

The officer at the other end was excited.

"That's it. Spot on."

Raynes turned to Fiona Stewart.

"You were right."

"I thought so."

Raynes asked, "How did she die?"

The officer at Oban was quite forthcoming.

"Multiple injuries consistent with falling out of a moving train. Severe bruising. Broken jaw. Seems to have gone out head first. Naked. You probably saw that bit in the paper. But we think she was probably strangled before she was pushed out. Clear marks on her neck. The surgeon's done his stuff and that's what he thinks." The voice at the other end was curious. "How d'you come to be in on this?"

Raynes gave him the background.

"I'm up here on holiday – just for the weekend. The Ellachie House in Mallaig. One of the guests has just given me a copy of the newspaper and said she thought she knew who it was."

Raynes paused.

"Yes. She thinks it's her assistant. She came up by air yesterday. Her assistant was on the train with all the luggage. Yes? We've got the luggage – but no assistant. Her employer was expecting to be met at Inverness airport. But there was no sign of her. Now she's worried that whoever killed Miss Graham might want to kill her. Bit nasty!"

Raynes listened to the voice at the other end.

"Her employer is a Miss Fiona Stewart. Investigative

journalist . . . You know her?" He turned to Fiona. "He knows you."

Raynes nodded thoughtfully.

"Of course. I'll put her on to you." He handed over the phone. "I think he wants you to go down right away to identify the body."

He walked over to the window and looked out at the beautiful scenery which surrounded the hotel. What a time – what a place – to be burdened with a real murder! The body in one place. The suspects in another. Of course, they might not be suspects at all. Jill Graham might have been raped and murdered by someone completely unknown. Perhaps by one of those Americans he had seen getting on the train.

She might even have been murdered by Fiona herself. They might have had a serious quarrel. They might both be lesbians. Jill might be blackmailing her employer. Fiona might be involved – right up to her neck. All this persiflage about someone wanting to kill her – pure moonshine. Raynes had no hesitation in including Miss Stewart herself among his list of suspects.

But, as she came off the phone, he gave her no hint of his thoughts.

"Did they want you to identify the body?"

"Yes. He asked me to go down right away."

Raynes nodded sympathetically.

"Have you got a car?"

"I hired one yesterday."

"It'll take you a few hours to get there and back."

Fiona Stewart looked doubtful.

"D'you think there's any point in coming back?"

The Inspector, who had been planning to examine the contents of her suitcases whilst she was away, was quite sure that she should return.

"I think it might look highly suspicious if you suddenly disappeared. It might look as if you had something to hide. As a result of what you've told me, I'm going to question all the people in Molly's crowd and see if there's anyone who has a connection with you and Jill – apart from Mr Potter . . ."

Fiona laughed coldly.

"Have you looked at her guest list?"

Raynes was not quite sure what she meant.

"Well, I've been talking to most of them for the past twenty-four hours. I have a fair idea of what they're like."

Fiona shook her head.

"You haven't the vaguest idea who they are. Each one of them's a blast from the past." She began to make herself clear. "They're all people I've done features on. There's that woman – Emily Andrews. She calls herself Lady Emily – but she isn't. She was the Director of the Poor Children's Trust. Milked them of a cool eight hundred thousand quid! Then there's that doctor's wife. Her husband killed at least three of his patients. Lethal injections! Once we'd exposed him, he committed suicide. And as for Suzanne Tempest; surely you remember her? She was the 'Two girls in a bed' scandal with the Minister of Commerce. He had to resign. She got £50,000 for her side of the story . . ."

"I remember that," said Raynes.

"Well, you should remember the rest. Kenny Savage was the owner of a haulage company which brought in hundreds of illegal immigrants, hidden in his lorries. He made a nice packet out of that. Thanks to us, he went bust!

"Canon Larkin – he was the one who admitted to entertaining a string of rent boys. Now he's got AIDS. Nice sort of character! Dear Mr Dixon is *the* Stanley Dixon who ripped off thousands of small savers in the Preston and General Life Insurance fraud. He was about to slip away to his bolt-hole in Cyprus but we tipped off the police. Caught him with his pants well and truly down!"

Fiona sounded exceedingly vindictive.

"Not to mention Gloria Markham-Jones!"

"She does crossword puzzles," said Raynes.

"She does more than crossword puzzles! She was the Matron of a private nursing home where they established a rather nice line in do-it-yourself euthanasia. Anyone who was coming to the end of their savings – or was proving extra hard work – just got bumped off. It took people a long time to twig. The staff got the blame, but it was Gloria's idea. She's a complete sadist."

Raynes was amazed at her revelations.

"So you are saying that there's not a decent one amongst them?"

"No. They're all nature's nasties. But what I find suspicious is that Molly's got them all together in one group. I find that very odd. Almost as if she were organizing a conspiracy against me."

"I understand your anxiety."

"They are all people who would have deep grudges against me. To see them all here – like a pack of wolves – makes one think."

Raynes thought quickly.

"All the more reason for you to come back. I could do with your knowledge. I feel that together we might give them a real roasting."

"I wouldn't be too sure. They're a slippery lot. Liars, cheats, murderers. It'd take a lot to pin any of them down."

She paused. "But it might be fun to see them squeal."

"Especially if you want to help me catch Jill's murderer?"

"Yes."

Raynes tried to look at the financial side – which might appeal to her.

"It should make a marvellous story. Net you a few more thousands."

Fiona shrugged her shoulders.

"If I live to tell the tale!"

"Have faith!" said Raynes. "I've never lost a witness yet."

It was a complete lie – but it impressed Fiona.

12. *Hunt the Thimble*

The information which Fiona Stewart had given Raynes caused the Inspector to re-assess all the characters he had met the day before in a new – and more jaundiced – light.

He had certainly recognized them to be an unusual bunch – but Molly herself was such a cheerful eccentric that one expected her choice of guests to be somewhat abnormal. But over the past twenty-four hours, they had blended together rather well.

He had never expected to encounter such a formidable cross-section of human wickedness – particularly as he had taken quite a liking to all of them. But now he would have to think twice before resuming his affair with Dorothy West; he would have to watch his wallet with Lady Emily; and if he saw Gloria Markham-Jones coming towards him with a syringe, he would know his number was well and truly up!

But, of course, he only had Fiona's word for it.

The first thing to do was to confirm that all these people had done what she said they had done. It would be useful to get the police national computer to check out their backgrounds and personal details. All their addresses would be in the visitors' book at reception. It would not take long to get the rest of the information.

After he had left Fiona, Raynes went to his own room and made a personal call to Detective-Constable Carlisle who was on duty in his absence. He gave him the list of names.

Even as he read them out, he could hear his junior colleague whistling with amazement. He was obviously a regular reader of the gutter press.

"You've got a right crowd there!" he said.

"I didn't realize it till this morning."

"And I hear you've got a body too?"

"Thrown off my train!"

Carlisle laughed.

"Begins to look like a classic case. I wish I was up there with you."

"Well, I could certainly do with some help. I'm supposed to be an impartial referee in this bloody murder game – and yet there's a real-life murder – and a real-life murderer – requiring my immediate attention."

"Who gave you all the guff?"

"Fiona Stewart. You've probably heard of her. She's an investigative journalist. Gutter rat!"

"Is she on your list of suspects?"

Raynes paused.

"Well, she says she was in London till yesterday morning."

"Put her on the list. She's bound to be involved."

"She's going down to Oban to identify the body."

"And what are you going to do?"

Raynes smiled.

"Well, actually, I was intending to go through all her luggage the moment she left, to see if there are any clues."

"So you do suspect her?"

"I'm beginning to suspect all of them. Even the one I slept with last night! You'd better put Molly Palmer on the list as well. She'll probably turn out to be a gun-runner for the IRA or someone working for Mossad."

Carlisle was pleased to note the healthy touch of cynicism which coloured the Inspector's conversation. It was always a good sign. Carlisle had often noticed that the more pessimistic he sounded, the closer he was to finding a solution.

"It won't be much fun interviewing them," he said.

"No," said Raynes. "If they're all what she says they are, they'll be lying through their teeth."

"And what about the body?"

"Jill Graham. You'd better check her out as well. She's been Fiona's assistant for the past two years. She describes her as a perfectly ordinary person – but you never know."

Raynes stood up.

"Well, there you are. Plenty to be getting on with. I'll have the addresses to you within the hour – but you can make a start on the more obvious ones. Perhaps you could give me a call at about 5.00pm – after I've finished quizzing the ungodly."

Confident that Carlisle would deliver the goods, Raynes

assumed his most benevolent expression and went down to the Highland lounge for coffee.

* * * *

Downstairs, in the lounge, Fiona Stewart's departure did not escape comment. Gloria Markham-Jones had seen her striding through reception with a set of car keys in her hand.

As she collected her coffee and a chocolate biscuit, she said to Stanley Dixon, "You know that woman we were talking about last night . . .?"

"The newshound?"

"Yes. She's just gone out."

"Gone for good?"

"No. She didn't have any suitcases. Just a handbag and a briefcase."

"So she'll be back. Making trouble for someone – that's for sure."

"Who'll it be this time?"

"Perhaps all of us. You remember what Molly said."

Mr Dixon stirred his coffee thoughtfully and watched Raynes crossing the room.

"Good morning, Inspector. Just allow us five minutes for our coffee and we'll be ready for the off."

He smiled.

"Splendid chap. Great fun. Really enjoyed his talk last night."

"Most instructive," said Mrs West.

* * * *

Raynes asked the hotel receptionist if he could have a word with the manager. It took about ten minutes for the manager to appear.

Raynes produced his police identification and explained why it was necessary for him to examine the names and addresses of all those taking part in the Murder Weekend. The manager was most helpful and Raynes soon had a full list of Molly's guests.

He put through a second call to Detective-Constable Carlisle.

The next part of his investigation was a little more delicate. When he was sure that all Molly's guests had finished their coffee and were assembled in the Highland lounge, he borrowed the manager's pass-key and went back upstairs to Fiona's room to conduct a full-scale search of her belongings.

He felt a little bit guilty about invading her privacy since she had been so helpful in giving him all the information about the murder. But he felt there might be some clue hidden amongst her possessions – and if there was, he wanted to find it. But Detective-Inspector Raynes was about fifteen minutes too late.

As he opened the door to her room, he saw that someone else had had the same idea. All Fiona's suitcases had been opened and their contents thrown out.

A very comprehensive search had taken place. Every cupboard and drawer had been inspected. And whoever had conducted the search had not only been through Fiona's property but Jill's as well. A sharp knife had been used to slit open each suitcase and bag. None could ever be used again.

Raynes decided that there was no point re-examining the debris. He picked up the phone and summoned the hotel manager.

Whilst he was waiting, he wondered if he should use his pass-key to enter the rooms of Molly's guests and see if any of Fiona's property had been stuffed under a mattress or hidden behind a wardrobe.

He decided that such a move would only rouse suspicions. No one would know that he had been in Fiona's room unless he told them. Much better to get all Fiona's luggage under lock and key and let her discover what, if anything, had been stolen.

Raynes looked at the mess around him. Whoever had done the search had been extremely thorough – and swift. It was less than half an hour since Miss Stewart had left the hotel.

He drew some comfort from the fact that every bag and every suitcase had been searched. If the thief had found what he or she was looking for, they would have stopped at some earlier stage. The fact that they had combed through the entire contents suggested that they had come away empty-handed. What on earth could they have been looking for?

The manager arrived.

"Good grief, Inspector! What a mess!"

Raynes shook his head.

"Not me. Someone got here before me. I don't think they found what they were looking for – but they've done the lot."

The manager bent down and looked at the suitcases.

"They've cut them open!"

"Yes, they've had it. What I would like you to do is to get two of your staff to collect everything together and put it into bags or boxes. They must wear gloves because the fingerprint people will need to examine it. When it is all packed up, it must be put under lock and key until this evening when I shall take it down to Inspector Cameron who is handling this case. It goes without saying that not a word of this must be mentioned. Your staff must exercise the utmost discretion."

The manager continued to look at the heaps of clothes and toiletries scattered across the floor. Then a serious thought suddenly entered his mind. He looked at the Inspector with some alarm.

"Does this mean . . .?"

Raynes nodded.

"It means that the person who murdered the girl on the train must be in the hotel. There may have been something connecting them with the murder hidden in her luggage – and they were looking for it. Whether they found it or not, I don't know. Probably not."

He looked at the manager's anxious face.

"Whoever it is – is dangerous, but will be no danger to your staff. I am sure they are quite safe. And now Miss Stewart's gone – she too is probably safe. Don't say anything about the murder to any of your staff; just treat it as a common act of theft. I'm sure you've had to cope with these things before. Just tidy up the room and make sure everything goes on as smoothly as normal.

"I shall immediately start questioning Mrs Palmer's guests. May I use the library? It's nice and secluded . . . perhaps one of your staff could be on hand to get me anything I need?"

The manager was pathetically anxious to do anything he could to help the Inspector. He immediately went off to organize the necessary staff.

Raynes again picked up the phone and dialled the Oban number and asked for Detective-Inspector Cameron. He did not mention the theft – but explained that Fiona Stewart was now on her way down to identify the body. Under no circumstances was she to be allowed to return to Mallaig. She must be kept in some local hotel.

After apologizing for getting mixed up in the case, he asked if it would be in order for him to question Molly's guests and do the preliminary spadework the inquiry would require.

Having received Detective-Inspector Cameron's whole-hearted approval, he was a much happier man. Finally, he asked if a police car could be made available for him some time after 5.00pm so that he could come down to Oban and report.

He put the phone down – and smiled to himself.

It was always better to be dealing with a real murder.

And this one was already on the way to becoming most interesting.

13. *Dumb Crambo*

"You're late!" said Molly. "I had to start them off without you."

"There's been a murder," said Raynes.

"Where? In the hotel?"

"No. On the train."

Molly looked blank.

"The train we came up in. The sleeper. One of the passengers was murdered and thrown off the train. It's in the local papers."

Molly still looked surprised.

"I don't see what it's got to do with us."

"Don't you?" asked Raynes sarcastically. "Does the name Fiona Stewart mean anything to you?"

"She's a reporter."

"So you have heard of her?"

"I've never met her. Was she murdered on the train?"

Was there a note of suppressed optimism in her voice?

"No," said Raynes, "she wasn't; but her side-kick was. The one who was bringing up all her luggage."

Molly passed a weary hand over her brow.

"I'm very sorry, Inspector, but I still don't see what it has to do with us."

Raynes could only believe that she was being singularly obtuse. Keeping his temper under control, he said, "We all travelled up on that train from London – on Thursday night. This young woman was also on the train. Possibly in the same coach. She was killed . . . and her naked body was thrown out of the train somewhere near Crianlarich. This means that all the people on the train are suspects. Any one of us – myself included – could have been her murderer."

"So . . .?"

Inspector Raynes decided to stick his neck out completely.

"I have no doubt that it was one of your guests who murdered her."

"Oh, don't be ridiculous! They're all thoroughly nice people. You've seen that for yourself."

Raynes shook his head.

"As the Queen of Sheba once said: 'Behold, the half was not told me . . .' I have now been informed that all your guests – with one exception – have been exposed by this reporter – this investigative journalist – Fiona Stewart.

"It appears that Lady Emily, Mrs West, Gloria, Kenny Savage, Stanley Dixon and Canon Larkin have all had their careers terminated as a result of exposés produced by her agency. And I have also been told – by the lady herself – that she was on the way up to Mallaig to expose Mr Bernard Potter."

"Whatever for?"

"Possessing cocaine. Organizing cocaine parties in his home. Not a very desirable activity for one of the civil servants in the Home Office who is supposed to be leading the war against drugs."

"That's absolutely ridiculous!"

"Is it?"

"I wouldn't know anything about his private life." She was beginning to get angry. "Really, Inspector! You mustn't believe anything that woman says. She's warped . . . twisted . . . She's just out to make money."

"But," said Raynes, "if she's right – and if all these people have been exposed by her agency – then surely every one of your guests would have had an excellent reason for murdering her? This is not a game. This is real life. One of your guests has committed a real murder."

"I'm sure there must be any number of suspects. She exposes different people every week. There must be hundreds of people longing to get their own back on her."

"Well," said Raynes, "that's a job for the local police. But I think we've got the murderer here. And instead of playing games, I think we should investigate this real murder. And I propose to do so."

"And what about our murder weekend?"

Molly looked tearful.

She could see all her hard-earned efforts being destroyed. People would be beastly to her. They would all want their money back. There would be much unpleasantness.

"What am I going to do?" she wailed.

Raynes could understand her feelings.

"Just go on with your different scenarios," he said. "Today and tomorrow. Carry on as normal. But count me out as a referee. I shall pay you for my train fare and my hotel bill, but I don't think I could play games with a crowd of murderers."

"They're not murderers! They're good, decent people."

Raynes looked at her.

"Apparently Gloria was Matron of a nursing home where several patients died . . . Lady Emily ripped off something called 'The Poor Children's Trust' . . . Mr Dixon defrauded hundreds of small investors with his Preston & General . . ."

"I notice you didn't mention Dorothy West!" said Molly sarcastically. "You'll protect her!"

"I shall not protect anyone," said Raynes, "whether I've slept with them or not. I shall question all your guests – one by one – till I get the truth."

"You have no authority to question anyone!"

"I have been on the phone to the detective leading this murder enquiry – Inspector Cameron. And it appears that we know each other from way back. Detective-Inspectors are a bit thin on the ground round here so when I offered my services, he was delighted to accept."

"And Fiona Stewart?"

Molly spat out the woman's name with contempt.

"She's on the way down to Oban to identify the body. She will not be returning to Mallaig."

Raynes looked at Molly thoughtfully. Why the venom? Was she more deeply involved with Mr Potter than he had imagined? Or was there something more to this that he didn't know?

"I think," he said slowly, "it might be interesting to know why all the people on your murder weekend happen to be people either exposed by Miss Stewart – or about to be. It is utterly beyond coincidence that you should have accidentally gathered together so many people who are likely to have a grudge against Miss Stewart. It looks as if you were all plotting some evil against her. But perhaps you killed the wrong person?" He looked at Molly. "You said you've never met Fiona – and I believe you. But if you didn't know what she looked like, you might be just the sort of person to kill the wrong woman. To look at all the personal luggage and assume it was Miss Stewart travelling on that train."

He looked at Molly's angry face.

"But, of course, you weren't on that train, so it couldn't have been you."

"No, it couldn't!" Again she spat out her words.

"And had you ever thought – clever Inspector – that Fiona herself could have been on that train? She could have killed her side-kick and blamed it on someone else. How did she get here?"

"She flew up to Inverness yesterday afternoon."

"I think you ought to double-check her movements."

Raynes nodded.

"I most certainly will. You may not believe me, but such a

thought had already crossed my mind. I shall consider everyone's movements . . ." He paused thoughtfully " . . . including my own. And with your help – causing as little inconvenience as possible – I would like to question all your guests one by one to see if I can find out what happened. You may disapprove. You may try to oppose me. But I think that if I could have your co-operation, we might be able to prevent your weekend becoming a complete disaster."

Put like that, Molly could hardly refuse.

"Would you like to start after lunch?"

It was an innocent question but Raynes immediately saw its dangers.

"No," he said, "I shall start now. With . . . Mr Potter!"

"You beast!" said Molly. "Picking on the weakest!"

"Just so," said Raynes.

14. *Vingt-et-un*

Raynes left Molly in the Highland lounge and went round to the rear of the hotel where "Chicago 1929" was being enacted. A fine old Silver Ghost had been borrowed from a local Rolls-Royce enthusiast; and the corpse lay artistically slumped against the running board – a row of bullet holes across his chest. More tomato ketchup!

The Inspector went over to Mr Potter and put a hand on his arm. "I wonder if I could have a word with you? A confidential matter."

"Of course."

Lady Emily viewed the Inspector's late arrival with some hilarity.

"Did you have a rough night, Inspector?"

"No," said Raynes chivalrously. "It was as smooth as chocolate!"

Mrs West's eyes twinkled knowingly.

"If you happen to like chocolate," she said.

"You must have swallowed the whole bar!" said Lady Emily crudely.

"Very nearly!" said Raynes.

He smiled. It would be a pleasure interviewing her. He might be able to get a little of his own back.

He escorted Mr Potter into the hotel.

"I think we might have a glass of something in the library."

"An excellent idea."

When they were settled, Raynes said, "When did you first decide to come on this murder weekend?"

"About two weeks ago."

"Did you see Molly's ad in the paper?"

"No. She phoned me up and asked if I would like to come and make up the numbers."

It sounded plausible.

"And you came up on the sleeper from Euston?"

"I did."

"Would you be kind enough to tell me which compartment you occupied in the train that night?"

"No. 8, I think." Mr Potter reached into his inside pocket and took out his wallet. He looked at his ticket. "Yes. No. 8."

"Do you know who was in No. 7 and No. 9?"

Bernard looked anxious.

"Is there any reason behind these questions?"

"Yes," said Raynes. "The police have just discovered that a woman was murdered on that train. Her body was thrown out of a window – or a door – and her body has been found on the track somewhere north of Crianlarich."

"Good heavens!"

Bernard looked genuinely surprised.

"The body was not discovered till yesterday afternoon, but it's in this morning's papers. Since all of us were on that train, I've been asked by the Inspector conducting this case to question people here about it."

"I see."

"The woman who died was working for Fiona Stewart – an investigative journalist. Do you know her?"

"I don't think I do."

Bernard's face coloured. His reply was obviously a lie, but Raynes decided not to challenge him at this point.

He continued blandly: "It appears that Miss Stewart was coming up to Mallaig to do a special article about one of Molly's guests. The sort of nasty little article which she writes quite regularly for the gutter press."

"How very unpleasant."

"However, it appears that – with one exception – all Molly's guests have previously been exposed by this wretched woman. Some have lost their jobs. Some have been fined – or gone to jail. They have no reason to love her."

"I would imagine not."

"So when her secretary's body was found, the police assumed that the murderer had intended to bump off Miss Stewart."

"I see."

"But because the murderer didn't know her from Adam – or perhaps I should say, in this case, Eve – he or she killed the wrong person. It seems likely that it was someone who had a deep-seated grudge against the lady . . ."

The civil servant nodded thoughtfully.

Raynes watched him.

" . . . Or someone who was fearful of having his evil deeds exposed in four weeks' time in some greasy tabloid. An exposé which could cause an important person to lose his job."

Raynes looked hard at Bernard.

He was beginning to fray at the edges.

He had got the message.

"Now when we met over breakfast here yesterday morning . . ." (How long ago it now seemed!) " . . . you told me that in the Home Office, you were part of a division dealing with drug prevention. You gave me the impression that you were quite high up in that division . . ."

Bernard nodded modestly.

"You are part of a major Government initiative to eradicate drugs. To pursue dealers. To give the police greater powers of search and entry. To uncover back-room chemists who are producing the stuff. And sifting information as to when carriers are bringing the dope into the country. True?"

"Yes. That's right."

"Well, how is it then," asked Raynes, "that you, a Government drugs enforcer, have cocaine stashed away in your house and apparently have permitted your house to be used for parties where cocaine was freely available?"

Bernard put the shutters up very firmly.

"I'm not going to say another word. Not until I have consulted my solicitor."

Raynes slid neatly round this difficulty.

"It's not me making this allegation. It's this woman, Fiona Stewart. She seems to have got detailed information from someone – I don't know who – that this has been going on. She was going to interview you here – and then write a damning article which would have cost you your job."

"I doubt it," said Mr Potter, sounding more confident. "I would have denied it completely. And if she had put anything in print, I would have sued her immediately."

"I'm sure you would; but by that time, the damage would have been done. You know as well as I do it's the smear, the innuendo, the suggestion of wrong-doing which does the damage. People are suspended whilst the matter is looked into. Everyone assumes they must be guilty. No smoke without fire."

Mr Potter nodded thoughtfully.

"Miss Stewart will not be interviewing you in Mallaig. She has weightier matters on her mind. But to the outward eye – my outward eye – this looks like a pre-emptive strike. Either someone is seeking revenge for an old injury – or else they were aiming to kill Miss Stewart before she could write that damning article. Which do you think it could be?"

Bernard was not going to fall into such an obvious trap. He was quite determined to express no opinion whatsoever. He was even wondering whether Detective-Inspector Raynes had any right to be investigating the case at all. He was off-duty. He was far beyond the bounds of his own police authority. He might do even more harm to his career than Miss Stewart.

"What force do you work for, Inspector?"

Raynes smiled.

He had followed the course of Mr Potter's thoughts.

"I did tell you yesterday morning. But I don't think this

murder is within the jurisdiction of the Home Office. It's a matter for the Scottish Office. And it so happens that the detective handling this case is an old friend of mine. He was quite willing to accept my help. But if you want me to pass things back to him, I will do so – most willingly."

There was an unhealthy silence for perhaps half a minute whilst both men considered their position.

Raynes decided that his best course was to shatter the civil servant's hope of sweeping the matter under the carpet.

"I'm afraid," he said, "the genie of 'cocaine' and 'cocaine parties' has got out of the bottle. We can't put it back. And if this proves to be the root cause of this young woman's death — and if you are involved – the truth will come out whether you like it or not."

"I certainly didn't kill her," said Mr Potter emphatically.

Raynes looked thoughtful.

"But others may have killed her to protect you."

"Why should they do that?"

"I don't know."

"With the exception of Molly, all these people are complete strangers."

"Yes," said Raynes, "that's true. But why are they all here – if not to present a united front against Miss Stewart? To turn this into a murder weekend with a real victim? A plot carefully thought out in advance. How did they know she would be coming to expose you? There's a lot of questions to which we should like answers."

"Well," said Mr Potter, throwing back the last of his drink, "you won't be getting any answers from me. I know nothing about the murder. I heard nothing. I saw nothing. I did nothing. And no one's going to pin anything on me."

Raynes smiled more confidently.

"You lied to me, Mr Potter. You lied."

"I did no such thing."

"Yes," said Raynes, "you did. You told me that you didn't know Fiona Stewart. But your face gave you away. You did know about this woman. You knew she would be coming up to Mallaig. That is why you are here. You knew she had evidence against you. None of these other people here have anything to lose – but you have.

"They have all been through the mud. They've seen their faces plastered across the tabloids. They've been booted out. Sent to jail. You're the only one still riding high. Fiona was about to finish you off. You knew that. What better motive could there be? You, a man with so much to lose. Why lie if you're innocent?"

Raynes looked him straight in the face.

"Only the guilty lie, Mr Potter!"

15. *Skittles*

It was not a very good start.

Mr Potter had been alerted to the dangers facing him. He would now have time to consider his defence, warn the other guests and put them on their guard. Before long, they would be buzzing around like a swarm of angry wasps.

Raynes sighed.

Fortunately, it was not his case. If anything went wrong, others would carry the can. But he had to confess that he found a real-life murder more challenging – and more satisfying – than Molly's make-believe, all of which he had been through twice before.

Who should he see next?

He decided on Gloria.

* * * *

"I must say I'm glad to have a break, Inspector. Gets a bit tiresome after an hour or so. I don't think I have much sympathy with gangsters and I'm too old to be one of their molls."

Raynes sympathized with her.

"You've heard what's happened?"

"Yes, indeed. Someone's taken a leaf out of the 'Orient Express'. I think it was daggers in that one."

"Well, it's strangling in this."
"Strangling? Must be a man!"
"You think?"
"Oh, yes. Poison points to a woman; strangling to a man."
"It was Fiona Stewart's assistant."
"Her? I thought I saw her sniffing around this morning."
"You're old acquaintances?"
"She lost me my position."
"And where was that?"
"Hastings. The White Cliffs Nursing Home for the Elderly and Incurable. Beautiful place."
Raynes wondered how far he could take Fiona's accusations. Rather delicately, he said: "They didn't stay incurable for all that long, did they?"
Gloria laughed.
A rather chilling laugh.
"No. Once they'd got beyond a certain point, we helped them on their way."
"The certain point . . . being financial?"
"You're a man of the world, Inspector. Yes."
"You don't seem to have any qualms about it."
Gloria shrugged her shoulders.
"Frankly, no. By the time people come into such places, their quality of life's pretty grim. They're incontinent. Often doubly incontinent. They've had strokes. They're deaf or blind. Senile, disorientated, severely depressed. They're an unending burden on their relatives. They moan. They complain. They spill food down their clothes. They have to be constantly cleaned up at one end or the other. If you think people want to go on living in that condition, you're a sadist!"
Raynes remembered that Fiona had called Gloria a sadist.
This was the view from the other end of the telescope.
"Did you use morphine?"
"I didn't use anything. I just recommended a suitable medication and my staff did what was required." She looked pityingly at the Inspector. "Morphine's a bit obvious. There are more subtle ways of . . . doing things."
"Did your staff object?"

"No. They got their cut."
"I see."
"Quite useful, an extra £500 – tax free."
Although Gloria sounded eminently reasonable, Raynes could sense a very chilling character coming through.
"So you were exposed by this woman?"
"Yes, one of the relatives shopped me. Quite unfair, really. We'd done more for her mother than most. We thought she'd be glad to get rid of the old bat. She probably was. But I think one of our care assistants must have rubbed her up the wrong way. So she phoned Fiona – she has a hot-line number – and once she got going, the shit truly hit the fan."
Gloria smiled.
"Fortunately, I got my money out in time. So, apart from my reputation, I didn't suffer all that much. Looking back, she probably did me a good turn. I've quite enjoyed being a lady of leisure. Handsome men take me to the Cote d'Azur." She smiled more warmly. "I think they enjoy living dangerously."
"Did you ever feel like killing Miss Stewart?"
Gloria laughed.
"At the time, such thoughts did go through my mind. I had an intense longing to hit back. I remember finding out where she lived – and where she worked. I thought about gassing her. 'Fixing' a bottle of gin. Loosening the bolts on the front wheels of her car. Putting petrol through her letter box. But I didn't do anything. After about three months, I was enjoying myself so much, I didn't really care."
Raynes listened thoughtfully.
"And which sleeping compartment were you in?"
"No. 1. Miles away."
"You noticed Miss Stewart was on the train?"
"Well, I didn't actually see her. But I saw all her luggage. Mountains of stuff – all marked F.S. Couldn't have been more obvious. The attendant carrying it into No. 9 . . ."
"Next door to Mr Potter?"
"Yes," said Gloria. "Makes you think, doesn't it?"
"But, of course, it wasn't Miss Stewart?"
"No. It was her side-kick. Probably an equally nasty piece of

work. You'd have to be, working for her. I've no sympathy. None at all. Good riddance to bad rubbish. That's what I say."

Raynes decided to move the questioning on.

"When did you decide to come on this murder weekend?"

Gloria hesitated.

"Quite a long time ago. I saw Molly's ad in the newspaper and I thought it might be fun. As you know, I love crossword puzzles and detective stories. I thought it might be just the ideal place to meet some like-minded people . . ."

"Like Stanley Dixon?" interposed the Inspector maliciously.

"Yes, like dear Stanley . . . but I didn't expect to be coming up here to Mallaig. I was hoping to go to the one in Cornwall. This is a bit remote from civilization."

"Perhaps that was the idea?"

"Perhaps."

"Molly didn't ask you to come on this particular weekend?"

Gloria hesitated.

"Well, no. It was my idea. But I think she said this was the first one that was free."

"An extraordinary collection of people?"

"Truly extraordinary. But all great characters – except for that wretched man, Potter. He's a typical civil servant. Colourless, grovelling, self-serving, false – I can't see what Molly sees in him."

Raynes ignored her criticism of Bernard, even though he agreed with her.

"You don't think Molly chose this venue because of the long train journey? The chance that Miss Stewart might be murdered *en route*?"

Gloria smiled sweetly.

"I'm sure we could've dealt with her when she arrived – much more easily. A sleeper compartment – even a first-class sleeper compartment – is a very constricted environment. Hardly room to swing a kitten – let alone strangle a full-sized bitch! If I was going to do something to Miss Stewart, I'd have waited till she was actually here."

"She's staying here now."

"Well, if I were her, I'd leave very quickly."

Gloria made her feelings abundantly clear.

"You think she is in danger?"

"Yes. Don't you?"

"But someone has already died . . ."

"That won't stop a really determined killer. If he got it wrong the first time, he'll make jolly sure next time . . . I would."

Her eyes glowed mockingly.

"But you have no burning hatred for Miss Stewart?"

"Not now." She smiled. "But for old times' sake, it wouldn't worry me if I had to wield a syringe!"

"Did you bring one with you?"

"No."

She laughed.

"I wasn't expecting anything dramatic to happen. But now that it has, it's much better than play-acting, isn't it? We're dealing with real people – not cardboard cut-outs. Real bodies, real blood."

"Perhaps," said Raynes, "a murder weekend is a good cover for such things?"

"Perfect," said Gloria. "Just perfect."

She looked at the Inspector.

"However, I think you're wrong about one thing . . ."

"What's that?"

"About Molly specially choosing Mallaig for the murder. I'm sure I heard her saying that she'd been up here last year – at about the same time. She thought the hotel was so good that it was worth travelling the extra distance."

"It is good."

"Superb cooking. Excellent service. And, if I may say so, Inspector, I thought your input last night was quite stimulating. I remember reading the case at the time, but I never thought I'd have it explained to me in such detail. She was quite a girl."

Raynes looked at Gloria.

"You are obviously a lady of very bloodthirsty tastes."

She smiled confidently.

"Inspector, to me, murder is just bread and butter."

The trouble was – she meant it.

16. *Noughts and Crosses*

There was time for just one more interview before lunch. Molly's guests would soon be heading for the cocktail bar.

Raynes had noticed that Canon Larkin had been strictly teetotal during the weekend – so he would not be missing anything. He asked Gloria to send him up.

Canon Larkin's face looked perhaps more sallow and cavernous than usual, but his manner was extremely cheerful.

"Well, Inspector, life imitates art! I must have seen the film four times – but I never thought I'd be living it for real."

"It isn't quite the same," said Raynes reprovingly. "It's Scotland – not Yugoslavia. It's high summer – not midwinter. It's 1989 – not 1929. It is a woman – not a man – that has died; and in this case, there was no murder weapon. The victim was strangled." He looked at the clergyman in a more kindly fashion. "And I am not Hercule Poirot!"

"That's not the impression I gained last night. I would have rated you higher than M'sieur Poirot. More patient – and more deadly."

"I like to think so," said Raynes modestly.

He looked down at his pencilled notes.

Alcohol was the first item on his list. It seemed sensible to tackle the issue head-on.

"I see that you don't drink. Is that because of your medical condition?"

Canon Larkin inclined his head.

"I had quite a severe drink problem. I had to go to a special clinic to get dried out. The doctors told me that if I drank another glass, my liver would pack up. It seemed sensible to take their advice."

"Is that why you lost your job?"

"Yes."

"It wasn't because of Fiona Stewart?"

Canon Larkin's lips moved in a silent curse as her name was mentioned.

"She was the one who did the dirty."

"She exposed you?"

"Completely – and utterly."

"And not just for the drink?"

"Inspector, how much do you know?"

In normal circumstances, Raynes would have bullied Canon Larkin into confessing his sordid deeds; but since this was not his case – and because he would still have to mix with Molly's guests – he adopted a gentler tone.

"Well," he said, "I was told that you were a very active – and promiscuous – homosexual, and that you used to have young men – rough trade – coming to your house. I can't imagine that that would go down very well in a Cathedral close. Was that why they chucked you out?"

"I think most of my colleagues were fully aware of what I got up to, but they didn't say anything. Too frightened of scandal. But, eventually, of course, that was what they got. Page after page of it."

"Did Miss Stewart come to see you?"

"She did. But, unfortunately, she came the wrong evening. I'd been out drinking most of the afternoon and I was as high as a kite. I thought she was doing an article about one of the boys I'd known. She seemed to think it was all a bit of a joke. Nothing serious. I responded in kind. Said far more than I should. I didn't know she'd got the whole thing taped. I assumed it was just a quiet chat – off the record. But with these people, you're never off the record. They're soaking it all up and by the time they've cut bits out – and stuck other bits together – they can make it sound far worse."

Raynes nodded.

He knew from bitter personal experience how devious the Press could be. Even a simple statement could be twisted to mean anything they wished. If they could trip you up, they would. Raynes always hated speaking to journalists. Whenever possible, he left the job to others.

"Do you bear Miss Stewart a grudge?"

Canon Larkin thought for several moments.

"If I am to be honest with you, Inspector; yes, I do. I hated the way she did it. It was so underhand. She led me completely up the garden path. I can't forgive her for that. But I suppose, looking back, I was fair game. And the Church is probably a much better place without me."

Raynes watched him closely.

"Did you hate her enough to kill her? Were you biding your time?"

Mr Larkin visibly relaxed.

"Of course not."

"But Molly provided you with a perfect opportunity?"

"It's been two years, Inspector. Two years and . . . four months." He counted on his fingers. "March . . . five months. I think that if I was going to murder her, I would have done so long before now."

"But part of that time you were in the clinic?"

"Just three months. But a lot of water has flowed under the bridge since then."

Raynes wondered if Canon Larkin was trying to tell him something.

"And are you in good health at this moment?"

"I know what you're thinking."

Raynes raised an eyebrow.

"Have you got AIDS?"

"No, but I'm HIV positive. Living on the brink, so to speak, But I'm not as ill as I look."

He took a leather notecase out of his pocket.

"That's what I used to look like about five years ago. Almost a different man."

Raynes looked at the photograph of a smug, plump-faced, smiling clergyman, radiant in self-righteousness. It was certainly nothing like the man sitting in front of him this afternoon. Even the eyes had changed.

Silently, he passed lack the photograph.

"Of course," he said, "Miss Stewart has not been killed."

"No."

"She's still very much alive."

"So I hear."

"And she's staying in this hotel."

"Very unwise."

"You think people are still gunning for her?"
"So I've heard – on the grapevine."
"You wouldn't care to mention names?"
"Well, if I don't tell you, someone else will. Kenny Savage will never forgive her for busting up his haulage business; and Lady Emily and Stanley Dixon both went to jail because of her. They're not likely to forget that."
"You think they are still waiting for revenge?"
"I would say so. Yes."
"And what about Mr Potter?"
Canon Larkin laughed.
"A fish waiting to be fried. Most entertaining. From what I hear, Molly's trying to protect him." He shrugged his thin shoulders. "I suppose attack is the best means of defence. Gathering all the wagons into a circle to resist the massed ranks of the Cherokee. It might even work. One Indian has already bitten the dust!"
He smiled.
"Yes," said Raynes. "And where were you when that Indian fell?"
"If what I hear is true – and the body was thrown from a fast moving train north of Crianlarich, then I was fast asleep."
"Which compartment were you in?"
"No. 6."
Canon Larkin surveyed the Inspector with dark, steady eyes.
"Was there something special about No. 6?"
"No. But there might have been about No. 8."
"Mr Potter?"
"Yes. I'm not here to protect him. But you might be interested to know that I saw him going into compartment No. 9 shortly after 10.00pm."
"You were in the passageway?"
"I was coming back from the toilet. I saw him going into another compartment. Out of curiosity, I went along to check. For a moment, I thought he might have been visiting Lady Emily in No. 10. But when I saw he had gone into No. 9, I was much amused."
"You knew who was in that compartment?"

"You could hardly fail to notice. All the luggage. You'd have thought she was about to climb Mount Everest. You didn't even have to look at the luggage labels. Her initials were embossed in gold on every suitcase."

"Were you expecting to see Miss Stewart in Mallaig?"

"A little bird did whisper that we might be expecting visitors."

"And what did you think Mr Potter was doing in No. 9?"

"Begging for mercy? Offering a substantial bribe? Telling her to call off the bloodhounds or else? Perhaps even biffing her over the head?"

"But it wasn't Fiona Stewart?"

"No. So what was the point?"

Both men were silent.

"Perhaps he thought she was Miss Stewart. A genuine mistake. He wouldn't know her, would he? All those suitcases with her initials . . . It was a mistake anyone could make."

Downstairs, the large brass gong sounded for lunch.

"One final question, Mr Larkin. Are you still a canon; or did you lose that with everything else?"

The cleric looked very deflated.

"Of course you're right, Inspector. You're very perceptive. I'm not really a canon any more. When you're defrocked, they take everything away. House, wage, titles – everything. I now work for a housing trust. I was going to be just plain Mr Larkin, but they thought a title would add distinction to their letterheads.

"So, for their sake, I resurrected my title. It pleased my mother. She was terribly upset by everything that appeared in the newspapers . . . At least she lived long enough to see me back on my feet again."

"When did she die?"

"Last Christmas," said Mr Larkin. "She was the only one I had left."

Raynes felt that he had had quite enough of Simon Larkin's self-pity for one day. He hoped that Dorothy West would have kept him a place at her table; but, unfortunately, the only empty table was set for two.

The Inspector sighed.

"I'm afraid," he said, "we're fated to sit together for lunch. Tell me about something cheerful. The joys of church music. The beauty of Truro cathedral . . ."

"Would you like me to tell you about Colin Dexter's latest novel?"

"If you must," said Raynes.

17. *Strip-poker*

After lunch, Raynes invited Suzanne Tempest to join him in the library. She had no desire to see the Inspector; but Molly persuaded her to go.

"It's safer if everyone goes," she said. "But be careful what you say."

Suzanne therefore came to the library in a very petulant mood and drummed her fingers impatiently on the arms of her chair.

Raynes could sense her all-consuming frustration.

"I don't think you're enjoying this murder weekend, are you?" he said.

"No. It's bloody boring. Cooped up in this sodding hotel. Pathetic people playing stupid games. No shops . . . no car . . ."

"So why did you come?"

"I was asked to come."

She crossed her long legs.

"By whom?"

"By Molly, of course!"

Suzanne wondered whether that was something she should not have said, because the Inspector immediately pounced upon her reply.

"And why did she want you to come? Did she think you might enjoy playing these 'stupid games'?"

Suzanne shrugged her shoulders.

"I don't know. I expect she invited me as a sort of thank-you."

"A thank-you for what?"

"For telling her about Bernard."

"And what did you tell her?"

"That Fiona was after his scalp."

"You know Fiona quite well?"

"I know her secretary. We used to share a flat."

"The girl who was murdered? Jill Graham?"

Suzanne looked thunderstruck.

"Jill? I didn't know it was Jill who was dead."

She started to cry.

Raynes realized that this was the first time he had mentioned the victim's name. He had called her "Miss Stewart's assistant", her "side-kick". Quite clearly, Suzanne had never imagined for one moment that the dead woman was her friend.

Raynes gave her his handkerchief and rang for a glass of brandy. Suzanne stared down at her knees, seeing nothing. She moaned to herself and tears ran constantly down her cheeks. When the brandy arrived, she gulped it down and tried to pull herself together.

"I'm sorry to have upset you," said Raynes, "but I thought you knew who had died."

Suzanne shook her head.

"Fiona works with several people. I thought it was one of the others. But she's fond of Jill – that's probably why she brought her up."

"You didn't see her on the train?"

"No. I was about the last one to arrive. They just threw me in – and slammed the doors. The whistle went – and we were off."

"Jill was in No. 9."

"I was in No. 2."

"If you had known she was there, would you have gone in to see her?"

"Of course I would. We'd probably have spent half the night yattering to each other. Catching up on all the latest gossip."

She shuddered and began to cry again. "That's awful. I can't believe it. Why should anyone have wanted to kill Jill?"

Raynes hoped that now Suzanne realized it was her friend who had been murdered – and Raynes was trying to discover her killer – she might prove more co-operative. He tried to be as gentle as possible.

"She was killed because someone thought she was Miss Stewart."

Suzanne hammered the arms of her chair again.

"But that's quite ridiculous! She doesn't look anything like her."

"No, she doesn't. But I think someone saw Fiona's luggage being loaded on to the train – and thought it was her. They knew she was coming up here to do one of her investigations – on Mr Potter – and they tried to stop her."

Suzanne began to see her own part in this tragedy. She sobered up very quickly.

"You think that because I warned Molly about Bernard all this happened?"

"Not the murder, no. But the precautions Molly took to protect Bernard. That provoked someone to attack Fiona. Unfortunately, they killed Jill by mistake. That's my reading of it."

"But who would have done that?"

"Well," said Raynes cautiously, "all Molly's guests have reason to hate Miss Stewart. They've lost their jobs. Some of them have been to jail because of her. If anyone really wanted to get rid of her, these are the prime suspects."

Suzanne was silent.

"I see what you mean," she said at last.

Raynes tried to be as tactful as possible.

"Weren't you the subject of one of Miss Stewart's investigations?"

Suzanne smiled.

"Oh, that was a giggle. We did it for publicity purposes."

"The Minister of Commerce?"

"He was an utter and complete sleazebag! You should have seen him! He'd been having it off with numerous women. Everyone knew about it. He liked to have them two at a time – even three at a time – in some London hotel room. He was just asking for it.

"Fiona got the whole place wired up – little cameras hidden

on top of wardrobes – mikes right up beside the bed – and we just hammed it up. Had him chasing us around stark-naked. Spanking our bottoms. Doing other naughty things. Lots of frolics on the bed. Plenty of saucy conversation.

"My friend serviced him just for the hell of it – and I joined in. Lots of moaning and groaning. Sounded terrific! When it came out in the papers, it was our photographs that people looked at. I can tell you, the telephone never stopped. Everyone wanted to see us. Snap more photographs. Take us out to dinner. After that, I never looked back."

"So Fiona did you a very good turn?"

"She did really."

"You didn't worry what it did to the Minister?"

"Hell, no. He lost his job, but he's still an MP. Probably picked up a couple of directorships and a new wife. He sold his story to some greedy publisher – like we did. Don't worry about him."

"And Fiona cleared – what? £50,000?"

"At least."

Suzanne clearly had no regrets.

Raynes looked thoughtful.

"Presumably she would make an equal killing from Mr Potter?"

Suzanne wrapped the handkerchief around her wrist.

"I doubt it. Drugs are not as exciting as sex. Everyone likes a good sex scandal. That's what people buy their Sunday papers for. The more juicy the better! But drugs are . . . different. It's sordid. In his case, it's sheer hypocrisy. How he can be fighting the drug dealers and at the same time using them, I just don't know. He deserves to be exposed."

"Cocaine, wasn't it?"

Suzanne nodded.

"It was his wife, really. She had these little tea parties for her friends. Only, of course, it wasn't tea they were tippling. It was vodka, Bacardis, Southern Comfort, Malibu, Blue Bols . . . But even that wasn't exciting enough. So they started passing round the cocaine – and I think she got hooked. Perhaps they all did. She was hiding it in little corners all round the house. It's probably still there. I think she's gone off to a private clinic."

"Mr Potter told me she'd left him."

"Well, perhaps she has. Good luck to her. I don't think he was much of a husband. Working late every night. Knowing what was going on behind his back. But not wanting to know. Pretending that he didn't know. Fat lot of good it's done him!"

"But, surely, now he's been warned, he'll be very careful what he says?"

"Fiona has a way with people like that. She exaggerates. Makes out things are far more awful than they are. People get so annoyed at her suggestions, that they start trying to correct her: 'You've got it wrong. It was nothing like that. This is what really happened . . .' And then she's got them. It's the passion to explain that does them – every time."

"You seem to know a lot about Fiona's techniques?"

"Well, Jill used to tell me. She was the person who went all wired up. Sat there with a little notepad on her lap. Wrote down the odd word. Everyone concentrated on Fiona. Never looked at Jill. But at the end of the day, she was the one who came home with the bacon." She smiled. "Straight from the horse's mouth!"

She smiled again; but then her eyes clouded over and she started shaking.

"Oh, this is awful. Poor Jill." She looked at the Inspector. "Could I have another brandy?"

"Certainly," said Raynes. "It's all on the house."

He rang the bell and gave the order.

"I just can't believe it. We met for lunch about a month ago – perhaps six weeks – and Jill was telling me what they were planning. She probably shouldn't have said anything to me, but she could be a bit indiscreet."

"But why did you tell Molly?"

"Well, Molly knows my mother. She knows everyone, doesn't she? I've known her for years – since I was a little girl. And we both go to the same hairdresser. It was just after I'd seen Jill. We were talking about drugs. Molly was saying she hoped I wouldn't be stupid and ruin my career by taking anything – and

I said I wouldn't touch them. And then I just found myself telling her what Jill had told me. I didn't know that she knew Bernard – but apparently she did." Suzanne hammered the arms of her chair once again. "It was so stupid . . . so bloody stupid!"

The second brandy arrived.

She gulped it down.

"Thank you," she said. "I needed that."

She looked at the Inspector critically.

"So you think one of them did it?"

"It's more than likely."

"It's probably that horrible Larkin creature. He's got a revolting face."

"He's quite ill."

"He looks evil."

"I don't think this is the moment to make accusations. We don't know the full story yet."

Suzanne laughed.

"It's just like one of Molly's games. You're waiting for the extra clues at the beginning of Round Two!"

The Inspector was glad she could see some humour in the situation. He thought it likely that she would break down later. Molly would probably look after her.

"Well," he said, "there's one thing we can be sure of. You would have recognized Jill on the train. You would have known she wasn't Fiona. I suppose that clears you of the murder."

Suzanne nodded dumbly.

"I would never have hurt her."

"Of course not," said Raynes.

But he was still left wondering if there was perhaps something Suzanne had not told him. He put a question mark beside her name.

18. *Snakes and ladders*

Kenny Savage burst into the library.

He looked angry.

"Have you been bullying that lovely young girl, Inspector? I saw her crying her eyes out downstairs."

Raynes shook his head.

"No. She's just discovered that the girl who was killed on the train was a friend of hers."

"You don't say!"

"Someone called Jill Graham. She worked for Fiona Stewart. She was her secretary."

Kenny's eyes narrowed.

"No one decent would work for the likes of her. She was a she-devil – and no mistake! A bitch to end all bitches. How she could ever sleep peacefully in her bed after what she's done to people passes belief!"

Raynes looked sympathetically at Kenny Savage.

"What did she do to you, Kenny? Tell me."

"Left me without a name! Left me without a business! One day I was running a fleet of lorries back and forth across Europe. Next day, I was bust. I just couldn't believe it. All because of that fucking woman! She ruined my life."

Raynes tried to get a more accurate picture.

"You set up a transport company . . .?"

"Twenty odd years ago. One man show for six months, then I took on my brother. We did quite well. One or two of our rivals went bust. We undercut them – to let you understand. But all's fair in love and war." He laughed nervously.

"We had low overheads; they didn't. So we took over their business. We also bought up their lorries for a song. Expanded. Decided that long-distance was where the money was. Went into Europe. Expanded again. Fleet of eighty lorries I had, Inspector. Well, seventy-eight, to be precise. Volvos, Mercs; only the best. They had to be when you think of the mileage they covered each year. Can't afford to have breakdowns in Poland or Bulgaria or some piss-awful little country. Got to be reliable."

Kenny paused for breath.

"Well, maybe I overreached myself, Inspector. Over-ambitious, perhaps. But I got carried away with the business. Invested constantly in new trucks. Built a new depot with a good repair shop. Properly qualified mechanics. Did it all myself. Took out bigger loans than I should. No harm in that if things had gone the way they should. I'd have paid back every penny. But I got greedy. I'll admit that, Inspector. I was willing to make a few quick bucks on the side.

"This Turk – I think he was a Turk – offered me a good deal if I'd carry a few of his fellow-countrymen into Germany. No fuss, no pack-drill. So I said I'd like to see his money up front. Cash! No messing about. Dollars or sterling. He was willing to pay good money; and like a fool, I took it.

"I had one or two of our trailers altered; put in false walls – beautiful job – and we did a couple of trial runs – no problem. Then we got going. Every week, we lifted about forty of the buggers in Istanbul and shipped them to Germany. The customs didn't twig. They knew our lorries were clean. We used busy crossings – at peak times. We were never caught. It seemed a bit of a lark, really. But someone must have talked – I don't know who – and that woman picked it up. Not only picked it up. Followed us. Took photos. Wrote a tissue of lies. Put me in Queer Street, she did.

"And what happened? I lost my HGV licence. The banks called in their loans. Our customers switched their business to other firms. I was finished. After that, I appeared in court. Fined. Jailed for six months. Came out – bankrupt! Now I drive taxis for my brother. Quite a good living – but nothing compared to what I lost." He sighed deeply. "I'll never forgive her. Never!"

Raynes was tempted to point out that if he had not been acting illegally, Fiona Stewart would never have had a story to write. But Kenny was so overcome by his downfall that he had to blame someone – and that "fucking woman" was the focus for all his bitterness and anger.

"How many years ago was this?"

"About four."

He sounder calmer.

"But you're still extremely bitter?"

"Very bitter, Inspector. I'll not hide it from you."

Raynes looked at him closely.

"Is that why you came on this murder weekend? Because you knew Fiona Stewart was going to be here? In this hotel?"

A shady look came over Kenny's face.

"Now you wouldn't expect me to admit that, Inspector, would you? Come on! It'd be as good as confessing my guilt."

"It's not Miss Stewart who's been murdered. It was her assistant. The murder's been done. Miss Stewart is still alive."

"More's the pity!"

Raynes looked at Mr Savage thoughtfully.

"Did you ever meet her?"

"Can't say that I did."

"Have you ever seen her photograph?"

"I may have done."

Kenny could see what the Inspector was getting at, but he wasn't going to help him. He knew what the police were like . . .

"If you had met Miss Stewart in the hotel, would you have attacked her?"

Kenny breathed deeply.

"It's difficult to say, Inspector. I'm a man of sudden moods and passions. I think that if I saw her – just walking through the entrance, like – I might be able to control myself. But if she opened her mouth or laughed at me, I'd let her have it. God knows, I've got nothing to lose."

"You're not the only one who feels strongly."

"No. Lady Emily's built up a fine head of steam. And so has Stan. I don't think Mr Potter'd be capable of lifting his hand. Too much of a wimp. But there's no telling. Some of these quiet guys – they just snap."

"Do you think that's what happened?"

Kenny looked uncertain.

"I really don't know, Inspector. I didn't think anything about that train till I heard this morning what had happened. I had a quiet night – slept well. I downed about six pints before I got on the train – six pints and a couple of nips!" He smiled. "Put me out like the proverbial light. Never heard or saw a thing."

"What compartment were you in?"

"Next to you, Inspector. No. 5."

Kenny smiled again.

"Bet you didn't hear nothing neither?"

Raynes acknowledged that he too had had a very peaceful and undisturbed journey.

He decided that Mr Savage, being a blunt and straightforward type of bloke, would find it difficult to lie. There was only one more question he wanted to ask.

"Tell me," he said, "when you were invited on this murder weekend, was there any plan mentioned? Any plan which might have involved an attack on Miss Stewart?"

"That's news to me, Inspector."

His face had a bland, frozen look. It had changed in a second. He looked at Raynes through thin, slit eyes. It was almost like a different person. His hands, too, which had been so open and expressive, were now hard and clenched. Raynes noted the change with interest. He had certainly touched a raw nerve.

Raynes continued in a friendly fashion as if Mr Savage's mood had remained unchanged.

"I'm not asking you whether you were involved in any plan. I'm just asking whether you heard that any other of Molly's guests were planning to attack Miss Stewart?"

But no one was going to make Kenny answer any trick questions. He looked the Inspector in the eye.

"You'll have to ask them."

"That means there was."

Mr Savage looked at the Inspector coldly.

"Well, if there was . . . remember! You never heard it from me."

19. *Ludo*

Lady Emily had been looking forward to being interviewed by the Inspector. She hoped it would be an interview for him to remember. To that end, she put on her most compelling, figure-hugging dress – which just happened to be in black velvet. The hemline was exceedingly high which showed her plump, juicy thighs to good advantage.

For good measure, she decided to dispense with any knickers – a formula which had worked rather well in thc past. She hoped to keep Raynes' eyes fixed on her lower parts. Perhaps that way, he would be too distracted to look deeply into her soul!

However, just in case he did concentrate upon her face, she made herself up rather nicely with a good deal of eye-shadow and mascara which made an otherwise plain face more exciting. Thus suitably prepared, she presented herself in the library.

Raynes was slightly taken aback. For a moment, he imagined that one of the other hotel guests had wandered into the library by mistake.

Lady Emily smiled happily at his confusion.

"The full chocolate bar!" she said provocatively.

"If you can't beat them, join them!" said Raynes.

"It amazes me how you men always go for the older women."

"I didn't realize there was any alternative."

"You never asked."

Raynes pointed to a comfortable chair.

"Would you like to sit down?"

Lady Emily sat down and crossed her legs slowly.

He thought . . . for a minute . . . but, no, he must have been mistaken . . .

But there was a mischievous smile on her lips.

Very quickly, Raynes realized precisely how she intended to handle the interview. She intended to distract him from the word go. When the questions got too difficult or too personal, she would lower her eyes, delicately cross her legs and try to unnerve him. And she would enjoy doing it.

But forewarned is forearmed and the Inspector made sure his eyes never left her face.

He raised his eyebrows.

"I see you're dressed to kill?"

"Bit late for that," said Lady Emily. "The deed's already been done."

"But not perhaps the victim you were expecting?"

"There's still time."

Raynes looked at her coldly.

"You're implying that if an opportunity arose for you to kill Fiona Stewart, you would still do it?"

"Might as well be hung for a sheep as a lamb. I've already served time because of her. I don't see why I should be deprived of the pleasure of bumping her off." Lady Emily smiled with exquisite sweetness. "Teach people like her that they can't get away with gutter journalism. Show them what it feels like to be threatened and bullied. Let them know that their poor victims can hit back and hurt them."

Raynes did not challenge her.

Instead, he said, "I believe you used to run a charity?"

Lady Emily nodded: "The Lady Cavanagh Trust for Poor Children. A Victorian foundation, completely out of touch with the twentieth century. It was designed for children whose parents had died of cholera or bubonic plague. They had to live within ten miles of Old London Bridge – long since dismantled and taken to America. Applicants were to approach the Trust through the clergy of a local church – bombed by the Germans and never rebuilt. It was a complete nonsense."

"So no one applied?"

"No one knew anything about the Trust. Not at least till I took over. It'd been accumulating funds for over a century, but no one knew how the money should be dispensed. Trusts are tricky things. I was employed as a research worker by the Trustees to find out how we could deal with it. Thanks to my efforts, I was made Secretary to the Trust. I appointed myself Treasurer; and when the other Trustees bowed out – they were both rather ancient – I took over as Patron and chief Trustee."

"And then proceeded to make the most of it?"

"Well, it seemed quite pointless leaving the money in the bank! I organized splendid parties. Had some wonderful trips. Bought myself a horse . . . a BMW . . . a rather nice flat – and even took flying lessons. And that was only on the interest. I never touched the capital."

Lady Emily's tone of voice suggested that she believed herself to have some moral standards.

"And how much did you spend?"

"Well, the Court said about £92,000, but it was a bit more than that . . ."

Raynes encouraged her to be more explicit.

"Well, over £800,000, I should think. It was all going rather nicely till that bitch came along and spoilt it. I didn't realize who she was. I'd been drinking rather a lot at a cocktail party and she came up to me – with her friend – and said: 'Do tell me about this marvellous Trust.' So I told her what I've just told you. How difficult it was to find claimants – and all I was doing to publicize the Trust. I should have kept my mouth shut."

Lady Emily shook her head sadly.

"I must have been really drunk. I told her the whole story. Everything. And she kept saying: 'I can't believe it. What a marvellous job!' And I just delivered myself into her clutches. I believe that's the way she traps everyone. That little bitch standing beside her was recording every word. Every bloody word! So how could I deny it? Once it appeared in the Press, I was sunk. The police arrived and questioned me. The Inland Revenue. Everything was confiscated. Even my flat. I had no money – no clothes. I spent a year in prison thanks to her." Her voice was hard and bitter. "You think I would pass up a chance to give her the chop?"

Raynes did not doubt the sincerity of her feelings. He could quite easily imagine her committing murder. There was a chilling sort of madness in her eyes.

He looked at her thoughtfully.

"Did you know that Fiona Stewart was coming up to Mallaig to do an exposé on Mr Potter?"

"Not till I saw the luggage sitting on the platform."

Raynes thought he detected a lie.

"You were in the next compartment to the woman who was murdered. You must have seen her. You would have known that she wasn't Fiona Stewart?"

"I knew it was somebody connected with her. You couldn't miss all the labels; they had 'FS Press Agency' printed on them – in gold. Pretty obvious."

"You hadn't seen Miss Graham before?"

"No."

"She wasn't the one with Fiona at the cocktail party?"

"No."

"Did you speak to Miss Graham on the train?"

"No."

"Not at all?"

"I was too busy fending off Stanley Dixon. He was being very persistent . . ."

Lady Emily smiled.

"Trying to sell you an insurance policy?"

"No. Trying to get me to spend the night in his compartment. But he's not my type."

"You prefer them rough?"

Lady Emily grinned.

"How did you guess?"

There was a sudden movement of the knees and an inviting whiff of *Ivoire*.

"Poor Stanley!" said Raynes.

"I wouldn't say that," said Lady Emily dreamily. "I think he's got his eyes on Molly. She's worth a bob or two."

Raynes raised his eyebrows.

That was a connection he had not considered.

Lady Emily laughed.

"Safer than your dear Dorothy anyway!"

"And what's wrong with Mrs West?"

"Well, I'm sure she's a good grind and all that – but she's a born killer. You didn't know that, did you?"

Raynes tried to look politely surprised.

"All the people her husband was supposed to have killed – it was her. She knows all about poisons and how to bump people off. Did it beautifully. Her husband accepted the blame – but he was covering up for her.

"She's a born psychopath. Selected her victims with great care and then wiped them out – with scarcely a trace. It took people a long time to realize what she was doing. Her husband was charged. She let him take the rap.

"But just before it got to court . . . surprise, surprise . . . he committed suicide. So neatly done. No one could point a finger at her. But who else could have done it? She's a dangerous creature, Inspector. You're playing with fire."

Raynes allowed that there might be some truth in Lady Emily's allegations, but he thought she was probably jealous.

He smiled.

"Well, I survived one night with her."

"Be careful what she gives you to drink! It might contain more than you bargained for."

Raynes immediately remembered drinking champagne the previous night. But he had opened the bottle. He had poured out the drinks. Dorothy had had no chance of lacing the champagne. But perhaps Lady Emily had a point. It was not the sex that was dangerous . . . next time, he might not be so lucky.

He thought that Lady Emily had neatly sidetracked him from his investigations. He returned – reluctantly – to the train.

"Well," he said, "you may not have spoken to Jill Graham, but you must have heard something."

"Oh, I heard quite a few things."

"Bumps and bangs?"

"No, mostly voices raised in anger."

"Male voices?"

"No. Female voices."

Raynes looked surprised.

"I'm told that Bernard Potter went to her compartment."

"I didn't hear him. He has quite a soft voice."

"Whose voice did you hear?"

"Suzanne's."

"Suzanne?"

"Yes. She was in there. Talking about money. Money she had been promised – but she hadn't got it. She sounded very angry."

"What time was this?"

"About an hour after we left London. It went on for about ten minutes."

"And you heard them talking?"

"Well, it was screaming mostly. Suzanne was shouting . . . she does shout rather a lot. Very temperamental creature . . . always bursting into tears. Means nothing. It's completely false."

"But you're sure it was Suzanne?"

"I didn't know who it was at the time. But I've heard plenty of her since. It was definitely her."

Raynes tried to imagine the scene.

Lady Emily watched him.

"You said 'voices' – plural. Who else did you hear?"

"Well, there was another person – about two hours later. I was almost asleep – but I heard the door bang. She had a very matter-of-fact voice – like Gloria. Calm but firm. She seemed to be telling her what to do. I actually thought it might be the bitch herself."

"Fiona Stewart? She wasn't on the train!"

"How d'you know? Just because she arrived in the hotel on Friday night – or Saturday morning? She could have got off the train – driven down to Glasgow – flown back to London. She could easily have fixed it."

It seemed very far-fetched to Inspector Raynes. But if Fiona had been involved, her movements could easily be traced through the airline records. Surely she would not be so foolish?

Raynes looked at Lady Emily.

"But why should Miss Stewart want to kill her assistant?"

"Betrayal."

"Betrayal?"

"Suppose that she discovered Jill had spilt the beans to Molly. Suppose that she discovered Molly had lined up all her enemies – all her ex-victims – and that she was walking into a pre-arranged trap. She might have been extremely angry."

"But she wouldn't have killed her!"

"I'm told that Fiona has quite a temper. Doesn't like being crossed."

"Who told you that?"

"Someone who knows her. Apparently she throws tantrums at work. Walks off in a huff. Sacks people for almost nothing. Throws their belongings out into the street. She probably fell out with her assistant. Lost her temper. Smashed her head against the wall . . ."

"She was strangled."

"Well . . . strangled her."

"And then waited five hours before she threw her body out of the train?" Raynes shook his head. "I think you're making it up."

"Perhaps she had an accomplice?"

"Kenny Savage? That would please you!"

"It would actually. He's a *real* man."

Raynes looked at her wriggling thighs. Even the mention of his name seemed to have got her hormones going.

"Perhaps you should take off your pants for him?"

"I was thinking of doing that tonight. He was too drunk last night – and, anyway, he was slobbering over Suzanne . . ."

"Not your favourite lady?"

"No. She's just a feather-brained idiot."

"Whilst you are a serious student doing business management at Oxford?"

Lady Emily smiled.

"Learning to do it properly – next time."

Raynes laughed.

"Well, I think Kenny could probably do with your help . . ."

" . . .Whilst you're dicing with death with dear Dorothy?"

Raynes shook his head.

"I think you're exaggerating. In fact, most of the things you have told me seem rather far-fetched."

Lady Emily adjusted her black velvet dress causing a final down-draught of *Ivoire*.

"I dare say you'll find a grain or two of wheat amongst the chaff."

"I hope so," said Raynes.

20. *Shuttlecock*

Raynes waited for his next victim to arrive.

He was rather surprised when Mr Dixon leapt into the library brandishing a hand gun.

"Hands up, Inspector! I've got you cold!"

Raynes did not react.

He said, "You're the bootlegger who pinches the car."

"That's very clever!" Stanley was full of admiration.

"I've been through it before."

"Ah, that explains it."

Raynes nodded.

"I wish it was as easy solving a real murder."

"Miss Graham, I believe the young lady was called."

Raynes looked him straight in the eye.

"An employee of Fiona Stewart."

Stanley Dixon sat down heavily in the chair recently vacated by Lady Emily. He shook his head sadly.

"Don't mention her! She caused me the greatest misery in my life. In fact, she destroyed it. Destroyed it completely. One moment, I was a highly respected businessman. The next, I was publicly declared to be a crook. No chance to defend myself. Set upon by a pack of wolves. Worse than wolves. Piranha! Tearing the flesh off your body. I don't know how I survived."

Raynes nodded sympathetically.

He could imagine that the collapse of the Preston & General Insurance Company would have been fairly dramatic. The anger of all the customers who had been diddled out of their savings; the anxiety of those who had suddenly discovered that their insurance policies counted for nothing. Whilst the man they had trusted had been living it up – on a private yacht, with a large Bentley, countless mistresses and a healthy account in a Swiss bank. Exposure must have come like a thunderbolt on a calm summer's evening. It was something Mr Dixon would never forget. But like most crooks, he put the blame on others.

"And worst of all, Inspector; she's still alive. Still making other people's lives a misery. She needs to be stopped." He thumped the arm of his chair. "Stopped before she does any more damage."

Raynes looked at him with curious interest.

"And were you going to be the one to stop her?"

"Me?" Stanley laughed. "What could I do?"

"You came on this murder weekend," said Raynes. "I believe you also knew Fiona Stewart was coming up to Mallaig – to expose Bernard Potter. You may not have known about Mr Potter; but you knew she was coming. I'm sure by now you are aware that everyone here has a grudge against Fiona Stewart. Every single one of Molly's guests – except Mr Potter. What other purpose was there in gathering all these people together if not to have a real murder and kill off the lady who has caused you all so much trouble?"

Stanley Dixon was upset at being asked so direct a question. He floundered unhappily.

"I don't think . . . In fact, I'm certain . . . No one had any intention of killing her . . . I certainly didn't . . . We could have made it very unpleasant for her . . . But angry as we were – are – I don't think anyone would have lifted their hand . . . I'm sure they wouldn't . . . we've already suffered enough. Well, at least, I have . . ."

Raynes let him tie himself in knots.

"Well, if you weren't going to punish her in some way, why come up here to Mallaig?"

"It was meant to be a pleasant weekend, Inspector. A few games. A bit of fun. Chasing the skirts. Meeting new people. Enjoying good Scottish food. And even better, Scottish drink. Your own splendid contribution. Up to this morning, I thought it was going excellently . . ."

"But now we have a real body!"

"Quite frankly, Inspector, I don't see what it has to do with us. Miss Stewart is still alive. No one seems to know this Miss Graham who was killed. None of us had anything against her. Why you should be picking on us, I can't imagine. You aren't the policeman in charge of this case. Why you should be getting yourself involved in something which doesn't concern you – seems to me . . . seems to all of us . . . quite absurd."

Raynes' eyes narrowed perceptibly.

"I am the man on the spot," he said quietly. "I assisted Detective-Inspector Cameron in identifying the victim – thanks to Miss Stewart – and he has asked me to help him. Since all of you seem to have a connection with Miss Stewart, all of you are prime suspects. Especially you. I have been told this afternoon, by one of your fellow guests, that you have a blinding hatred against this woman and that you will never forgive her. Is that true – or not?"

Stanley Dixon took a deep breath

"It's true."

"Thank you," said Raynes courteously. "Now perhaps you see why I am making these inquiries. To establish the truth, I need your help."

Mr Dixon nodded his head in agreement.

"Well, first of all, when did you book to come on this murder weekend?"

"About five weeks ago."

"Was it your idea to come – or was it suggested to you?"

"It was suggested."

"By whom?"

"Gloria."

Raynes noted the connection with interest.

"Have you known Gloria for some time?"

Stanley's face coloured a fraction.

"We used to do business together."

"I see. At the White Cliffs Nursing Home?"

"And elsewhere."

"To your mutual advantage?"

"Naturally."

"And did Gloria suggest that this weekend might be to your mutual advantage?"

"She said that Fiona Stewart was expected to gatecrash a murder weekend that was being held up in Scotland and would I like to get a bit of my own back."

"And you said yes?"

"Immediately."

"Did you expect that this would involve murder?"

Stanley Dixon shook his head.

"I can tell you quite truthfully that the thought didn't cross my mind. I imagined that we might do something pretty nasty to her – tie her up, beat her, take some compromising photos, humiliate her in some public place, perhaps even hold her to ransom – but not murder."

"And would you have been quite happy doing these things to her?"

"Most certainly. It would have given me great pleasure."

"Did Gloria tell you that this was what was planned?"

"She didn't say anything had been planned. The things I mentioned were my own ideas."

"Did you communicate these ideas to anyone else?"

"To be perfectly honest, Inspector, I did mention them to Molly."

"And did she favour your proposals?"

"I think she thought I was joking."

"But they might have given her some ideas?"

"They might." Stanley looked a trifle shifty."But even if they did, she hasn't done much about them. Miss Stewart still stalks the globe like Hercules Unchained."

Raynes looked at him.

"But for the murder of Miss Graham, it might have been a different scenario?"

Mr Dixon smiled. "Mallaig 1989?"

He picked up the hand gun. "Boom! Boom!"

Raynes smiled indulgently.

"But someone jumped the gun? Someone couldn't wait till they got up to Mallaig? They took their revenge . . . on the night sleeper. What compartment were you in?"

"No. 7."

"Next door to Mr Potter?"

"So I believe."

"Did you see much of him?"

"I saw him wandering about – but I had no idea who he was until we were introduced."

"Did you go and speak to Gloria?"

"As a matter of fact, I did."

"And did you have any dealings with the lady in No. 9?"
Mr Dixon looked flustered.
"Well, of course I was curious. Who wouldn't be? I guessed who it was. I even looked into her compartment whilst they were loading in all her luggage. But the woman I saw wasn't Fiona Stewart. I must say I felt somewhat relieved."
"Why?"
"Why? Because I was itching for a fight."
"Did you speak to the young woman?"
"Briefly. I asked her where her boss was."
"You expected her to be somewhere on the train?"
"When I saw all the luggage, I thought it was very likely she was somewhere close by."
"But Jill Graham told you Fiona was coming up later?"
"She did."
"And you backed off?"
Stanley looked rather sheepish.
"Well, not immediately. I actually offered her a drink."
"In your compartment?"
"I told her I was in No. 7. I suggested she might like a little nightcap before we settled down for the night."
"Did she accept?"
"Well, I thought she was going to say yes, but this other bloke came in . . ."
Raynes moved forward in his seat.
"And who was that?"
"Mr Potter. As I say, I didn't know who he was. But he came in, said he was a personal friend and asked me if I would mind leaving. They both looked at me. What else could I do?"
Raynes smiled at Stanley's misfortune.
"Then you went to see Gloria?"
Mr Dixon nodded his head.
"Inspector, you are very perceptive."
"You went to tell her that Miss Stewart was not on the train?"
"I did."
"And what did you do next?"
"I went back to the young woman's compartment . . ."
" . . . to see if Mr Potter was still there? And was he?"

"He was. I could hear them talking in low voices. I think they knew I was outside. They shut the door. After that, I didn't see any more of her."

"And then you moved on to No. 10?"

Stanley laughed.

"You know too much!"

"No. Lady Emily said that you had been pestering her."

"Pestering? I wouldn't say that. She was all over me. Very dominating. Mark you, Inspector, I like dominating women."

"So you offered her a nightcap?"

"I did. And if I am to be honest, Inspector, we spent the entire night together."

"In which compartment? Yours or hers?"

"In mine."

"Are you sure? Lady Emily specifically said that she spent the night in No. 10."

"Well, she didn't. She spent it with me."

Raynes thought: "One of them is lying!"

To Stanley he said, "Were you aware of anything else that was going on in the other compartments during the rest of the night? Any voices? Any sounds of breaking glass?"

Mr Dixon smiled.

"After a couple of rounds with Lady Emily, I was totally bushed. Not to mention the three double whiskies. Must be beginning to feel my age."

Raynes smiled in return. "I think we all have that experience from time to time. One final question: Was Lady Emily still in your compartment when you woke up?"

"Indeed she was. Snoring like billy-ho! Can't stand women who snore."

The Inspector looked at him with a wicked glint in his eye. "Perhaps Mr Savage would be less particular?"

21. *Black Maria*

"Well?"

Raynes looked at Dorothy West.

"Last – but by no means least! I won the bottle of claret for 'Chicago 1929'."

"It was the coloured waiter."

"No one else got it."

"Congratulations. Now you'll be able to help me with this one."

"Is it proving difficult?"

"I think I've got the broad outline – but the reason for the murder escapes me. It was perfectly clear that Fiona Stewart was not travelling on the train. Even if people wanted to kill her, why make a pre-emptive strike and kill the wrong person?"

"Perhaps they thought she was as much to blame as Fiona?"

"She'd only worked with her for two years."

"You can make a lot of enemies in two years."

"When did she run the feature on your husband?"

"Two years ago this November."

"So Jill Graham was part of the investigating team?"

Mrs West nodded.

"I see," said Raynes. "So you're one of those who had no cause to love her?"

"Like mistress, like dog."

"Was it painful – the muck-raking?"

"Extremely. As I told you, it drove my husband to an early death."

Raynes was acutely aware of all that Lady Emily had told him, but he had no intention of repeating it to Dorothy.

"You said that he died after an injection. Self-inflicted."

"That's right. You have an excellent memory."

"Why did he feel he had to take that step?"

Dorothy West regarded the Inspector with a pitying look.

"I'm sure Fiona Stewart told you the whole grisly story."

Raynes was instantly defensive.

"All she told me was that your husband had killed three of

his patients. Injections seem to have been his preferred method."

"It causes the least distress to the patient."

"Were they mercy killings?"

"Depends what you call a mercy killing!"

Mrs West's eyes twinkled mischievously.

"Tell me," said Raynes.

"My husband had a partner. In fact, he had two. One full-time, one part-time. The full-time partner, Dr Clark, had a very attractive wife – Valeric. A vivacious redhead. My husband was very fond of Valerie; but his love was completely unrequited. She wouldn't have anything to do with him. That's what he said.

"But I think they had a brief affair which didn't work out. Dr Clark didn't get on very well with his wife. They slept in separate rooms. I don't think he was very interested in women. Much more interested in his work. He was a good doctor."

Raynes listened carefully.

"Valerie had to take what she could get – elsewhere. She was fairly discreet, but my husband found out whom she had been seeing. He was jealous." Mrs West paused. "Partly jealous, partly sorry for his colleague. For what she was doing to him. When the occasion arose – and one of these gentlemen fell ill – he didn't get better."

There was a chill tone to Dorothy's voice.

"It was revenge – but administered with great discretion. When the first one died, Valerie was naturally distressed. When the second one died, she was surprised. When the third one died, she became suspicious. She examined the practice records and noted that each of her suitors had received an injection from my husband before he died. She couldn't see what the injection was. Like most doctors, my husband's handwriting was quite illegible. But the hieroglyphics looked similar.

"She didn't accuse him to his face. She didn't mention it to her husband. She phoned up Fiona – on her hotline number – and told her of her suspicions. Next thing we knew, Fiona Stewart was examining our practice records. Taking photographs. She interviewed the men's families. Encouraged them to make an official complaint to the General Medical Council. She confronted my husband and accused him of killing these three men. She suggested that it was me who had been having affairs with them.

"My husband said it was Valerie. Fiona laid into her. She denied it. Dr Clark announced he was getting a divorce. The practice was thrown into complete chaos. All three of them were plastered across the tabloids. My husband was charged with murder. Rather than face trial and public humiliation, he took the quick way out."

It was a tragic story.

"And of course, once he died, Fiona Stewart ran the story all over again – so she got two bites at the same cherry. She made a lot of money out of it; but my husband died."

Raynes asked innocently, "And what happened to Valerie?"

"She was drowned."

"How very convenient!" said Raynes.

Even if he had not entirely believed Lady Emily's determined attempt at character assassination, there were enough dead bodies lying around – and enough unanswered questions – to give one pause for thought.

He looked at Dorothy.

She seemed to be following his train of thought.

"Did she die in Woodbridge?"

"Yes. It was a boating accident. Very sad."

"Fiona didn't investigate that one?"

"No. It was quite straightforward."

Raynes turned back to his immediate problem.

"This murder weekend," he said, "seems to have been arranged almost entirely with Fiona's investigation in mind."

Mrs West said nothing.

Raynes continued. "Suzanne Tempest was apparently a friend of the dead girl. Shared a flat with her. Jill Graham told her in an unguarded moment that Fiona was about to do the dirty on Bernard. Suzanne also knew Molly quite well, so she told her what was going to happen. Molly seems to have some protective urge to spare Mr Potter. Or perhaps she saw this as an excellent opportunity to dish Fiona.

"So she chose a very distant setting – a hotel which she had used once before. This meant that Fiona would be confronted on ground of Molly's choosing, surrounded by her friends – who are, *ipso facto*, all Fiona's sworn enemies.

"She contacted Gloria. Gloria enlisted Stanley Dixon – and probably Lady Emily as well. Canon Larkin, Kenny and yourself were invited because you had also been her victims. Mr Potter was then encouraged to put his trust in Molly's protection; and I was invited – presumably to protect Molly. Finally, Suzanne was brought in to make the numbers up to eight – to give it an appearance of a normal murder weekend."

The Inspector looked at Mrs West.

"Does that sound fairly accurate?"

"Molly certainly invited me. I didn't know why. But your explanation seems to square with the facts."

"How long ago were you invited?"

"About three weeks ago."

"I think this has been brewing for about six weeks. Molly has had plenty of time to prepare her ground. Book the train and everything."

"Perhaps even to plan the murder?"

"Yes," said Raynes, "but which murder?"

"A good question!"

Raynes proceeded to think aloud.

"Everything points towards Fiona Stewart facing a very unpleasant encounter in Mallaig. According to Stanley Dixon, she was to have been put in some very compromising situation - tied up, humiliated, photographed, blackmailed – if not actually murdered. Everything was very carefully arranged. And yet it didn't happen. Some quite innocent person was killed in her place – apparently at the wrong time – even before the curtain was due to rise. Everyone was waiting for the murder plan to begin – but surprise, surprise – it had already happened!

"Has someone upset a carefully prepared apple-cart? Or was the planned humiliation of Fiona Stewart simply a cover for a completely different murder? Was Jill Graham the intended victim? If so, why?"

The Inspector looked at Mrs West, hoping to detect some flicker of response in her eyes. There was none.

"And why was Bernard Potter in her compartment? Why did Suzanne Tempest have a row with an old friend? And where was Fiona Stewart whilst all this was going on? And where was Molly?" He paused for a moment.

"Come to that, why was Jill Graham in compartment No. 9? Why was she not in No. 10 or somewhere else on the train? Do you have the answers to any of these questions?"

Dorothy West shook her head.

"I'm afraid I can't help you with any of that. But I can give you one piece of information you may find interesting." She smiled. "I am trying to be helpful. You might like to know that, before she went to work with Fiona Stewart, Jill Graham worked in the Home Office . . ."

" . . . with Mr Potter?"

"So I've heard."

Raynes took a deep breath.

"That is very interesting."

"I heard Suzanne Tempest talking to Stanley Dixon. They were speculating as to whether she had been his mistress."

"Was she?"

"They weren't sure."

"But it would make all the difference."

"She would have known about his wife . . . about the cocaine parties . . . So, if Fiona wanted the lowdown on Bernard's private life, Jill could have supplied it."

"But then perhaps she had second thoughts? Regretted what she had done? Tried to mitigate the damage?"

"That would explain why she talked – so indiscreetly – to Suzanne about what Fiona was planning. Trying to prevent a successful exposé taking place. It might also have been part of a plan to get rid of Fiona?"

"That's an interesting thought."

"It might have given Fiona an extremely good motive for getting rid of her secretary."

"But surely not to murder her?"

Raynes' mind was racing ahead.

Mrs West watched him with some amusement. Give the dog a bone and he will play with it for hours. She was surprised that no one else had given him this information about Jill.

Dorothy waited till she felt the Inspector must have considered every possibility before she interrupted his thoughts.

"In return for this vital information, might I perhaps count on a repeat performance later this evening?"

Raynes rapidly returned to reality. He was suddenly aware of all that Lady Emily had said about Mrs West. The accidental death of Valerie Clark was not to be forgotten. If the doctor's wife was a serial killer, it might be quite lethal sleeping with the enemy. On the previous night, she might have been willing to use him . . . but now he might be surplus to requirements. If she was as dangerous as had been suggested, he would have to say no.

Raynes therefore smiled innocently.

"I'm not quite sure of my movements this evening. I will have to go down to Oban to see Inspector Cameron who is conducting this case. I may have to stay there overnight. I don't know. May I take a raincheck on your offer?"

Mrs West looked disappointed.

"So we're not even having a talk this evening? Last night was fascinating. Everyone enjoyed it. But . . ." and here she licked her lips sensuously, " . . . the 'afters' were even better. At least I thought so."

"So did I," said Raynes. "But until this inquiry is over, I shall have to be very careful. I can't afford to show any favouritism." He paused, wondering if he should say more. "In fact, I've already been accused of trying to protect you."

"I don't need protecting!" said Mrs West indignantly.

"Others perhaps see it differently."

The Inspector looked at his watch.

"You'll be missing your gin."

"I prefer champagne."

"So do I."

22. *Shuffling the Pack*

Detective-Inspector Raynes was only just in time to receive the pre-arranged phone call from Detective-Constable Carlisle in Grasshallows. His colleague had worked hard all day and the call was a long one.

Raynes listened carefully as Carlisle read out all the details he had been able to find about Molly's guests – and Raynes supplied, in return, the extra information he had received during the interviews.

None of what Carlisle said changed his opinion about the characters involved, nor the extent of their past crimes. It was clear that Stanley Dixon and Lady Emily were nothing more than greedy opportunists who had seen their chance of making a quick buck and had grabbed what they could – whilst they could. They had not been guilty of any other serious offences.

Kenny Savage, as he had admitted, had been a fool. He had tried to make a bit of extra money on the side, bringing Turkish immigrants into Germany. It was a senseless crime which had led to his complete bankruptcy and a spell in jail. Kenny had quite a lengthy list of motor vehicle offences on his record but was otherwise clean.

Gloria Markham-Jones was undoubtedly a murderess – but although substantial allegations had been made against her in court, most of the evidence was circumstantial. There was no physical proof that she had killed anyone. Most of her victims were long since dead – and cremated – so it was difficult for the jury to find her guilty or the judge to convict. Gloria had denied everything. As Fiona had said, it was the staff who took the blame. Gloria had not ended up in prison.

"But watch her!" said Carlisle.

"I'm watching all of them," said Raynes. "Especially Dorothy West!"

"It was her husband who did the murders."

"Not according to Lady Emily. She says he covered up for his wife – and then she killed him off before he could change his mind." Raynes laughed. "There was also a boating accident you ought to look into. In the River Stour at Woodbridge. A Valerie Clark. A doctor's wife. She was the one who leaked the story to Fiona Stewart in the first place. She died soon after. Drowned. It sounds very suspicious to me."

"When was it?"

"Within the past two years. Some time after November 1987. Her husband was Dr West's partner. I don't know if he's still around. He was intending to divorce his wife, but she may have died before the divorce went through. Even if Mrs West didn't kill off her husband's patients, I suspect her of this one. When she told me about it, she seemed to be almost challenging me to believe she did it. It was most odd."

"Not a nice lady."

"She is in some ways."

Raynes smiled to himself.

It would be fun to shock Carlisle who was very much a family man. Casually, he added: "I slept with her last night. She was quite good."

"Well, don't sleep with her tonight!"

"Don't worry! I'm moving out of the hotel later tonight. I'm going down to see Cameron to discuss the case. They're sending a car up for me. I shall be quite safe."

Carlisle was looking down his list.

"If you're thinking of sowing any more wild oats, you'd be safer with Suzanne Tempest. She's not killed anyone. I must say her high jinks with the Minister of Commerce were most amusing. There was far more in the police report than appeared in the papers."

"Don't let it corrupt you."

"There's nothing much against her. Just a couple of R.T.A.s. One drunk and disorderly. Nothing serious."

"What about Simon Larkin?"

"Not very good. Quite a large number of convictions for drunkenness, drink-driving, one for assault. Hit a fellow clergyman with a bottle. He has a number of minor sex offences – mostly with young men. He's been in a drying-out clinic for three months. Since then, he's been involved in some housing racket. A couple more drinking offences. That's all."

"He's also HIV positive."

"We haven't got that."

"He looks horribly ill. Very drawn. Yellow appearance. Liver failure, I should think."

"On the way out?"

"Temporarily in remission, he says. He also likes Inspector Morse . . ."

"Definitely on the way out!" said Carlisle.

"I'm also told he's a cat lover."

"I see. Perhaps I should note him down for bestiality?"

"Well, it would probably make his case notes more interesting. Who else is there?"

"I haven't been able to find out anything about Bernard Potter. There's nothing about him on our computer. I tried to bring him up on the Home Office staff list, but I got blocked off. He's in the 'restricted' category."

"He's in the drug squad."

"That explains it."

Carlisle moved on.

"And nothing about Jill Graham."

"Nothing?"

"Not under that name anyway."

"I wonder if she was married."

Carlisle was deep in thought.

"What about Fiona Stewart? Did you get anything on her?"

"Plenty – and quite colourful."

Raynes could hear the rustle of paper as Carlisle searched through his notes.

"Here we are. Arrested for soliciting at 17! Theft at 20. Shoplifting. Assault on a police officer. Road traffic offences by the dozen – mostly speeding. It's a wonder she still has a car! Defamation of character. Criminal libel. Deported from the United States. Involved in several punch-ups. More libel. Caught bringing excess spirits into the UK. Defrauding the Inland Revenue. Is that enough for you?"

"No murder?"

"Not yet! Oh – and by the way, she's been disqualified for the past year. October 1988."

Raynes raised his eyebrows.
"Well, she's driving a hired car at the moment."
"Must be in someone else's name."
"Probably Jill Graham's."
"A very unscrupulous woman."
"They all are. What about Molly?"
"Well, there was nothing interesting on her; but I found her ex-husband in *Who's Who* and he told me one or two little snippets. Apparently, she likes cocaine. Doesn't go overboard. Just now and again, she likes a snort. And these murder weekends – apparently she makes about £2500 a time on them – and never declares them. Her ex thinks that over the past few years, she must have diddled the Inland Revenue out of about £20,000. Could be nasty . . ."
Raynes was not worried about tax. It was not his problem.
" . . .The cocaine?" he said. "That's interesting. Bernard's wife's into cocaine parties. In Tunbridge Wells, of all places! That's what set the whole thing off. Fiona Stewart's using his wife's drug problem to try and nail him. Amazing that she and Molly have the same habit. I wonder if she knows Bernard's wife? She told me she knew nothing about Mr Potter's private life. Could be a lie."
"D'you want me to check up on the wife?"
"Why not? If we don't, Fiona will. She's called Rebecca Potter. Some address in Tunbridge Wells. There must be quite a few ladies involved. It's worth finding out."
"Anything else you want?"
"Not at the moment. You've been most helpful. Excellent work!"
Raynes felt very pleased with his younger colleague. He was most adept at sniffing out useful information.
"When are you going to be back?"
"Tuesday or Wednesday – depending on how this business goes. See you then."
Having decided to move out of the hotel, Raynes got down his suitcase and zipped it open. Facing him was a neatly ironed and folded white handkerchief, lying on top of his spare pair of trousers, which he had left in the case. It was definitely his

handkerchief – but why was it there?

The rest of the handkerchiefs were in the top left hand drawer of the dressing table. If the handkerchief had been returned, why had it not been added discreetly to the others? It had been deliberately placed where he would see it. Someone wanted him to know they had been in his room. They had probably examined the rest of his property whilst they were there.

Where might he have left a handkerchief?

The only place he could think of was the previous night with Dorothy West. He had used his handkerchief to mop up the champagne that had run over his fingers – but he didn't remember putting it down anywhere. He was sure he had put it back – wet – into his pocket.

He sighed deeply.

So Mrs West had been in his room. Had she also been in Miss Stewart's room? He had thought it might have been someone else. It seemed that they had a pass-key. There had been no damage to Fiona's door – and there were no marks on his. Who could have obtained a pass-key in such an out-of-the-way place like this? It must be Molly. She had been in the hotel on a previous occasion. Had she had a copy made? And why?

Raynes suddenly felt vulnerable. He was not safe. Even with his bedroom door locked, they could still get in. And they wanted him to know it. It was perhaps as well that he had decided to leave that night. With people like Gloria and Dorothy around, no one was safe. There could easily be another murder.

He piled his clothes into his suitcase and waited for the police car from Oban to arrive.

23. *Passing the Parcel?*

Detective-Inspector Raynes was given a warm welcome by his Scottish colleagues. First of all, he was taken to a local hotel and given a drink. Then he was given a decent meal. During the meal, Inspector Cameron explained how Jill Graham's body had been found.

"We were called in on Friday morning. The driver of a local train saw the body lying beside the track – naked. It might not have been noticed at night – but it was fairly obvious in daylight. He stopped to check. It was female – and it was dead. He called us when he got to the next station.

"We came up by helicopter because the area is a bit inaccessible. We took photographs. Lifted out the body and started wondering how she got there. The nearest road is a couple of miles away – so it was more than likely she had fallen out of a train. But which train? We thought about the overnight sleeper to Mallaig – but no one had reported anyone missing.

"Our surgeon had a look at the body. He didn't have to look very far. Strangled. Various other cuts and bruises consistent with being pushed out of a moving train. But she was certainly dead before she was pushed out. Time of death – after midnight. Time the train passed through Crianlarich – about six. That was as far as we got before your call this morning.

"At last we had a name. Jill Graham. We checked her dental records. Correct. Miss Stewart came down and identified the body. Said it was definitely her secretary. Looked very upset. Said she feared Jill had been mistaken for her.

"Apparently, she suspected some plot to kill her whilst she was up in Mallaig. Sounded a bit paranoid, if you ask me. But she said she couldn't think of any reason why someone would want to murder her secretary. We took a statement.

"This afternoon, we had a look at the train. Miss Stewart said that Jill was travelling in her name in compartment No. 9 - which carriage, she did not know. The station master at Mallaig told us that the sleeping car attendant had found compartment No. 9 unlocked – but the luggage inside intact. They had it taken off the train – and it was collected later in the day. No mystery there.

"At this moment, we're trying to get in touch with the sleeping car attendants who were with the train on Thursday night. They're bound to have seen or heard something. We're hoping to receive a list of their names – and then get a statement from each of them; particularly the attendant in carriage D.

"That's as far as we've got." He looked at Raynes with optimism. "And you think some of these people in Mallaig could be responsible?"

Inspector Cameron poured out a second cup of black coffee from the cafetière.

Raynes explained how he came to be taking part in Molly's murder weekend. He gave Cameron a detailed description of each of Molly's guests, supplemented by information Carlisle had gleaned from the police national computer.

Without mentioning Mr Potter specifically by name, he indicated that one of the guests had a wife severely hooked on cocaine and that Miss Stewart was an investigative journalist who made it her business to expose the failings of others.

She had been on her way to Mallaig to make mincemeat of this individual, who would undoubtedly lose his job. Detective-Inspector Cameron instantly put two and two together,

"You mean this civil servant, Potter?"

"Yes," said Raynes.

"So d'you think Potter planned this attack? Would he have known this Stewart woman?"

"I think it extremely unlikely. He would certainly have known her assistant – the murdered woman. As I said, she used to work for him in the Home Office. She may also have been his mistress."

"Don't you think he might have been so angry at her being involved in this business that he lost his temper – and lashed out in blind rage?"

"He isn't that sort of person," said Raynes. "He's very wishy-washy. A wimp. Not the sort of person who would hurt a fly. There are far more aggressive characters in the hotel. Kenny Savage and Stanley Dixon have both expressed their undying hatred for Miss Stewart. Gloria Markham-Jones said that she might willingly kill her 'for old times' sake!'

That's why I advised you not to let Miss Stewart return to Mallaig. Most of them know Fiona by sight. They wouldn't have mistaken Jill for her. The clergyman, Canon Larkin, is dying of cirrhosis of the liver – at least it looks like it. I can't see him attacking a woman."

"He's an ex-alcoholic, you said?"

"He has quite a string of charges. Drunk and disorderly; drunk driving. He has one or two charges for assault – but not just recently. His attacks were on men – not women; if you call clergy men!"

"We do round here," said Inspector Cameron – very firmly. "We have a great respect for our ministers. A fine body of men. I won't hear a word spoken against them." He smiled at Raynes. "You obviously see things differently."

"We won't argue about it," said Raynes, back-pedalling rapidly. "The other thing I wished to mention to you was Miss Stewart's luggage. I've brought it down with me. It's in the back of the car. This morning, just after she left the hotel, someone got into her room, slashed open the sides of her cases with a sharp knife and went through all her clothes and belongings."

"Have you any idea what they were looking for?"

"No. I think that – whatever it was – she must have taken it with her. But she'll need to go through it to see if anything's missing."

"Fingerprints?"

"If there are any, they should still be there."

"We'll look after them."

Raynes wasn't sure whether this meant that his involvement with the case was now at an end. He had no jurisdiction outside Grasshallows and he had already poked his nose more deeply into the case than was really permissible. Now was the moment when he ought to withdraw gracefully. However, he thought he might chance his luck a little further.

"You've been very kind letting me help you with things. Would it be possible for me to have a word with Miss Stewart?"

He looked at his watch. "It's a bit late tonight . . . tomorrow morning, perhaps?"

Inspector Cameron knew exactly what Raynes was thinking. He smiled. "In for a penny, in for a pound. I know you're desperate to be involved. So would I be if I was in your position." He patted Raynes' arm. "Don't worry," he said, "we're in this together. You've done all the hard work up to now. You know how these people tick. Keep up the good work!"

"I have to get back by Wednesday," said Raynes, stretching his long weekend by an extra day. "I'll give you all the help I can till then."

"So long as you leave us to do the arrest, we won't quarrel."

He looked at Raynes.

"Have you any idea who did it?"

"Not yet," said the Inspector. "But I feel I'm getting closer. Perhaps closer than I think."

"Well, in that case, I shall certainly leave it to you. Miss Stewart's in this hotel. I'll make sure you see her first thing tomorrow morning."

Raynes was more thankful than he dared to admit.

24. *Shadow Boxing*

Fiona Stewart had just finished her breakfast. A policeman had told her that Inspector Raynes was also staying in the hotel and would like to see her. Without much enthusiasm, she made her way to the manager's office. Raynes stood up politely when she came in.

"You've seen the body?"

"Yes. It's Jill. I thought it was."

"Was she badly marked?"

"Not as much as I expected. She looked as if she was asleep."

"Inspector Cameron tells me that she was probably pushed out of the window in the door at the end of the carriage."

Fiona felt such action was completely pointless.

"Why didn't they leave her where she was?"

"I should have thought it was perfectly obvious," said Raynes. "The murderer wished some time to elapse before the body was discovered. The greater the delay, the less likely the connection with the people at Mallaig. If you hadn't told me, I wouldn't have made any connection."

"But you do now?"

"Most certainly. I have interviewed all Molly's guests and found that everything you said about them is true."

"Were they plotting to kill me?"

"Nobody has actually said what they were proposing to do. Stanley Dixon wanted to see you placed in some humiliating position, to be photographed – and thereby punished. But I think Kenny Savage, Lady Emily and Dorothy West all bear you enormous ill will. Any one of them might have attacked you. I think it is much safer for you to be down here."

"What about my luggage?"

Raynes sighed.

"I've brought it with me. But I'm sorry to say that no sooner had you left the hotel than someone broke into your room and ransacked all your belongings. Unfortunately, they used a knife to get into your suitcases and bags. They've been completely destroyed. The police are testing them for fingerprints."

"Is anything missing?"

"You'll have to tell me. I don't know what you had with you. They went through all Jill's things as well."

"Beasts!"

Fiona Stewart looked very annoyed.

"What did you take with you when you left Mallaig?"

"I brought my make-up, the typewriter and my business file. That's about all. Oh . . . and a couple of dresses."

"They were probably after your business file."

"Well, why didn't they take it on the train?"

"Jill had it?"

"Jill had everything. Surely, if they were interested in the file, they'd have taken it then?"

"Yes," said Raynes, thinking fast. "But perhaps it was a different person who broke into your room. Someone who knew what he was looking for . . . but the murderer didn't."

Fiona sighed – a long, deep sigh.

"I've told you before. It's a conspiracy. They're all in it. All of them!"

"I think you may be right. But if I am to pin them down, I shall need your help."

"I'll help you in any way I can."

"You already have," said Raynes. "But for you, I wouldn't have got this far." He looked at Fiona. "The whole thing seems to revolve around Bernard Potter ."

"I told you that."

"Yes, you did. But it seems to me, it was your investigation into Bernard Potter which opened up this can of worms. Until you began investigating, everything was quite peaceful. Even Jill herself must have been affected."

"Why?"

"Surely you know that Jill used to work for Mr Potter?"

"She said she was an administrative assistant in the Civil Service. She was bored stiff. She wanted to do something more exciting; that's why she applied to work with me."

"Well, whether you knew it or not, she worked for Bernard."

"Who told you that?"

"Dorothy West."

"She may be lying."

"We'll soon find out."

Fiona looked at her nails. They needed painting.

"Interfering bitch!" she thought. "How could she know about Mr Potter? Molly must have told her."

Raynes continued. "She may even have been his mistress."

"Probably!" said Fiona sarcastically.

"Well, if she was close to Mr Potter, it may explain why she felt a conflict of loyalty. Jill talked to Suzanne about what you were planning to do. Suzanne spoke to Molly. That's the way the whole thing seems to have begun."

Fiona looked across the desk at the Inspector.

"You are perfectly right in your suggestions; but you are wrong about one thing. It was Jill who gave me the story about Bernard. She told me about his wife and her cocaine parties. If she hadn't told me, I wouldn't have known anything about them. Don't feel sorry for her. It was her idea."

Raynes smiled.

"D'you think she may have had second thoughts?"

"Why should she? She had no feelings for him. Even if she was his mistress, he sacked her."

"Because of her disloyalty to him!"

"Look!" said Fiona. "I told you before. Bernard is a bully. When he's got power on his side, he's a complete bastard. You're seeing another side to him up here. You see him as a wimp. At the moment, he's full of self-pity. But he's not normally like that. He's a swine. Jill had got absolutely fed up working for him . . ."

"She passed you a few stories?"

"Yes, she gave us a few pieces."

"And he sacked her? Surely he had to?"

"Well, you know what civil servants are like. Tight-lipped. Tight-arsed. You mustn't penetrate their ivory tower. But people need to know what's going on. They have a right to know who the drug-pushers are. Jill did the right thing. Bernard didn't like it – but who cares? Jill had a conscience – she's a clergyman's daughter – she felt these things should be public knowledge. I think she was right."

Raynes changed tack.

"How long ago was this investigation planned?"

"About five or six weeks ago . . . not all that long . . ."

"And how long has Jill been working for you?"

"Two years."

"I wonder why she waited so long to expose him?"

"We've been thinking about it."

"For two years?"

"Longer. I think it was probably because his wife left him – or he threw her out. We're still not sure which way round it was. But I think it was that which made us decide to go in for the kill."

"But you say it was Jill's idea?"

"It was."

Raynes stared hard at the torn and battered blotting pad on

the desk in front of him – as if it was hiding some closely-guarded secret.

"Knowing what was coming his way – having been told by Molly that you were going to do an exposé – and that his career was up the spout – d'you think it could have been Bernard who killed her? He couldn't get at you. He was frightened to get at you – so he attacked her instead?"

Fiona nodded.

"It's possible."

"It's more than possible. One of Molly's guests saw Bernard going into her compartment. Another of her guests was actually in her compartment at the time – chatting her up. He got frozen out. Later, he came back to try his luck again, but Bernard was still there. He shut the door on him because he thought he was listening to their conversation. So they were definitely in contact with each other on the train."

"Just like old times," said Fiona, "I don't think!"

"The trouble is," said Raynes, "that we still don't know whether Jill was killed because she was Jill or whether she was mistaken for you. If she's only been working for you for the past two years, there are quite a few of Molly's guests who wouldn't have known who she was. To people like Lady Emily, Kenny Savage, Stanley Dixon, Gloria or Canon Larkin, she'd have been a complete stranger. They'd have seen your luggage, but they would've known she wasn't you."

Fiona nodded.

"Stanley Dixon was the one who went in and tried to chat her up. He specifically asked her if you were on the train. When she said no, he went and told Gloria. So I can't see why any of these people should have attacked her. There were only three people on that train who really knew her: Suzanne, her former flatmate, Bernard and Dorothy West."

When the Inspector mentioned Dorothy's name, Fiona's eyes narrowed. "A very dangerous woman!"

"That's what Lady Emily said."

"Well, for once, she's right."

Raynes looked thoughtfully at Fiona.

"There was a Valerie Clark?"

"Yes. She died in a so-called boating accident. We're still trying to prove she did it."
"I think she did."
"So do I. It was pure revenge."
Raynes smiled.
"I'm surprised to find you agreeing with Lady Emily. She actually named you as Jill's murderer."
"And how could I do that? I wasn't even on the train."
"Lady Emily thought you were. She was sure you did the deed and then rushed back to London to make sure you had a good alibi."
Fiona shook her head.
"If you'll believe her, you'll believe anything. She's a complete liar. When we were doing our investigations, she told us five mutually incompatible stories. Five! In court, the explanations she gave were pure fantasy. If someone else asks her who killed Jill, she'll probably tell them it was you – and she'll believe it. Extraordinary woman."
Raynes looked at her closely.
"Why didn't you travel on that train?"
Fiona looked him straight in the eye.
"First of all, I prefer to fly. Secondly, Thursday night's one of our busiest nights. That's when we get our stories to Press – for Sunday. Thirdly, Jill had done the booking. The train was full – only one compartment was left and that was in the middle of Molly's crowd. Far too close for comfort. Finally, instinct. I thought something was brewing and I was right. Would those be good enough reasons, Inspector?"
"They'll do. Lady Emily also said you had a violent temper."
Fiona bit her lip.
"That's true."
"Apparently you once assaulted a policeman?"
Fiona's eyes opened wide.
"Fancy bringing that up! That was years ago. I expect you've got the rest of the crap?"
"Enough to splash a good story across the tabloids!"
Raynes laughed.
"Don't worry. Nobody's going to say anything. There are

just three things I would like you to do. Firstly, to go through your luggage and see if anything is missing. Secondly, I would like to see your business file – now – in your presence, so we can see what it was the thief was looking for. Thirdly, I would like you to stay here just a little longer – in case we roll up the inquiry fairly quickly.

"If we can do that before Tuesday night, I may have to ask you to come back to the hotel in Mallaig. But don't worry; both Inspector Cameron and I will be there. You should be quite safe."

Fiona looked at him with amused contempt.

"Now who's telling porkies? Safe with that lot? Never!"

25. *Checkmate*

Raynes went up with Fiona to her room. It was much less impressive than her suite in the north-eastern corner of the hotel in Mallaig. In fact, it was quite pokey.

"Not up to your usual standards!" said Raynes.

"No," she said, feeling a little ashamed. "I shall be glad to go home."

She went over to the wardrobe, unlocked the door and brought out a black briefcase.

Raynes sat down on the one easy chair and pulled up a small coffee table, badly chipped and scored. Fiona put the briefcase down on the table and gave him the key.

"I'll have to ask you to respect my privacy in what you're about to see. It's not pleasant."

"I'm prepared for the worst."

He opened the case.

Inside were a series of plastic files. The thickest one – on top of the pile – was entitled: *BERNARD POTTER*.

Raynes opened the file.

Among the documents it contained were a full chronology of his life; pictures of his home, his office, his wife and car; photographs of his grown-up children; photocopies of his birth certificate and marriage certificate; statements from neighbours, friends and colleagues; lists of questions that Fiona intended to ask him.

There were actual photographs of drug pushers selling cocaine to his wife, Rebecca – taken with a hidden camera. There was a list of the personnel employed in his department in the Home Office together with their backgrounds and phone numbers.

Someone had been through the family photograph album because there were snaps of Bernard from his childhood right up to his marriage.

There were sample headlines chosen for the article: *Drug-buster Busted! Home Office Scuttled! Cocaine – It's Official! Goodbye, Mr Potter!*

There was even a little plastic envelope containing some white substance. Neat handwriting declared it to have been found in a bedside unit in Mr Potter's home in Tunbridge Wells.

Raynes looked up.

"Did Jill put this together?"

Fiona nodded.

"And how did they get all the family photos?"

"She got a key to the house."

"Not from Bernard?"

"No – from Suzanne." She sneered. "A family friend!"

"Some friend!" said Raynes bitterly.

He fingered the plastic envelope.

"Is this what I think it is?"

"Of course. We have to have proof."

"You're not frightened of being charged for possessing it?"

"No. The moment the story takes off, we shall hand it over to the police. We don't keep it."

Raynes passed the file over to Fiona.

"Well, I can see why Mr Potter would be interested in getting hold of that. It's damning."

"Even if he did get hold of it, it wouldn't have made any difference. We've got a second file locked away at the office. And another sample of cocaine. Pinching the file wouldn't save him."

She sounded cold and cruel.

Raynes made a mental note to keep well away from all investigative journalists. Perhaps he should make sure his own private photographs were kept under lock and key.

He reached for the next file: *MOLLY PALMER*.

Not quite as thick as Mr Potter's, but equally comprehensive. A full CV; marriage certificates; divorce documents. Raynes noted that Molly had been divorced twice. There were two photographs of her in bed with different men. It seemed to be the same bed so it was probably taken in her own home.

There was a full list of all the murder weekends she had organized over the past five years; photocopies of the advertisements which had appeared in the quality newspapers promoting the events; and copies of her bank statements for the corresponding period. There was a list of those taking part in the Mallaig weekend. All that seemed to be missing were the questions and the family photographs.

"No cocaine?" said Raynes.

"We know she does it. Suzanne told us."

"Suzanne's been very useful to you."

"An unconscious helper. She told Jill a lot of things. I'm sure she never expected Jill to make use of them."

"Don't you think that Suzanne would have been furious with Jill if she'd known about this? After all, she and her mother have been Molly's friends for years."

"Another suspect? Yes, I suppose she would have felt betrayed. But it's all part of the job. No sentiment. Every piece of information is worth money. After a little while, people forgive . . ."

"But they never forget!"

"No."

Fiona put the file to one side.

She looked at the Inspector.

"Of course, you probably know – Suzanne had a brief fling with Bernard – after Jill, but before Molly. It didn't last long. Probably no more than a one-night stand. But it helped Suzanne to get into his house – and get us a key. After that, it was easy. You can't accuse us of breaking and entering when we have a key!"

Fiona bestowed a twisted smile.

Raynes returned to the brief case. He picked up the next file – and then stopped. He was transfixed by the file underneath.

"I've never seen that one before," said Fiona.

Raynes put down the file he was holding and reached out for the slim plastic file which said: *RICHARD RAYNES.*

It looked as if his day of judgement had already dawned.

The Inspector looked at Fiona.

"I'm telling you the truth. I've never seen it before."

Raynes said, "Well, if it's anything like the rest . . ."

"Jill must have put it together herself."

From an objective point of view, she had done it extremely well. The chronology of his life was detailed and accurate. She seemed to have got all the dates correct. He noted the stages in his promotion. The reasons for his departure from one or two of the forces he had worked for. Comments on his character. Doubts about his integrity and morals.

He recognized the source of most of the police material. But how had she managed to gain access to all this information? Some disaffected officer must have helped her. Raynes had made many enemies in the past; but which one would have risked his career to make all these facts available?

He hardly dared to turn the page for what he might see next. But he could imagine what was coming.

His two ex-wives! Prime witnesses! Splendid photographs of them "as they are today". Photographs of both weddings. Ghastly pictures in which he looked awful. They had obviously given Jill the worst ones. Looking at their most recent pictures, he noted that his ex-wives looked happier and more cheerful than he ever remembered them. Revenge is sweet. Perhaps they were glad to dish the dirt on him?

His first wife accused him of being a serial adulterer. She was probably right. His second wife described her misery living with a compulsive workaholic who had no time for her or his family. That was also true. Oh, God! There was an interview with Lucy from Manchester!

He had never thought of anyone getting in touch with her. This was dynamite. She described him as a "disgusting pervert" and explained why. If this got out, he was finished.

He took a very deep breath and moved on.

There was also an interview with a Mrs Jacqueline Foster, a staff nurse at Grasshallows Royal Infirmary, spilling the beans about his relationship with Debbie May, whom she described as "a common prostitute".

Debbie would not enjoy that.

There were pictures of Mrs May with several men – mostly in hotel bars – again taken with a hidden camera. There was a picture of her basement flat – together with her address and telephone number. A draft headline: *P.C. 69!*

There was an interview with a Commander Kenworth: *My kinky nights with the Inspector's Mistress*, and an article by Rosalind Hayman: *The Richard Raynes I Knew.* Neither were to be counted among the Inspector's greatest admirers. The damage was well and truly done.

He fingered through the press reports of his most successful cases: *The Royal Kidnap – Prince Released! Inspector Nails Psychopath!* and *Vigilante Murders Uncovered By Police.* But against the deluge of innuendo, it amounted to very little.

There were pictures of himself at various police functions – not the photographs he would have chosen. In almost all of them he was either laughing or grinning a smug smile of satisfaction. How galling such pictures were! What a rotten impression they gave!

In the file, there were a few pleasant surprises. There was a beautiful picture of Debbie at her first wedding when she was seventeen. He had never seen that photograph before. And there was her later wedding. Both her husbands had treated her so badly that she had vowed never to marry again. She was probably right.

Raynes realized very quickly that if this appeared in the Press, he would be a laughing-stock – not only in Grasshallows – but also right through the force. No police committee would ever dare to employ him again. The very suggestion would be laughed out of court. The career he loved would be over. He was finished.

And if he lost his job, how could he afford to pay off the

expensive mortgage on his new home? It would have to go. He might hang on to his car. And what about Debbie? She cost him a lot. He couldn't expect charity. Perhaps he would lose her too?

For the first time, he understood something of what Mr Potter must feel. The fear. A sense of desperation. The approaching end of a distinguished career. The feeling of failure and frustration. The anger. The very real desire to hit back at the people who had accumulated all this filth.

Certainly it was the story of his life – and in parts, it was pretty sordid. But such things should be private – not a source of public humiliation. He could feel something inside him building up to fever pitch. Hatred, leading to an intense desire for revenge.

He hardly dared to raise his eyes.

He stared at the file for several minutes before he looked at Fiona. She could see tears in his eyes. There had been tears in the eyes of many of her victims. It left her completely unmoved.

"I told you I'd never seen this file before."

Raynes looked at her long and hard.

"If this ever appeared in the Press, I would kill you!"

"That's what they all say."

"But I mean it."

Fiona and the Inspector eyed each other – neither giving way. Which one had the greater determination? Fiona nodded.

"I believe you."

"I have no wife," said Raynes. "If this appears, I shall have no job. I would lose my house. There would be nothing to live for. I would personally make it my vocation to kill the person who did this to me as swiftly and as painfully as possible. And I wouldn't care if I was tried and jailed. I would make sure I got complete revenge."

"Perhaps you understand the feelings of the murderer?"

"I do. And perhaps I now feel a great deal more forgiving. If she was capable of doing this to me – and to other people – then she deserved to die."

Fiona said quietly, "We do it all the time."

Raynes gave her one of his most chilling looks.

"Well," he said, "be careful which victims you choose. Not all of us are wimps. Some of us would bite back. I wouldn't give much for your chances."

Fiona shrugged her shoulders.

"It's a risk we have to take."

Raynes looked at her with scorn.

"Would you like people to know you were soliciting on the streets at the age of seventeen?"

"I knew you were going to bring that up!"

"But I have no intention of making it public. I shall never tell anyone about you. Can you promise me the same privacy?"

Fiona shrugged again.

"We weren't planning to do an exposé on you. I certainly wasn't. But Jill obviously got our research team to do a profile on you. Just in case, I suppose. We'd have made a few thousands on it. But, as you say, it's worth more than a few thousands to you."

"That sounds like blackmail!"

"I have no intention of blackmailing you. We never do deals with our subjects. Even if I were to give you this file, there's bound to be a second copy in the office – plus all the research material that goes with it. You'll just have to trust me."

"If I'm saving your life," said Raynes quietly, "both now and in the future, I think the least you can do is to shred it. Every page of it. And if it was Jill's doing, let it die with her."

Fiona Stewart was silent.

She didn't like giving way to anyone. Especially not to a policeman. She had always hated the police. They had caused her the most humiliating moments in her life. They reminded her of of times when she could not hit back. Times when she herself had been exposed as a little scrubber – a thief.

But, as someone had once said, knowledge is power. Power was very comforting. Having files on so many important people gave her a feeling of power which she relished. To give up any of that power meant loss of face. Something which was completely unthinkable . . . in normal circumstances . . .

But she had to concede that the Inspector had done

everything he could to help her. He had immediately put her in touch with the police and helped them to identify Jill. He had made a determined effort to find her killer. He had not done anything personally against her.

In fact, as she had decided at their first meeting, he was the only sort of man she could respect. A man who was willing to be as ruthless as she was. A man who was prepared to kill. To kill her! A man who was prepared to play for the highest stakes even if it meant losing everything.

She looked at him.

"It's a deal. I give you this file. I shred the rest. But you let me get Potter. I'm not losing two of you in one day!"

Fiona Stewart and the Inspector solemnly shook hands on the deal and Raynes took possession of the wretched file.

He had no doubt now what the thief had been looking for in Fiona's room in the hotel in Mallaig.

He had been looking for *his* file!

26. *Solitaire*

After his devastating encounter with Fiona Stewart, Raynes could not endure the thought of remaining in Oban for a moment longer. There was nothing more he could say or do down there. He made his apologies to Inspector Cameron and said that he must return immediately to the hotel in Mallaig. His colleague imagined that he must have had some flash of inspiration – or been given a vital clue. He had willingly lent him a car.

But Raynes had had no flash of inspiration. His mind was numb. He felt – more than anything – an overpowering need to get away from the whole sordid business. To be out in the fresh air. To have the freedom of the open road. To be surrounded with beautiful hills. To recover from the shock of seeing his name on that file – and realizing that his whole life and work stood on the brink of disaster. He needed to repair the damage which had been done – personally – to him.

The file was now lying on the seat beside him. He kept

looking at it with a sort of revulsion for what it contained. He could not imagine how a complete stranger – someone he had never met – someone he had never even heard of till yesterday morning – could have constructed such a comprehensive and damning report on his life – with every intention of using it and exposing him.

Fiona Stewart had said that she was not involved in its construction. He believed her. So it must have been Jill Graham. But why should she have been targetting him, when everything he had heard suggested that Bernard Potter was "the victim"?

Had she been commissioned by someone else to produce the report? Ever since he had seen the wretched file, he had been thinking about Dorothy West and her casual references to his past cases. How he had congratulated her on doing her homework so well before coming to the murder weekend. She must have known about the file. She had read it. She knew the sort of man she was dealing with. She knew all his weak points. Even his sexual preferences . . . And she had used that information.

There must therefore be some connection between Jill Graham and Mrs West. But what?

And what sort of person was Jill Graham that she could get involved in a thing like this? His first impression was that Fiona Stewart was the relentless newshound and that her assistant was a mere cipher, a typist, the passive bearer of recording equipment who sat in a corner with a shorthand pad, making the odd note. But it was not like that at all.

Jill was an organizer of material. A director of research. She had put together the file on Bernard Potter. She had acquired the key to his home by devious means; she had plundered his family photograph album; searched his room; neatly labelled the plastic envelope containing the cocaine; assembled useful information about all the people he worked with; and had even suggested possible headlines which could accompany his downfall.

What sort of woman was she who could do things like that? Did she have a massive chip on her shoulder? A deep-seated bitterness against the world in general? Surely even Bernard could not have hurt her so much that she could have turned on him so viciously? But it wasn't just Bernard. It seemed that she could willingly turn out similar material for a whole host of other people.

It was her chilling efficiency that appalled Raynes.

The sort of soulless organizing ability which had sent six million Jews to the gas chambers; or the public prosecutor on the Committee for Public Safety who had dispatched thousands of French aristocrats to the guillotine. "A clergyman's daughter," Fiona had said. But what sort of clergyman could produce a daughter like that? Was her father aware of the sort of job she was doing?

Raynes could not help admitting to himself that if he had known Jill Graham was carrying such an incriminating file about him on the train, he would have spared no effort to get it from her. True, he would not have known about the second file locked away in Fiona's office, but he would definitely have threatened her, bribed her – even assaulted her – to recover his file. The Inspector asked himself whether in all honesty he would have killed her. Perhaps not – at that stage.

But he would certainly have threatened her as he had threatened Fiona. He had meant every word he had said.

But whoever had killed her had not taken away the file. It seemed that they had not known of its importance. Perhaps they had assumed that Fiona would keep the most important documents with her; but the black brief case with all its dangerous contents had been in Jill's sleeping compartment.

No one had broken into it. No one had stolen it. And yet, for any potential victim, that file was dynamite. It seemed incredible that on the train, her belongings had remained intact. Had Mr Potter not even guessed?

It seemed therefore that whoever had killed Jill had been unaware of the importance of those files – just as he had been. It suggested that she had been killed for some other reason. Until now, it had not seemed that she was a person whom anyone could hate; but when one considered her part in Fiona's organization, Raynes could see that she was a person whom many people might fear.

Might not Fiona herself have reason to be anxious? Raynes had no reason to believe such a thing – but it was certainly worth considering. Jill undermining her own boss. But if she was, why kill her? Why not just sack her?

Raynes ran these questions continuously through his mind. As he thought about them, his car ate up the miles, running through the pass of Glencoe, Ballachulish and Fort William. By the time he calmed down, he found that he was only twenty miles or so from Mallaig.

He looked at his watch. They would all be having lunch at this moment – presumably before picking up the final threads of Molly's third scenario: "Desert Island Deaths". How corny it all seemed!

The first thing he must do was to get his own personal file sealed away in an envelope and locked in the hotel safe. Then he must concentrate single-mindedly on Molly's guests to try and find answers to all his questions. He felt sure that one word – one slip of the tongue – would give him the clue which would enable him to wrap up this sordid case.

Perhaps he had already heard that word spoken – but had missed its significance? He needed to hear it again. Perhaps, at last, all would suddenly be revealed?

27. *Contraband*

Molly's guests seemed surprised to see the Inspector return. His presence revived unhappy memories. And no one could fail to notice the grim look on his face.

When he said, "Mr Potter, I should like to see you in the library – immediately," few could doubt that it was the prelude to a very unpleasant afternoon.

However, once they were in the library, Raynes showed himself more gentle and compassionate.

"I think you must have found this a very unpleasant weekend."

"Quite dreadful, Inspector. Much as I like and admire Molly, it's just not my scene."

"It was arranged for your benefit."

"So I'm told."

"They were aiming to protect you from the scourge of Fiona Stewart. In that at least, they appear to have been successful."

"So far."

Raynes nodded.

"You are right to say 'so far'. I'm afraid Miss Stewart is still on your trail. I have seen the personal file which she has built up on you. I can only say that I found it quite nauseating. She even has a sample of cocaine found in your bedroom at home."

"Oh dear!"

Bernard wiped a weary hand across his forehead.

"You have my complete sympathy," said Raynes. "I don't think anyone deserves to undergo such public humiliation."

"Thank you for being so understanding."

Raynes looked at the unfortunate civil servant.

"I wonder if you are aware that the person who put this profile together was not Fiona Stewart – but Jill Graham?"

It was difficult to tell whether this was news to Mr Potter. He looked tired and drained.

"She was your secretary?"

"For four years."

"And when did she leave?"

"Christmas 1986."

"You remember the date?"

"Exceedingly well."

"She had also been your mistress?"

"Do we have to discuss that?"

"No. But it might make some material contribution to the case."

"I doubt it."

Raynes was pleased to note that Mr Potter was being more forthcoming than at his previous interview. He thought it was probably because he had adopted a more conciliatory approach. He must keep it that way.

"The parting was unpleasant?"

"Sad."

"In what way?"

"We seemed to get on so well. She was the best secretary I ever had. Superbly well-organized . . ."

"But disloyal?"

"I'm afraid so."

"She couldn't be trusted?"

"Not at all."

"She had an affair with someone else?"

"It wasn't that which worried me."

"What did worry you?"

"The fact that she was leaking high security material to that woman."

"Fiona Stewart?"

"Who else? I can't tell you when it first began – but suddenly there was a story about a man in Devon who was bringing drugs into the country. He was collecting them from a boat about thirty miles off the coast, shipping them into a small creek, transferring them into a van and running them up to London.

"We'd been watching this man for several months, hoping he would lead us to the bigger fish. Only a few of us knew about it. When we saw it in the paper, we realized there had been a terrible breach of security.

"We didn't say anything, but we concocted a highly-coloured follow-up to the case – completely bogus – and waited to see what would happen. Miss Stewart's agency couldn't resist it. So we knew it was Jill."

"You had to sack her?"

"Of course. But we didn't know what else she had disclosed. We eventually realized that she had given the agency a complete picture of our work in Southern England, the names of all the people we suspected, the places where we thought synthetic drugs were being made, the contacts abroad. We slapped an injunction on the agency to prevent it revealing any of the more sensitive stuff, but Miss Stewart made very good use – very profitable use – of the rest of the information she received."

"And Jill Graham went to work for her?"

"Looking back, I think she must have been working for the

agency for quite some time. In fact, she may have come into the Civil Service for precisely that purpose – to see what she could ferret out. That's probably why she became my mistress, to lull my suspicions – which she did most effectively."

"A clergyman's daughter?"

"A Canon's daughter, no less. Of course, she had done all this before. She did the same thing to Stanley Dixon. Wormed her way into his company. Found out everything she could about his business; then shopped him to the agency."

"Stanley didn't tell me about that."

"He's still feeling pretty sore about it."

"I'm not surprised."

Raynes looked at Bernard in a more friendly fashion. Another link had been established. Another suspect. Another motive. He continued.

"That perhaps explains why both of you were speaking to her on the train?"

"I didn't know who he was. I didn't know about his side of things till last night. We got talking; discovered our mutual connection. Stanley said he hadn't seen her for seven or eight years.

"At first, he thought she was one of Molly's guests; but then he saw the luggage and realized that she was still working for the agency. He was really angry about that. He went and warned Gloria so that everyone would be on their guard."

"And what were you speaking to her about?"

"I told her I thought her behaviour was despicable. She had already deceived me. Now she was working with that wretched woman to destroy me. I'd never done anything against her. Why pick on me? She said it was a good story – and there was money to be made."

He shook his head sadly.

"I never realized that she was such a dirty, money-grubbing little bitch. I think it's working for that agency which corrupted her. She had no personal feelings. None whatsoever."

Raynes could imagine that Mr Potter's feelings closely resembled his own.

"Did you threaten her?"

"Only with legal action, Inspector. I believe in going through the correct channels. We've already had to deal with Miss Stewart several times. If necessary, we'll take out another injunction."

"You didn't threaten her with death?"

"I don't think she'd have taken any of my threats seriously. She knew I wouldn't lift a hand against her."

"What about Stanley Dixon?"

"That's a different story. I think she had much more to fear from him. After all, she put him in jail. He's not likely to forget that!"

"Revenge is sweet."

"Very sweet, Inspector."

Raynes smiled at Mr Potter.

"I wish you'd been as co-operative at our previous interview. It would have helped me a great deal."

"To tell you the truth, Inspector, I didn't trust you."

Raynes raised his eyebrows.

"I saw you with that woman. You seemed to be hand in glove with her. We were all terrified."

"Terrified?"

"You didn't seem to realize what sort of woman she was."

"It seems to me that Jill Graham was infinitely more dangerous. You thought you could trust her – but she deceived you utterly. At least, with Miss Stewart, you know where you are."

He looked at Bernard.

"One final question – yes or no. Did you, yesterday morning, go into Miss Stewart's room, cut open her suitcases and search through her belongings?"

Raynes had hoped to catch Mr Potter unawares. To lead him gently up the garden path – and then hit him with a direct question. He hoped that his victim would blush and hesitate. But Bernard did neither.

Instead, he looked at the Inspector with some amusement.

"I did no such thing. As I've told you several times, I always go through the correct channels."

Raynes was disappointed.

Another of his choicest suspicions had bitten the dust.

28. *Consequences*

Raynes had hoped to see Molly next, but she was too busy organizing the next murder scenario. She was in the middle of Round Two. In her place, she sent Suzanne.

The Inspector noticed that she seemed to have taken death in her stride. She was looking much more cheerful.

Suzanne agreed.

"I cried a lot last night but I feel better today."

Raynes said, "There were one or two things you didn't tell me about Jill."

"I thought I told you quite a lot."

"You didn't tell me that Jill used to work for Mr Potter. That she was his secretary . . ."

"You didn't ask me."

"But you knew that?"

"Of course."

"And you didn't tell me that she was also his mistress."

"She didn't enjoy it very much."

"Is that why he got rid of her?"

"Probably."

Raynes shook his head.

"You're not being as helpful this afternoon as you were yesterday. She was sacked because she disclosed confidential information to Fiona whilst she was working at the Home Office."

"I didn't know that."

"Genuinely?"

"No, I didn't know that. I thought he just got tired of her."

"And who took her place?"

"As his secretary? I don't know."

"No. As his mistress?"

"How should I know?"

"I was told it was you."

"Me? I wouldn't touch him with a bargepole."

Suzanne looked quite horrified.

Either she was a good actress – or Fiona had given him duff

information. Which was it?

Raynes looked at her thoughtfully.

"Miss Stewart definitely told me that you had had a brief affair with Bernard . . ."

"That's not true!"

". . . That you went down to his home in Tunbridge Wells, got a copy of his key, so that Fiona could get into his house and search it for cocaine."

Suzanne was white-faced.

"That's an absolute lie. Jill had a key. I know she had one because she told me. She went down there – but not until his wife went into the clinic. She said that Fiona wanted factual proof for her story. But she didn't have far to look. There were little packets everywhere. In fact, she gave me a couple. But I'm not into drugs so I gave them to a friend."

Raynes wondered which friend that might be. Molly, perhaps?

To Suzanne, he said, "Do you think Jill enjoyed doing these investigations?"

"Oh, I think so. First of all, the money was good. As I told you, Fiona liked Jill. She paid her big bucks. She did well out of it. But I think she also liked the detective work involved – finding out about other people's lives. How they came to be the sort of people they were. I think she found it fascinating."

"Even if it was used for destructive purposes?"

"That was Fiona – not Jill."

"What would you think if she had done a profile on one of your own friends?"

"I don't think she would do that."

Raynes paused – wondering how much he should say.

"Were you aware that she had done an investigation on Molly?"

"On Molly?"

Raynes nodded.

"I didn't know that."

"I've seen it. It doesn't make very pleasant reading. Some of the pictures are fairly lurid. And I'm told that it was you who provided most of the background information."

Suzanne was about to say, "That's absolute rubbish!"

But then she remembered several conversations she had had with Jill over the past few months. Jill had asked her a lot of questions about Molly. She hadn't thought there was any sinister purpose; but there had been a lot of questions about Molly's private life – and she had answered them without thinking.

Raynes noted her hesitation.

"You did tell her things?"

"Yes, but I didn't think . . ." Suzanne's voice trailed off.

Looking back, it was rather strange how much they had talked about Molly. Suzanne had thought it was simply because she was trying to find out more about Bernard. Both of them knew he and Molly were seeing a lot of each other.

Jill had kept saying, "I can't see what she sees in him."

And Suzanne had talked quite freely about Molly's previous affairs which her mother had told her about.

She blushed deeply. This was terrible.

She looked at Raynes.

"But why should she want to do that?"

"Perhaps she was going to do a public exposure of Molly at the same time as Bernard? Or soon after? She'd even got hold of her bank statements – to show that she hadn't paid any tax on her murder weekends. There were copies of them – and her divorce papers. I think she had gone quite a long way down the line. All that was missing was a series of questions for Fiona to ask her . . . "

Raynes sighed deeply.

" . . . and you gave her most of the ammunition."

Tears came to Suzanne's eyes.

"That's rotten! Even to suggest such a thing."

Raynes gave her one of his penetrating looks.

"But you know it's true. You don't want to believe it, but you're remembering things . . . things you said . . . things she asked . . ."

Suzanne nodded.

"She used you – like she used everyone else. Did she have any loyalty to anyone?"

"I thought she did." Suzanne rubbed away her tears. "I'd never do anything to hurt Molly. She's a lovely person. I couldn't bear to see her splashed over the papers."

"Or having to pay £30,000 back to the Inland Revenue?"

Raynes exaggerated the total to make it sound worse.

Suzanne looked glum.

"I can't believe she would do that."

Raynes said thoughtfully, "I'm beginning to wonder if she was loyal to anyone. Even to Fiona? If it came to the crunch, might she have stabbed her in the back?"

Suzanne shook her head.

"No, she wouldn't have done that. They were too close."

"But," said Raynes, "you thought she was your friend. You shared a flat with her. But she used you."

Suzanne looked exceptionally sad.

"Well, she's dead now. Nothing's going to bring her back."

"True," said Raynes, "but Fiona's still got Molly's file. There's no saying she won't use it. The question is, did anyone tell Molly about the file? And did anyone try to get it back? You say you knew nothing about the file . . ."

"I didn't."

"But if you had, you'd have moved heaven and earth to get it back, wouldn't you?"

"Of course."

"Well, someone did."

"Bernard?"

"He denies it."

Suzanne looked puzzled.

She wasn't very good at these murder games. She felt a fool. No one was who you thought they were. Everyone told lies. Good people got hurt. Fresh allegations were constantly being made. One minute you were an innocent bystander. The next, you were a prime suspect. It was all very confusing.

Suzanne was not to know that even the Inspector was casting a small red herring across her path. It was not Molly's file that mattered. No one was going to kill anyone because of that.

What was of consequence was her own part – in trusting Jill. In putting a loaded pistol into that young woman's hands. A pistol that might have destroyed at least three other people. And Suzanne would never have known.

But she did now.

Once again, tears came to her eyes.

Poor Molly! It was so awful. And it was all her fault.

29. *A quick rubber?*

The Inspector looked at Dorothy West.

"They say that the female of the species is more deadly than the male."

"A gross understatement." Mrs West was still her sparkling self.

"I think you have a lot to answer for."

"On the contrary, my dear Richard, I have done absolutely nothing."

Raynes was embarrassed that she should still be using his first name.

"This is a professional murder inquiry," he said.

"You mean I should address you properly? The time of intimacy has passed?"

"Long since," said Raynes shortly.

"What a pity!" said Mrs West. "And to think of such depths still unplumbed."

"That's primarily what I want to talk to you about. You said to me – at lunch on Friday – that you had done your homework before you came on this murder weekend. I took that to mean that you had asked a few people if they knew a policeman called Raynes. What I didn't realize was that there was a fairly lurid file about me in Miss Stewart's possession."

"Is there?"

"Don't play the innocent," said Raynes. "No one would have remembered my part in the royal kidnap case. It must be at least ten years ago. But I noticed that the file contained full details of that and other cases. Do you deny seeing it?"

Mrs West smiled.

"I was given a privileged peep."

"So what was the purpose of the file?"

"Well, I would imagine it would have been a natural sequel to the one exposing Mr Potter. People might want to know a little bit more about the splendid sleuth who had been employed to protect him from the devilish wiles of the Press; who had either succeeded so brilliantly – or utterly failed. I imagine that at some significant moment, it might have appeared in its own right."

"It's not going to appear at all."

"What a pity!" said Dorothy. "Did you succumb to blackmail? How much was it worth to you?"

Raynes ignored her barbs.

"Do you realize," he said angrily, "the damage a piece like that could do? I could lose my job, my home – everything."

Mrs West smiled.

"There's always a place for you down in Suffolk. I could do with an accomplished lover on a permanent basis. That is, if Mrs May could spare you?"

Raynes realized that he was being deliberately provoked. He instantly controlled his temper.

"You've seen the file?"

"I've read parts of it. I haven't seen the whole."

"Have you seen Mr Potter's file?"

"No."

"You weren't given 'a privileged peep' at that?"

"No."

"Well, why were you shown mine?"

"I suppose . . . to give me some idea of the sort of detective who was going to supervise our murder weekend."

"I don't believe you."

"Why should you? Everyone round here is telling lies all the time. It's all part of the game."

"Dorothy, this is not a game!"

Mrs West raised her delicate eyebrows.

"'A professional inquiry' I think you said?"

"I'm sorry. It just slipped out."

Raynes inwardly cursed himself. Then he returned to his preceding question.

"What I want to know is why you should be so privileged as to be allowed to read this document?"

"Well, if you must know, one of the reasons was because I wanted to know precisely what sort of man I was going to share my bed with. What his tastes were – what would turn him on . . ."

Raynes looked surprised.

"Was it intended that you should make love to me?"

"Yes."

"It wasn't a spontaneous act of lust or affection?"

"I'm afraid not. It was all arranged."

"But why?"

"If you haven't worked that out yet, you must be dimmer than I thought."

Raynes cast his mind back to his night of passion with Dorothy West. To those things which had appeared inexplicable at the time. The champagne; the glasses; the handkerchief . . .

He looked at Mrs West.

"You moved your glass away from mine!"

"Your memory's improving."

"Fingerprints."

"Getting much warmer."

Raynes at long last saw the picture. Like Mrs West, he was surprised he had not seen it before.

He said slowly, "I thought we'd all been brought together to protect Mr Potter. I hadn't realized we had all been assigned particular roles."

"They do say that the best form of defence is attack."

Raynes was immediately reminded of Valerie Clark. Had she also been part of Mrs West's defence strategy?

To Dorothy, he said, "I think I've got it now. You were all waiting for Miss Stewart to arrive in Mallaig to do her investigation on Mr Potter. You were all prepared. Miss Stewart would be attacked – silenced – perhaps even done to death. Something unpleasant anyway.

"The local police would then be informed. And when they arrived, they would find – apart from the body – a bottle of champagne (empty) and a couple of glasses (both containing a few drops of champagne) with a certain person's fingerprints prominently displayed on bottle and glass."

He smiled sadly.

"There would also be a well-used handkerchief – and a rather juicy file outlining all the exciting moments in that policeman's life. Everything neatly suggesting that the aforesaid policeman had been the subject of an aggressive interview by Miss Stewart. He had lost his temper. Biffed her over the head. And gone back to his room carelessly leaving vital evidence behind him."

Mrs West smiled broadly.

"You describe it most elegantly."

"And I was to be your stalking horse?"

"In a manner of speaking, yes."

Raynes was suddenly reminded of a crossword clue Gloria had uttered to Molly on Friday afternoon. He hadn't been able to grasp its meaning.

"A penny drops in autumn. Seven letters." He guessed it now. "Fall-guy."

Had she mentioned that it was two separate words, hyphenated, he might have got it right away. The clues had been right under his nose.

At least he had got it now.

"So your part in this was to obtain the necessary evidence?"

Mrs West smiled again.

"I enjoyed doing it."

"So did I," said Raynes more warmly. "I presume others were to wield the blunt instrument?"

"Or the syringe?"

"I see."

Raynes did see – much more clearly. It was a blessing that Jill had been killed on the train. That Miss Stewart had been unable to do her interview with Bernard. If she had, he would have been in deep trouble.

"But it all went wrong?"

"Yes. It was a great shame."

"You didn't need the fingerprints or the file?"

"No."

"All your efforts had been in vain?"

"I wouldn't say that." Her eyes twinkled mischievously. "I'm still hoping for a repeat performance."

Raynes ignored her brazen proposal.

"So someone had to recover the file from Miss Stewart's luggage in double-quick time – because Fiona knew nothing about it? Was that part of your job?"

"D'you think I would have left such a mess?"

"No," said Raynes. "It was obviously someone with a complete lack of finesse. It was quite pointless too, because the files were in Miss Stewart's personal business case."

"Is that where they are?"

A distant look came into Mrs West's eyes.

"I expect so," said Raynes nonchalantly.

He was determined to give nothing away. He still had the nasty feeling that Dorothy could read his mind. He would not put it past her to bribe the hotel manager to open the safe and seize the file. He changed the subject quickly.

"So when was this charming little plot hatched?"

"About four weeks ago."

"And you were part of the organizing committee?"

"I was consulted."

Raynes' eyes narrowed.

"I take it that Miss Stewart's assistant was also involved – since she put together the contents of the file?"

"I think you'll have to ask Molly about that."

"To each his own?"

"Something like that."

"I presume," said Raynes, "that having been so involved in the main plot, you must also have some ideas about the sub-plot where someone was actually killed?"

"I'm sure we all have our pet theories."

Raynes smiled.

"What I was meaning was – do you have any private information about Jill's death on the train? Would you have any idea who the murderer might be?"

"Inspector, I understood you perfectly the first time. I think it is reasonably obvious who the real murderer was; but the big question is, who pushed the poor woman into eternity? It may not be quite the same person."

"It wasn't you?"

"Strangling is not exactly my trademark."

"No," said Raynes brutally. "Drowning is more your style."

Mrs West's eyes did not twinkle.

"You mustn't believe everything you're told!"

30. *Puppet show*

Molly was still unavailable. Raynes was beginning to wonder whether she was deliberately trying to avoid him. With some reluctance, he agreed to see Lady Emily again.

Most of what she had told him during her first interview had been complete lies. However, rather surprisingly, she had opened his eyes to the true nature of Mrs West and for that she deserved some credit.

She was dressed in tight fitting red cords and a white cotton top which the Inspector found much less overpowering than her previous ensemble. However, her manner remained provocative.

"You took my advice then?"

"If you mean that I slept elsewhere last night, the answer is yes. I was in a hotel in Oban."

"Bet the food wasn't as good! Is that why you came back?"

"The food was quite acceptable. But I came back because I wanted to wrap up this case. To find out who killed Jill Graham."

"Well, I've told you all I can."

"About the 'voices'?"

"Voices?"

"Last time, you told me you heard voices in compartment No. 9. Voices raised in anger. Voices demanding money. Suzanne, I think you said it was."

"I'd forgotten that. Perhaps I did."

"Or perhaps you didn't? Because, I am told, you spent very little time that night in compartment 10."

"I didn't?"

"No. You were elsewhere."

Lady Emily grinned.

"Perhaps I was with you?"

"No, you weren't," said Raynes. "I think I should have remembered that."

"I might have been," said Lady Emily wistfully. "They wanted someone to stay the night with you. It was either her or me. They probably chose her because they knew I wouldn't keep my mouth shut."

"You mean, it was all planned in advance?"

Raynes spoke as if the fact was new to him.

Lady Emily put her hand to her mouth.

"I shouldn't have said that."

Raynes calmed her fears.

"Don't worry about it. Mrs West's already told me."

"Thank God for that! It was supposed to be a secret."

Raynes laughed.

"Well, I think I've penetrated most of the mysteries round here. It's what happened on the train that I'm interested in. You told me that you spent the whole night in your compartment but another guest has said that you spent the whole night with him."

"Dear Stanley, he's so sweet – and rich. I believe he's just got a new job. He wouldn't tell me anything about it – but it sounds really exciting. He's going to make oodles of money."

Lady Emily relished the word "oodles".

Raynes remembered that the last time she had spoken to him she had been less kindly disposed towards Mr Dixon.

"Didn't you tell me he was pestering you . . .?"

"Did I? Well, perhaps I like being pestered by rich men with oodles of cash."

"I believe he enticed you into his compartment for a brandy?"

"Yes, I remember that. But it was more than one brandy. I can't really get going till I'm 100% tanked up."

The thought of Lady Emily 100% tanked up was quite mind-boggling. The Inspector laughed.

"So you really got going?"

"Yes. We had a great night."

"And you are Stanley's alibi?"

"Am I? Yes, I suppose I am. He couldn't have done much that night, could he? Perhaps he'll marry me. Make a respectable woman out of me." She giggled.

Raynes said, "I thought you had designs on Kenny Savage? You can't have both of them."

"I haven't really got either of them. It's all in the mind. But I suppose I'll have to make a decision one day. Perhaps Bernard would be the best choice."

Raynes found himself floundering in Lady Emily's rich fantasy life.

"The murder . . ." he said. "Have you had any fresh thoughts? Last time you accused Miss Stewart of being the murderer – even though she was not on the train."

"Oh, things have moved on quite a bit since then," said Lady Emily airily. "Most people now think it was you."

"Me?"

Lady Emily's voice sounded rich and convincing.

"Most people think that only a man of your skill – and genius – could have pulled off such a superb trick. To be sleeping alone in compartment No. 5 – only four doors away – you have to be a prime suspect; and yet you've been accusing everyone else. Some might say it takes a brass neck. I think it's brilliant!"

"And why should I, a complete stranger, want to kill off Jill Graham?"

"Well, of course it may be pure hearsay, Inspector, but the rumour going around is that the poor bitch had done an investigation into your background – highly-coloured, quite racy, I'm told – which you were only too anxious to recover. You pinched the document out of Jill Graham's luggage on the train, but then you made a mess of Fiona's room just to make everyone think it was one of us. What d'you say about that?"

"It sounds deliciously plausible."

"You were in Fiona's room?"

"I was."

"You recovered this damning document?"

"I did."

"And you don't have an alibi, Inspector?"

"I'm afraid I don't."

Lady Emily waved a reproving finger in Raynes' direction, "Well," she said triumphantly, "people in glass houses shouldn't throw stones!"

* * * *

Lady Emily was once again followed by Stanley Dixon.

"I hope you didn't believe a word that girl said, Inspector. She has an incredible imagination. She lives in a world of complete make-believe."

Raynes smiled indulgently.

"She's just accused me of murdering Jill Graham."

Stanley laughed.

"Well, I'm sure that would solve everybody's problems. What is it the Prayer Book says? 'A happy issue out of all our afflictions'?"

"She was kind enough to point out I had no alibi."

"A dangerous position to be in, Inspector."

Raynes looked thoughtfully at Mr Dixon.

"Fortunately, Lady Emily will vouch for you."

"Did myself a good turn there!"

"Trouble is," said Raynes, "who would believe her?"

Mr Dixon agreed.

"She's a slippery customer. But quite good fun . . . especially when the lights are out!"

Raynes smiled disarmingly.

"Was Jill Graham 'quite good fun' when the lights went out?"

Stanley suddenly realized he was on very dangerous ground.

"Jill Graham?"

"Yes. I think she once worked for you." He paused. "In a horizontal capacity. You never told me."

"Well, Inspector, it doesn't always pay to admit that one knew a murder victim . . . especially to a knowledgeable person like yourself. It might raise suspicions."

"Indeed. But it makes me even more suspicions when people don't tell me."

"Who told you?"

"Mr Potter. He said you'd both been talking about it. Shared experience and so forth. She wormed her way into your affections and then used private information to her own personal advantage."

"It's a long time ago. Nearly eight years. A lot of water has flowed under the bridge since then. To be honest, I hardly recognized her. She'd lost her youthful good looks."

"Don't you still have a grudge against her?"

"Not as much as I do for Fiona. If it wasn't for people like her – paying out large sums of money – there'd be no market for people like Jill. It's not the small fry who make the big bucks. It's her ladyship who rakes it in. That's why I hate her so much. If she'd been in that compartment, I tell you, I'd have done something nasty."

"You said, last time, you were 'itching for a fight'."

"I was. I was all ready to lash out; but when I saw Jill, it sort of defused things."

"Was she glad to see you?"

"I don't think so. I think she preferred that creep Potter. She certainly spent more time talking to him."

"Why did you go back to her compartment later?"

"Well, I think I told you before. I was going to offer her a drink." He laughed apologetically. "Don't tell Lady Emily . . . she was my second choice!"

* * * *

"We meet again," said Gloria.

"I'm afraid so," said Raynes. "But I know a little bit more than I did yesterday."

"I did try to help you, Inspector. I told you that it was much more sensible waiting till we got up here to give that bitch her quietus – rather than trying to do something stupid on a train."

"That was the plan?"

"It was something people had considered."

"No," said Raynes, "that won't wash. There was a definite plan. People have told me that events were arranged beforehand. Mrs West was primed to seduce me. And a rather lurid document was concocted – outlining my life and achievements! Please don't say you knew nothing about it. A lot of hard research had gone into it."

Gloria licked her lips delicately.

"Well, since Miss Stewart is still alive and well, it's probably safe to say that certain possibilities were considered."

"By whom?"

"By everyone. Not Mr Potter. He didn't contribute anything. He was just told what he should do – and did it with extremely poor grace. Considering the whole thing was being done for his benefit, I feel he could have tried harder to enter into the spirit of things." She looked at the Inspector. "Two words – four and six. 'A Dali of the drains'."

"I get you," said Raynes. "And I agree with you. But I didn't particularly like the part you had prepared for me."

"We all have unpleasant things to do in life. Count yourself lucky you were spared."

"I have no doubt," said Raynes, "that you were the brains behind all this. I don't think Molly . . ."

". . . has the little grey cells to mastermind such a plan?"

"No. As you said yesterday, you're the sort of lady who likes her murders clean and tidy."

"Years of experience," said Gloria with a smile.

"I didn't realize," said Raynes, "that you were an old friend of Stanley Dixon?"

"Known him for years."

"You invited him to this murder weekend?"

"I believe I did. It's always good to have a trusted friend on board."

"He told me that he had suggested quite a few nasty things that might be done to Miss Stewart – stopping short of murder."

"Yes, he told me too. Bondage, I think it was. Cutting off her hair. Whipping her. Pulling out her nails. Very unpleasant. But if you're going to deal with a person like that, you have to do it properly."

"You mean poison – or an injection?"

"Yes. And disposing of the body in some distant location

where it will never be found." Gloria looked out or the window. "This is a perfect place. Miles of uninhabited moors. Hardly any population to speak of. The scope is enormous."

"Wouldn't Jill Graham have said something?"

"If she'd lived to tell the tale she might, but we'd have found ways of silencing her."

Raynes began to appreciate how utterly ruthless Gloria Markham-Jones really was. To her, murder was not just a game but almost an act of artistic endeavour. But how far was she involved in Jill Graham's murder?

The Inspector looked at her – a long, penetrating look.

"It seems to me that when you are engaged in such things, you leave the dirty work to others."

"It's much the best way."

"Would you have delegated someone else to do the murder on the train?"

"If I had been so foolish as to organize a murder on the train, I would certainly have delegated it to others. But I've already told you, I disapproved of the whole thing. Whoever did it was an impulsive fool . . ."

"That suggests Bernard Potter."

"He's number two on my list."

"And who is number one?"

Gloria smiled.

"Well, actually, you are, Inspector. You had the motive and the means. And who would suspect an officer of the Law? Molly may have told you that Fiona Stewart had you in her sights. That she was anxious to add a police scalp to her collection. She might have given you some indication of what was coming your way. Naturally, you responded. But, of course, you didn't know what Miss Stewart looked like. You didn't know, did you?"

"No."

"Nor Miss Graham?"

"No."

"So you were the most natural person in the world to make the mistake – and kill the wrong woman. All of us here knew one or other of them. None of us would have made such a stupid mistake. You were in compartment No. 5. I'm sure we can find a witness or two to say that you were seen coming out of compartment No. 9."

Raynes smiled.

"Now I see where Lady Emily got her story."

"She's already told you? Excellent! She's a born communicator."

"She's a born liar!" said Raynes.

"Don't judge her too harshly."

"She's wrong," said Raynes, "and so are you."

But Gloria was quietly confident.

"We shall see."

Raynes decided to change tack.

"Perhaps," he said, "you could tell me who ransacked Miss Stewart's room?"

Gloria shook her head.

"Call yourself a detective! Think, man, think! A panic reaction. An understandable panic reaction."

Raynes nodded.

"Thank you. I've got it."

"By rights, of course, you did it yourself. That's probably why there was such a mess."

"At that stage, I wouldn't have known what I was looking for."

Gloria looked at Raynes with shrewd eyes.

"But once Fiona left the hotel, you were going to search her luggage, weren't you?"

Raynes admitted that he was.

"But somebody else got there first."

"You know so much," said Raynes. "I don't suppose you know who killed Jill Graham on the train? It would be a great help."

Gloria shook her head.

"The *deus ex machina* . . . something one can never predict. If the thing had been part of our plan, I would certainly have known about it. If it was the proceeding of a rational mind, I might just be able to guess. But I just cannot see what anyone had to gain by killing her – and leaving Miss Stewart alive."

"You are suggesting it was the work of some blundering fool?"

"I think I am."

"In that case, it was . . ."

"Kenny Savage!" Gloria and the Inspector said his name together.

But still a doubt remained.

31. *Snap!*

Raynes was determined that Molly should not escape his questions. He knew she would be reluctant to face him but, using such imaginary powers as might have been given him by Detective-Inspector Cameron, he insisted that she come to the library and see him. There was some delay whilst she decided what she should wear, but eventually she decided to come as she was – in a dark blue satin top, black flared trousers and her usual quota of gold chains and bangles.

The Inspector looked at her sadly.

"I think you've been avoiding me these last couple of days."

"I've been very busy."

"Has the weekend gone well? The games and things?"

"Very well. But small thanks to you."

"You think I spoilt the . . . ambience?"

"Totally."

Raynes gladly accepted the blame for spoiling things.

"Last time we met, you said that the murder had nothing to do with any of your guests. I hope you would now agree that statement was completely untrue?"

"Not at all. I still maintain that the whole thing was arranged by that wretched woman. She was determined to spoil our weekend."

Raynes raised his eyebrows.

"I don't think you can honestly hold that line much longer. It's quite clear from what the rest of your guests have said . . ."

"You're hand in glove with that scheming bitch!"

"I most certainly am not!"

Molly looked at her nails. They needed touching up.

Raynes sounded much colder.

"You know perfectly well that this whole weekend was arranged with two things in mind. The protection of Mr Potter. And, secondly, a revenge attack on Miss Stewart – in which Jill herself was involved."

"Who told you that?"

"Gloria."

Molly was silent.

"I don't blame you for doing it. I think you were perfectly right to protect Bernard – and I can quite understand why you wanted to hit back at Fiona."

Molly said nothing.

"Gloria told me that you conceived this plan of getting everyone together. Others suggested attacking Fiona whilst she was here."

"Who suggested such a thing?"

"Stanley Dixon. He told me he had suggested a whole list of unpleasant things you could do to her . . ."

"Sadistic fantasies!"

"But you planned to go further. Mrs West said . . ."

"Her!"

"Well, if you don't believe her, let's go back to Gloria. She said quite categorically that there was a plan – discussed four weeks ago by you, her and Dorothy West – perhaps with a few others, which involved killing Fiona Stewart once she arrived in Mallaig. You had it all worked out – who was going to do the murder, and when.

"Mrs West was to produce the incriminating evidence. Jill was to supply the motive – a highly embarrassing profile of my life which, if sold to the Press, would destroy my career. A brilliant idea.

"I would be tied up in knots trying to prove my innocence whilst you lot walked away. Bernard safe; Fiona gone. A highly successful murder weekend."

Molly was disappointed that so many of her trusted guests had blabbed to the Inspector. He had obviously got the whole picture. There was no point denying it.

Raynes continued.

"You invited me up here to referee some light-hearted games. You didn't tell me that you were going to use me as a fall-guy for someone else's murder."

He looked at Molly.

"Is that the way to treat an old friend – and lover?"

Raynes hoped he might touch her conscience or some other sentimental part of her nature – but Molly brushed it aside.

"It was only a one night stand – and I didn't particularly enjoy it."

Raynes laughed.

"That's not what you said at the time."

"Politeness sometimes demands a lie."

"It strikes me," said Raynes, "that you do nothing but lie – to yourself and other people. When I asked you about Bernard Potter, you said you knew nothing about his private life. And yet you have been having an affair with him for several months; you knew all about his wife, about the cocaine parties, about the break-in at his home in Tunbridge Wells." He looked at Molly harshly. "You were even given some of the cocaine they found there. Jill gave it to Suzanne. And Suzanne says she gave it to you."

In fact, Suzanne had not told Raynes any such thing. She had simply said that she had given the cocaine to a friend. But having discovered that Molly herself was partial to the drug, it seemed a connection worth making. And it appeared that he was right.

No other statement he had made proved quite so devastating to Molly Palmer. She visibly crumpled. She breathed heavily and stared at the carpet. She didn't admit to anything. She would never dream of admitting anything – but her body language told the Inspector all he needed to know.

He continued.

"Now about the suitcases . . .? Miss Stewart's luggage . . .?"

Molly said nothing.

"You attacked them with a knife? Mrs West's dagger?"

"I'm not saying anything."

"Well, other people say that you did it. They say it was a

panic attack . . ."

"A panic attack?"

Molly bristled with anger and then sank back in her chair.

"Yes. When you heard about Jill's murder, you put your plan rapidly into reverse. You got rid of the champagne bottle and the glass. Mrs West returned my handkerchief. But you had to get your hands on that file – the file which Jill had made up about me. Fiona Stewart knew nothing about it. If you had managed to get hold of it, you would have destroyed all the evidence – all the evidence that there was any plot to kill Miss Stewart. You could legitimately have said: 'What plot?'"

Raynes smiled coldly.

"You had the key to Fiona's room. The pass key."

"I had no such thing!"

"You lent it to Mrs West when she returned my handkerchief."

Raynes could see that any mention of Mrs West's name was like a red rag to a bull.

She snorted angrily.

Raynes pressed home his attack.

"You obtained it from the hotel last year when you came up for your previous murder weekend. It's probably still in your handbag. Shall we go and look?"

Raynes looked at her face.

Guilt stood out in every line.

"I thought so. You had the key. You attacked the luggage. A very stupid thing to do. It made me realize that there must be something of great importance in Fiona's luggage. And because you slashed open every piece, it seemed that whatever it was, you had failed to find it. My natural curiosity was aroused. So when I went down to Oban, I examined Miss Stewart's business file – and there it was."

"It doesn't prove anything."

"Oh yes, it does. It proves that Jill was working with you. She prepared the material – incriminating material that was to be left beside Fiona's body, pointing the finger at me. That's what it proves.

"It also helps to explain the murder on the train. It may be that Fiona discovered that her employee was working with you – against her – and she may have found out – again from one of your guests – what was planned."

Molly bristled.

"Nobody would have said anything to her. They all hated her!"

The glimmering of an interesting idea formed in the Inspector's mind. How fascinating! It might even be the missing link. He put it aside till later.

To Molly, he said: "Who would have believed that Jill would turn against her employer? But she's done it twice before, hasn't she? She deceived Stanley Dixon. She betrayed Bernard. Miss Stewart was fair game. What was she going to get out of it? The agency?"

"I have no idea."

"Quite a dangerous little lady, this Jill Graham. Perhaps it's as well she was murdered. Otherwise, if your plan had gone ahead, both of you might have ended up in the dock!"

"There's nothing I can say."

"Of course not," said Raynes in a kindly fashion. "Your silence says it all. The fact that you denied that any of your guests were involved. The fact that you tried to prevent me interviewing them. The fact that you got me up here on false pretences. The fact that you have been diddling the Inland Revenue – not declaring your income from these weekends in your tax return. The fact that you are into drugs. The fact that you are committing adultery with Mr Potter, the fact that you organized this whole weekend with a view to committing murder." Raynes watched her anger steadily mounting. This was the moment to catch her out. "The fact that your fingerprints . . ."

"I used . . ."

She choked back her words.

"You used gloves. Yes, I know you used gloves. There were no fingerprints. But it's nice to know you were responsible."

"You tricked me!"

"And you tricked me," said Raynes. "Snap!"

"You deserved it!"

Raynes shook his head.

"This attitude is not going to help you. If you're not careful, you're going to end up with some very serious charges being laid against you. Possession of drugs, tax evasion, breaking and entering, attempted murder – for a starter . . ."

He paused.

". . . For all I know, you may also be responsible for Jill's murder."

"Don't be ridiculous! Why should I want to murder her?"

"What you mean is," said Raynes, "one murder was quite enough."

He stood up.

"Let's go and look at that handbag."

32. *Leap-frog*

Raynes smiled at Canon Larkin in a friendly fashion. His smile was that of a hungry tiger who sees an unarmed keeper enter his cage just before lunchtime. To bite – or not to bite?

"Have you enjoyed this weekend, Canon Larkin?"

"It's had its moments."

"Indeed it has. Were you party to the subplot?"

"I beg your pardon?"

"The plan to murder Miss Stewart when she arrived in Mallaig?"

Canon Larkin's complexion changed from yellow to a pale orange. (But perhaps it was just the Inspector's imagination.)

"You were aware that there was a purpose to this trip to Mallaig?"

"I heard that there was a plan to protect Bernard from a very dangerous lady."

"Against whom you also have a grudge? And perhaps more than a grudge?"

Canon Larkin shrugged his shoulders.

"I told you all I knew last time I saw you."

"You said to me that a little bird had whispered certain things to you. What I want to know this afternoon is whether you were part of the working group which prepared all this?"

"No."

"Thank you," said Raynes. "That clears one point. The next is – how did you come to be on this weekend? Did you reply to an advertisement or did Molly phone you?"

Canon Larkin hesitated.

"I don't think there was an advertisement. As you say, I was invited."

"By Molly?"

"Yes."

Raynes registered a lie.

He thought about it.

"How long before the weekend were you contacted? Two weeks? Six weeks?"

"About three weeks, I should say."

"Molly had your number?"

"She must have done."

Canon Larkin began to look uncomfortable.

"And why d'you think you were invited? Because of your 'grudge' against a 'very dangerous lady'?"

"Probably."

"They felt that in the event of anything unpleasant happening to Miss Stewart, they could count on you?"

"I expect so."

"In fact, you had a very good idea of what was going to happen? You knew Fiona was going to be attacked and I would be the person left holding the baby – in this case, the corpse?"

Since Canon Larkin knew that Fiona was still alive, he felt able to answer this question more honestly.

"I'm afraid so."

"You didn't warn me?"

"Inspector, I felt you were quite capable of handling any situation. I was sure – like Houdini – you could wriggle out of it. As indeed you have."

Canon Larkin managed an ingratiating smile.

It did not last long.

"But perhaps you did do a little something to help?"

"Me?"

Raynes nodded.

"Perhaps you were the little bird that whispered in Miss Stewart's ear? Told her that Molly was planning an unpleasant surprise up in Mallaig? Miss Stewart told me that she had had an instinct that things might go wrong. Perhaps it was more than instinct? Perhaps she knew in advance that things would turn nasty? That's why she flew up to Inverness? Didn't come up by train?"

"I've no idea."

Raynes brought the full weight of his personality to bear on the unfortunate clergyman.

"But you told her?"

"I . . ."

After trying for several minutes to think of a way of avoiding the question, Canon Larkin decided to come clean.

"Yes," he said. "I told her."

"But why?" asked Raynes. "Here was a woman who had publicly humiliated you – exposed you, lost you your job, your home, your title, your wage. Why lift a finger to save her?"

Canon Larkin swallowed.

It was difficult to tell the Inspector the truth without revealing himself as a double-crossing little shit. The Inspector would despise him. But if he tried to lie his way out of it, it would probably be even worse.

"I will try and explain it to you. It's not a pretty story . . ."

"I appreciate that."

Canon Larkin put on the best gloss that he could.

"When I was in the drying-out clinic, I thought about all the clergy I knew. Their vices. Their failings. I made a list. I discovered it was quite a long list. Much of it I knew at first-hand but I'd also heard lots of gossip. And I thought to myself it would make quite an interesting book."

"Totally scandalous."

"Totally. So I set about writing it. It's almost finished and I thought I would get it privately printed. I doubt any publisher would take it on. Far too hot." Canon Larkin smiled sadly. "My plan was to insert copies into the shelves of public libraries. Send copies to lots of top people. Cause as much trouble as possible. I had nothing to lose."

Raynes raised his eyebrows.

"Wouldn't it be terribly dangerous? Libel writs would be piling up at your front door!"

"Well, I wasn't planning to hang around. Once the music started, I was planning to go and live in France with my two cats – Purcell and Schumann. I know it's a dirty trick. I know it's an act of revenge. But when I think of what some of my ex-colleagues got up to – and got away with – it makes me sick. By comparison, some of my own failings don't seem quite so bad."

"So?" said Raynes.

"Well, this is the difficult part. I know that Fiona Stewart is a sworn enemy. I know she did me down. But she's agreed to publish extracts from my book. She's going to give me a handsome advance to get the book printed. It'll also help me to get somewhere to live in France. It's my only chance. And she's promised to expose all those bastards. She'll make a packet – but so will I."

Raynes said quietly:

"Thirty pieces of silver."

Canon Larkin sighed deeply.

"I knew you would despise me – but I'm determined to get my own back. It's the only thing that's keeping me alive."

Raynes thought that that was probably true.

"Have you sent her some of the extracts?"

Canon Larkin nodded.

"And she liked them?"

"She was delighted with them. Right up her street. She's already given me a couple of thousand."

"Has she?" said Raynes.

He thought about it.

There was more to this than met the eye. More than just a sordid commercial deal.

Canon Larkin watched the Inspector's face. He could see his mind moving inexorably to the inevitable question. He had not got there yet. But he would.

"Did this deal precede your invitation to Mallaig?"

"No. It came after."

"I see."

"It was very much to our mutual advantage."

"Yes, I can see that. But I'm wondering why Miss Stewart's being so generous. From what I hear, she normally gets all she wants for nothing."

So there must have been something . . .

He looked at the clergyman.

One of his deep, penetrating looks.

"Did she ask you to do anything in return?"

Canon Larkin nodded unhappily.

"She asked you to kill Jill Graham on the train? Am I right?"

"Yes. But I didn't do it."

"But she asked you to do it?"

Canon Larkin nodded again.

"And what were you supposed to do? Strangle her?"

"I couldn't do that."

Raynes looked at him.

"She gave me a pistol; but I've never used one before. I should probably have made a muck of it." Canon Larkin sighed deeply. "Anyway I didn't shoot her. Someone stole it."

"The pistol?"

"It was pinched from my compartment."

"By whom?"

"I don't know."

"One of Molly's guests?"

"Perhaps. But they didn't use it."

"Too noisy."

"Well, at least my conscience is clear."

"Some conscience!" thought Raynes.

To Canon Larkin, he said: "But the intention was there?"

"It was."

Raynes was curious.

"But why should you want to kill an unknown woman?"

"She wasn't exactly unknown."

"You knew her father? Canon Graham? Of course!"

Why hadn't he thought of it before?

"He was one of those bastards at the Cathedral! A

sanctimonious hypocrite!" All the cleric's hatred came pouring out. Canon Larkin could scarcely control himself.

When he eventually calmed down, he said, "I've known Jill for years. She's always been a sneaky little bitch. Telling tales. Getting people into trouble. She had a wicked tongue. She was the one who was stabbing Fiona in the back. She was part of that group who were planning to murder her in Mallaig. If I hadn't warned her, they'd have done it, sure as eggs is eggs. Don't weep for her, Inspector. She was a nasty piece of work. She's not worth shedding tears over."

"I'm not weeping for anyone," said Raynes. "I'm only interested in the truth."

"Well, you've got it."

"Most of it," thought Raynes.

There was one final piece needing to be added to the jigsaw – apart from the missing pistol.

"How did you know Jill was planning to stab her employer in the back? Did Molly tell you?"

"Well, I should think it is obvious, Inspector."

"Tell me."

"It wasn't Molly who phoned me."

Raynes now saw clearly.

"So," he said, "it was Jill who invited you to join the party. She told you what was going to happen. She thought you would be glad to get your own back on Miss Stewart. But you hated Jill – and her family – more than you hated Fiona. So you decided to double-cross her – and tell her boss precisely what was going on. And then you received your reward. Is that it?"

"One double-cross deserves another."

Raynes shrugged his shoulders.

"That's a matter of opinion. But from the moment you told her, Fiona was out to get Jill. Not directly – but through someone else so that the finger of suspicion would not point at her."

"I'm afraid I let her down."

Raynes laughed coldly.

"We've only got your word for that. Even if you lost the pistol, you could still have done it. Bitterness and hatred can

carry one a long way – especially if you're getting paid for it."
"Well, I didn't do it."
"If you didn't, it must be another of Molly's guests. Perhaps the one who took the pistol."
"I don't think Fiona would leave anything to chance."
"No," said Raynes – thinking back to the hard-faced woman he had met down in Oban. "When she means to attack someone, nothing'll stop her. To her, you're just a pawn. An expendable pawn. And there are seven other pawns still on the board."

33. *The last domino to fall*

Before Raynes set off to find Kenny Savage, he received a message from the hotel manager. Detective-Inspector Cameron had been trying to get in touch with him.
Raynes had been so involved in his final bout of questioning that he had quite forgotten that others were also busy on the case.
Cameron sounded quite excited.
"We've found Stevens."
Raynes was puzzled.
"Who's Stevens?"
"The attendant, man! The sleeping car attendant."
Raynes mind rushed ahead.
"Did he see anything?"
"He thinks he did."
"Where is he now?"
"On his way up to Glasgow. We're flying him up and then bringing him over to Oban by car."
"That's excellent news."
"You'll want to see him?"
"Of course."
"We'll see him together."
"Naturally."
Raynes realized that this was Cameron's first "break" in the case. Up to this point, he had had all the luck. He must make

sure he gave the local man his place.

"What time will he arrive?"

"About seven."

Raynes looked at his watch.

It was just coming up to five.

"I'll be there."

"Are things going well at your end?"

"I'm just about finished. Just one more person to see. But I think I've got the picture. I know who planned the murder, but I'm still not sure who pulled the actual trigger. It'll be interesting to see if Mr Stevens can give us the final clue."

"Well, it's worth trying."

"See you soon."

* * * *

Kenny Savage was sitting alone in the Highland Lounge with a pint of Carlsberg Special on the table in front of him.

"Ah, Inspector," he said, "just the man. We've been doing this ridiculous charade – 'Desert Island Deaths.' I was killed off quite early on. But I ended up being the murderer! The game's over, but I still can't understand it."

Raynes smiled.

"Agatha Christie played the same trick in one of her novels. In one version, the survivor ended up marrying a pretty girl. Perhaps the same thing'll happen to you."

Kenny took a sip of his beer.

"I'm working on it, Inspector. I think she's begun to appreciate my rough charms."

Raynes was sorry to cast a damper on Kenny's hopes.

"When I last saw her – about an hour and a half ago – she was thinking of marrying Stanley Dixon."

"Was she? That's a pity. Still, he's a good bloke. Sensible, straightforward chap – just like me."

"Except where a certain lady's concerned?"

"Don't mention her, Inspector! I've had it up to here – all weekend. People have talked about nothing except Fiona bloody Stewart. I'm tired of hearing her name."

"You'd have been happier if the plan had worked?"

Kenny's eyes narrowed.

"What plan, Inspector?"

Raynes laughed.

"I know all about it, Kenny. I know Molly, Gloria, Dorothy and you all met together to plan this weekend. I know that you aimed to kill Miss Stewart and put the blame on me. I've seen the profile. I know all about the fingerprints on the glass and bottle. It's no secret. I even know whose idea it originally was."

"It was Molly's idea."

"No, it wasn't. It was that girl who was murdered on the train. She prepared the profile. She bought the tickets. Even though she worked for Miss Stewart, she was gunning for her as well."

"Good for her."

Raynes said, "I think you're missing the point, Kenny. She was killed because Miss Stewart found out about the plan. That was why she died. Miss Stewart gave one of Molly's guests a pistol so that they could shoot Jill."

Kenny seemed to have difficulty taking it in.

"She was killing her own employee?"

"Yes."

"So whoever killed Jill on the train was working for Fiona?"

"Precisely."

"Bloody hell!" said Kenny. "What a woman! She'd go for anyone." He downed more of his Carlsberg and wiped his mouth.

"I can tell you this, Inspector. None of us – none of us – would lift a finger to help her. Talk about being 'once bitten, twice shy'." He laughed bitterly. "And she's not even content with one bite at the cherry. Stanley told me – in confidence, you understand – that she was about to have another go at him. Him! After all he's suffered already! It doesn't bear thinking about."

Kenny shook his head.

"I tell you this. The only one who's escaped her clutches is that pompous ass, Potter. He's never suffered. He's used us to get her off his back. I wouldn't put it past him to be in cahoots with her."

"It's worth thinking about," conceded Raynes.

"I'm told he was in that girl's compartment for quite some time, gassing away. Stanley wanted to see her but she froze him out good and proper. Now I ask you, Inspector, what was he doing in that compartment? A good, strong bloke who was capable or carrying a body down the corridor and turfing her off the train. Not a chap like me, half-tiddled on five pints of beer."

"Last time you spoke to me, it was six."

"Well, six pints."

"You mustn't change your story!" Raynes smiled. "Mark you, we only have your word for it that you were half-tiddled. That could be a red herring."

"Well, I still say it's him. He was the last one to speak to her."

". . . And she had been his mistress."

"Well, there you are! Why blame any of us? She deserted him, didn't she? So I've heard. He could've been pretty cheesed off. They had an argy-bargy; came to blows; he grabbed her by the throat. Might have done the same thing myself."

"You're a man of sudden moods and passions?"

"I am. And I tell you this, Inspector – a woman who plays around is asking for it. She's asking for all that comes to her." Kenny finished off his beer.

"If anyone's hand in glove with that bitch, it's him. This whole weekend has been a cover-up so that he could bump off his ex. He wanted it. She wanted it. They knew what they were doing. We were just the bloody extras! Stands to reason none of us were involved. We've been play-acting. And a right old farce it's been!"

Raynes felt that there was a lot of truth in what Kenny was saying. Bernard Potter was a bitter man. He had been hurt by the way his wife had behaved. He felt Jill had betrayed his confidence. He was aggrieved that she had used private information to expose his private life. He and Miss Stewart had both been betrayed.

The Inspector smiled.

"Kenny," he said, "you're getting too old for these things!"

"Too old? I'm only forty-eight!"

"You need a sweet little number to keep you young."
"I thought you said she was spoken for?"
Raynes laughed.
"I'd still keep trying."

* * * *

Raynes left the hotel and set off back to Oban.
Kenny Savage sat on in the Highland Lounge for another few minutes trying to calm his nerves – and deciding whether to treat himself to another pint.
"Too old!" he said. "Me? Too old?"
He laughed.
"Thank God he didn't ask me about that pistol! I might not have been able to keep a straight face."

34. *Chemin de fer*

The unfortunate Mr Stevens felt like a Daniel in a den of lions. The police station at Oban was not large and four police officers were crammed into one small room. Three of them were in uniform. The other was dressed casually – and had a slight smile on his face. But Gerry Stevens had no doubt. He was one of them!
It was the climax to a rather alarming day. He had been woken up at 1.30pm in his little flat in Peckham by loud knocking at the door. He had come off duty at 8.30am but had only managed three hours of sleep. The knocking continued.
He had struggled to the door. Two policemen were there.
He wondered what on earth he had done. Had there been some trouble on the estate? Another murder? His mother hadn't said anything about it.
He let the policemen in. He was conscious that the flat looked a bit of a mess. They took some time to come to the point.
They asked him his age, his family background, his job . . . Of course, they mentioned his brother. (They knew all about

him!) They asked how long he had worked for British Rail; how long he had been a sleeping car attendant. They explained to him that there had been "an incident" on the specially chartered overnight sleeper to Mallaig on Thursday August 10th. He was needed as a witness.

He thought, "Oh, bloody hell!"

Gerry imagined that he was being asked to go down to the local police station to make a statement. But, no! He was required in Scotland.

"In Scotland?"

"Now!"

Mr Stevens protested loudly. He'd only just come off duty. He'd hardly had any sleep. His mother was out working. She was expecting him to make the tea. He had a darts match booked . . .

But the police were adamant. They had their orders – and their orders were to get him up to Scotland as quickly as possible. To take him to Heathrow; to put him on a flight to Glasgow, where he would be met. He could leave a note for his mother. He could phone his friends to say where he was going – but he was needed urgently.

So he had got dressed. It looked like a collar and tie job, so he put on his best suit. He left a note for his mum. He phoned Betty at the pub. He gave his shoes a quick brush and straightened his tie. He was ready to go.

It was amazing how smooth the arrangements were.

Straight out to Heathrow. No trouble about tickets – or queueing. Driven out on to the tarmac to the foot of the steps, where he was joined by a man in plain clothes. He talked about the weather, about football, about his brother . . . ("How long was he away for this time?")

Then he went on about whisky. Not that Gerry knew much about whisky. He was strictly a beer drinker – preferably draught special.

They had a meal on the plane. A nice one. Proper china. Metal knives and forks – none of your plastic rubbish. A can of Carlsberg, which was welcome. Then out of the British Airways jet . . . another police car . . . goodbye to the man in

plain clothes . . . a warm welcome from his new escorts . . .
"Where am I going?" he asked.
"Oban."
"Oban?" It was in the middle of bloody nowhere. Why the hell was he going there?

* * * *

So this was the moment of truth.
What was it all about?
The older policeman introduced himself.
"I am Detective-Inspector Cameron and this is Detective-Inspector Raynes . . ."
Gerry looked at Raynes.
"I've seen that bloke somewhere before," he said to himself.
". . . I'm sorry we've had to bring you up all this way to Scotland but we're anxious to speak to you about an incident on the overnight train to Mallaig on Thursday August 10th. You were on duty that night?"
Gerry nodded.
"Carriage D?"
Gerry nodded again.
"It was a specially chartered train."
Gerry remembered it. He also remembered where he'd seen the man called Raynes.
"You were on that train," he said.
The Inspector smiled.
"You have a good memory for faces."
"Well," continued Detective-Inspector Cameron, "what can you tell us about that journey?"
Gerry Stevens cast his mind back.
"It was a special. Chartered, like you said. Folk going up to their estates. Shooting – and such like. A lot of luggage. Plenty of toffs. We were a bit late getting off . . ."
"What time did you leave Euston?"
"About 9.30pm. We were following the Fort William . . ."
"Which leaves a bit earlier?"
"At 9.00pm."

"You followed it?"

"Well, we went non-stop to Glasgow. The service train goes via Birmingham. Stops at Crewe. Part of it divides up for Stranraer. We got to Glasgow about an hour ahead of them."

"What time did you leave Glasgow?"

"About ten to four."

"Crianlarich?"

"About six."

"Fort William?"

"Just after eight."

"And what time did you arrive in Mallaig?"

"We got there about half past nine. We had to stop at Corpach to let the up train go through. It's a single line, you see."

"Quite a long journey. And how did you occupy your time?"

Gerry Stevens had spent many boring hours going up and down the West Coast main line.

He shrugged his shoulders.

"I read the paper . . . Had a chat with the other attendants further up the train."

"There were three of you?"

"Well, there was also the guard."

"You had a chat with him?"

"Well, you've got to fill the time in somehow."

"Quite."

Detective-Inspector Cameron smiled a friendly smile.

"Did you get any requests from the passengers?"

"Not many. They slept most of the way."

"You took in an early morning tray to each of them?"

"At 7.30am. Just before we got into Fort William."

"Were all the passengers in their own compartments?"

"Well . . ." Gerry Stevens found that he had a fairly accurate memory for that particular train.

"There was no one in No. 10."

"Lady Emily," said Raynes.

"She was in No. 7 with a bloke. Fast asleep. He was awake."

"Stanley Dixon," said Raynes.

"No. 9 was empty."

"You didn't see her in another compartment?"

"Didn't see her nowhere. She had a lot of luggage. Tons of it. Expensive stuff. Leather."

"Her compartment was empty at 7.30am?"

"It might've been empty all night, for all I saw of her. I did reckon she might've hopped it at Euston. I didn't see her from the moment she got on. I helped her load her luggage in – then I had to hump it out at Mallaig. Bloody nuisance, I can tell you. Mark you, she did give me a fiver. I remember that."

"Can you describe her?"

Gerry Stevens screwed up his face.

"Not really. Brown hair . . . small . . . cream suit . . . brown shoes . . . She left them behind too."

The significance of these questions began to dawn on him.

"You think she was bumped off?"

Detective-Inspector Cameron was kind but firm.

"Let's just keep to what you remember."

Mr Stevens felt much happier. It was no fault of his that was being investigated. It was a missing person – probably dead. He tried to be more co-operative.

"Yes. She left her clothes on the bed . . ." It was all coming back to him. ". . .There was a tall bloke who came in to see her. Chap with a beard. He asked a lot of questions . . ."

"He came into the compartment?"

". . . At Mallaig. I opened the door for him. He wanted to know where she was. 'I don't know,' I said. 'Search me. She's skipped it. Gone for an early morning bathe!' I was just joking. He insisted on checking all the compartments."

"All the compartments?"

"All six carriages. He didn't find her."

Detective-Inspector Cameron looked at Raynes. He said nothing.

"Can you remember what her compartment looked like?"

"Well, like I said, there was a lot of luggage. All piled up. Not all that much room."

"Had it been moved – during the night?"

Gerry shook his head.

"No. It was pretty well where I put it. There was her handbag."

"And where was that?"
"On the bed."
"Had the bed been slept in?"
"No. I think she'd sat on it. But she hadn't been in it. You know what I mean. It was all still tucked up. But I think she'd been lying on it. Turned round the pillow. There was a book on the floor."
Gerry wondered if he should say any more.
"There was another odd thing . . . She had stuffed her underwear into her handbag."
"How d'you know that?"
"The big man looked inside her handbag. I saw she'd stuffed away her bra and pants."
"So all her clothes were still in the compartment?"
"As far as I could see."
"And you never saw her from the moment she got on the train?"
"No."
"You didn't even see her going to the toilet?"
"No."
Mr Stevens sounded uncertain.
"You don't seem quite sure?"
"I'm quite sure. But there were one or two other people roaming about. Chap with a yellow face. Nasty piece of work . . ."
"Canon Larkin."
"And a real glamour puss in a red nightie. Model or something . . ."
"Suzanne Tempest."
The sleeping car attendant looked at Raynes.
"I think you may have been . . ."
"Yes. I went to the toilet twice."
Gerry Stevens was proving a very good witness.
"Was there anyone else you particularly noticed?"
"Chap in a blue dressing gown. He went into the toilet about sixish. I saw him going in just as I came through the connecting passage. I'd been chatting to Les. He shut the door pretty pronto. I did wonder if he was alone. Might've had some bird with him." He smiled. "You know, people get up to all sorts of

tricks. Had a chap in with two of them the other night. Both middle-aged. Just in their knickers, smoking pot." He laughed. "Not a pretty sight."

"That wasn't on the Mallaig train?"

"No – the Aberdeen. Tuesday night."

Raynes smiled.

"Was there anything else in the compartment that you noticed? Any blood? Any fluid of any sort? Scrap paper in the bin? Rope? Cord? Light bulb missing? Signs of a fight?"

Gerry scratched his head thoughtfully.

"Can't say as I remember anything. Nothing except the luggage. And that bloke asking questions. I thought he was a detective. Sounded like one. He seemed worried . . . I was hoping he might give me a hand to get all that luggage off the train – but he never lifted a finger."

"Bernard Potter," said Raynes. "That'd explain why he was late."

Detective-Inspector Cameron looked at Mr Stevens. "So you moved it?"

"Every frigging piece. Got it all down on the platform and took it into the office. Too small a joint to have a left luggage. Left it at the ticket office. It was going to some hotel . . . El . . . Ell . . ."

"Ellachie House?"

"Yes. That's right. Fiona someone."

Cameron nodded his head.

"And you saw nothing else?"

"Not really."

Gerry Stevens wished there had been more to report. But as he had said, it was a very boring journey. Virtually no calls all night. They'd had their early morning trays. For once, they'd drunk their tea. Eaten their biscuits. Sometimes they left them untouched. A further thought came into his mind.

"There was an empty bottle in that yellow-faced chap's compartment."

"Gin?"

"Whisky, if I remember. I should think his liver must be packing up."

There was a long silence whilst the police waited to hear more. But there was nothing else to report.

Eventually, Raynes said, "What time would the train have been crossing Rannoch Moor?"

"Rannoch Moor? You don't mean Rannoch station?"

"No. Rannoch Moor."

Mr Stevens did a rough calculation.

"About twenty minutes or so after leaving Crianlarich."

"And you left Crianlarich at six?"

"Give or take ten minutes. On the Fort William train, we normally get there just before seven, but this was a special."

"Quite so," said Raynes.

"And what did you do after you had unloaded the luggage?"

"Had a spot of breakfast. Went back to Glasgow. We had to wait till the local train arrived – about half past ten. Then we got the hell out of it. The return train's supposed to be picking them up tomorrow night."

"You can join it at Glasgow."

Gerry Stevens was relieved to know that he was not being detained.

"However, we shall be needing your services tomorrow morning." Cameron's slow Scottish voice could sound intimidating. "You will stay in the local hotel overnight. Tomorrow morning, we want you to come with us to a hotel in Mallaig . . ."

"The Ellachie . . .?"

"Precisely. There you will required to identify certain people. After that, you're free to go. We shall make sure you are suitably reimbursed for your services."

Mr Stevens nodded happily.

If that was all that was required of him, he was glad to be of service. Quite obviously, the lady passenger had been bumped off. Disposed of on Rannoch Moor, about the same time as he had seen a man in a blue dressing gown going into the lavatory. He could swear that he had seen three bare feet! What a pity he'd been in such a hurry. If he'd hung around, he might have seen a lot more.

"Sergeant McAlister will take you over to the hotel."

After Mr Stevens had gone, Raynes gave Detective-Inspector Cameron a very full report on all the interviews he had conducted that afternoon and showed him how the picture was steadily falling into place.

"You've not exactly been keeping the Sabbath, have you, Mr Raynes?"

"I think the pursuit of the ungodly is a very worthy activity on the Sabbath."

Cameron's eyes twinkled.

"Especially as most of them are English folk!"

"You've got a point there!" Raynes laughed.

"But you think you know who the murderer is?"

"I'm fairly sure. But I'd like them to incriminate themselves out of their own mouths."

Rather hesitantly, because he was a visitor, Raynes suggested that when they went back to the hotel the following morning, he should give an exposition of the case, leading up to the dramatic moment when the murderer was revealed.

The idea appealed to Cameron.

"You've done all the work, man! As long as I get an arrest; that's all that matters to me."

"Well, you'll certainly get an arrest," said Raynes confidently. "But I shall need your help."

He explained what was needed.

"And we shall have to take Miss Stewart up with us. She's heavily involved. And you'd better provide some extra officers for her protection."

"You think it's as bad as that?"

"You haven't met them. They hate her like poison."

Detective-Inspector Cameron looked at his assistant.

"Better get a couple more lads over. At least Mr Stevens won't need protecting. I shall be interested to see who the man was going into the lavatory wearing a blue dressing gown. He sounds a bit suspicious."

Raynes smiled.

"We could dress up Mr Stevens as a waiter. He could do the rounds whilst they're having breakfast. They'd never notice."

"And while he's doing that, we could check and see who's

got a blue dressing gown."

Raynes' eyes brightened.

"I've got Mrs Palmer's pass-key. We can get into any room. I think we should arrive just before breakfast."

Cameron looked at his watch.

"That means an early start."

There was a knock at the door.

McAlister re-appeared.

"Excuse me, sir. A final thought from our friend at the hotel. He thinks he saw *three* bare feet going into that toilet on the train. He thinks the bloke may have been carrying the body. He didn't like to tell you here. Thought you might think he was pulling your leg! But it's been troubling him."

"Thank you, McAlister."

He turned to Raynes.

"As you said, it's all falling into place. Fancy carrying a naked body down the corridor! Just asking to be caught!"

Raynes smiled.

"Well, I'm sure he'd have preferred to shove her out through the window, but it's a bit difficult with metal frames and double-glazing. The door was his only option."

Detective-Inspector Cameron rubbed his hands.

"It's getting easier all the time. You get me an arrest and I'll be a very happy man."

35. *The games people play*

Once again, Raynes stood in front of the stone fireplace in the hotel library. There was an overwhelming sense of *déjà vu*. Only three nights before, he had entertained an eager, friendly audience with the story of one of his most celebrated cases.

This morning, the numbers would be much the same – about sixteen, including four police officers, Gerry Stevens and Fiona Stewart – but this time, no one was there by choice.

Fiona Stewart sat close to Detective-Inspector Cameron. It seemed to be the safest place in the room. It was certainly nearest to the door.

As they came into the library, Molly's guests looked at her – some with curiosity and amusement, others with contempt and hatred. Raynes made sure that, once in the room, they were kept well apart.

And there was another difference. The last time the Inspector had spoken, he had had the benefit of a fine malt whisky; but this time, there was not even a cup of coffee.

It was strictly business.

Before he started, he looked at each of their faces. They registered little emotion – not even interest or fear. The atmosphere was cold and sullen.

"When we were last here," said Raynes, "we were discussing past history. This morning, I am speaking to you about events in which we ourselves have been involved.

"Over the weekend, you have taken part in three murder scenarios, so you may find it difficult to distinguish between fiction and reality. This, unfortunately, is real. In the course of your play-acting, you have often discovered how difficult it is to get at the truth. Things are not always what they seem. That has been my experience up here in Mallaig.

"About three weeks ago, I received a charming invitation from Molly Palmer inviting me to another of her splendid murder weekends. I have been to two others and enjoyed them both. I assumed that this one would be much the same. A chance to meet new faces, to have a lot of fun, to enjoy some excellent cuisine and have a thoroughly relaxing weekend. So I promptly accepted her invitation.

"The first twenty-four hours went much as I had expected. But, on Saturday morning, I was accosted by an unknown lady in the reception area of the hotel. She told me that there had been a real murder on the sleeper train which brought most of us up to Mallaig.

"I had not heard about it – but there it was in the paper. The naked body of a woman had been found beside the railway track just north of Crianlarich. The unknown lady told me that she believed the murdered woman was her assistant, Jill Graham.

"I asked her who she was. Her name meant nothing to me,

but I gathered that she was an investigative journalist who supplied lurid articles to the Press. I volunteered to help her get in touch with the police who were in charge of the case. Detective-Inspector Cameron was delighted to receive her information and asked her to come down to Oban to identify the body.

"Shortly after Miss Stewart left the hotel, someone went into her room, slashed open her cases and ransacked her possessions. What they were looking for, I did not know; but the fact that they attacked every item showed that they failed to find what they were looking for."

Gloria smiled.

"By this time," Raynes continued, "I had gained a clearer picture of the situation in which I found myself. Because of her role as an investigative journalist, Miss Stewart was able to tell me who you all were. To my surprise, it appeared that almost all of you had – at one time or another – suffered at Miss Stewart's hands. You had lost your jobs, your property and even gone to jail because of her disclosures in the Press. I found it difficult to believe that all of you could have come together just by accident. There must be a reason.

"I soon discovered what that reason was. Among the guests was a prominent civil servant, Mr Bernard Potter, who works in the Home Office and specializes in catching people who bring drugs illegally into the country. Miss Stewart was intending to publish an article about him. Not because of anything he had done, but because his wife, Rebecca, had got hooked on drugs and had been organizing cocaine parties at their home in Tunbridge Wells.

"It seemed a handy peg on which to hang another sensational story: *DRUGBUSTER BUSTED!* It would almost certainly have brought an end to Mr Potter's distinguished career."

Bernard shook his head.

"You may disagree, but that was how Miss Stewart's agency saw it. They had personal reasons for promoting his exposure. Mr Potter's former secretary – indeed, his former mistress – had been sacked for leaking highly sensitive information to Fiona's agency and this was her revenge. As you all know, it was this woman who was found dead beside the track.

"Apparently, this was not the first time Jill Graham had used private, privileged information for financial gain. When she was working for Stanley Dixon at the Preston & General, she had discovered financial irregularities in the company, which she promptly forwarded to the agency. This had drastic results for Mr Dixon's company. However, in that case, I would say that she had some justification in doing what she did."

Stanley Dixon sat with his arms folded, looking at the ceiling. It was not difficult to guess what he was thinking.

"But in Mr Potter's case, it seemed like an act of personal revenge. She and Fiona discussed the matter at length before a plan was finally hatched.

"Unfortunately, despite her many talents, Jill had a tendency to gossip. No sooner had the investigation been launched than she told her ex-flatmate, Suzanne, what was afoot. Suzanne happened to know that Bernard was currently a close friend of Molly Palmer; so she passed on the news to Molly who decided that the best means of defence was attack.

"If Miss Stewart was going to go for one of her friends, she would meet her head-on. And who better to support her than other victims of Miss Stewart's vicious pen?

"Molly spoke to Gloria, who in turn contacted Stanley Dixon. Kenny Savage, Dorothy West and Lady Emily were also brought on board. Canon Larkin and Suzanne were added to make up the numbers and I was invited to be the referee. With this formidable collection of talent surrounding her, Molly felt able to protect Mr Potter and face down Miss Stewart. This was the background to my invitation to Mallaig.

"During the first twenty-four hours of the murder weekend, I was quite unaware of any deep undercurrents of hostility. To me, everything seemed perfectly normal. But once Fiona had told me who you all were, the scales fell from my eyes. I soon discovered that there were some very strong passions lurking beneath the surface.

"Protection for Mr Potter was one thing; but plans had also been laid to attack Miss Stewart. Several of you said that it would be most unwise for her to stay in the hotel. This suggested that something nasty had been arranged.

"What I did not realize at that time was that I myself had been accorded a privileged place in those plans. Miss Markham-Jones told me, in her own oblique way, that I was to be the 'fall-guy'. I was to enjoy a romantic night with Mrs West. In the course of our entertainment, we would broach a bottle of champagne together. My fingerprints would be left on both glass and bottle. When Miss Stewart had been dealt with, these items would be placed in her room – together with other helpful material – so that the finger of suspicion would point directly at me."

Raynes paused.

"A fine way to treat a guest!"

But no one showed the slightest glimmer of remorse.

(Not that he had expected it.)

Raynes continued.

"As I say, I was completely unaware of this, even though I did notice my glass being isolated as if it contained some poisonous germ. I understood things a little more clearly when I discovered my own personal profile in Miss Stewart's business file. It too was extremely revealing. But Fiona told me that she had never seen it before.

"I believed her. It seems that the profile was put together by her assistant, Jill Graham – working in the best traditions of the agency – to assist the sub-plot being arranged by Molly and her friends. Apparently, this profile was also to have been left in Miss Stewart's room – along with the corpse, the glass and the champagne bottle – to suggest to any interested observer that the reason for the reporter's death was not because she was pursuing Mr Potter, but because she was pursuing me! The police were to think that I had discovered what she was up to; I had lost my temper and killed her."

Raynes took a deep breath.

"It was a clever plan. It could have worked. And but for Jill's untimely death – and Fiona's rapid departure from the hotel – it would have been carried out quite ruthlessly – with no thought as to the damage it might do to myself and my career."

He looked at them.

No. They didn't care a damn about him.

"What all this did prove was that Jill's death on the train was not part of the plot. At the time I was being 'entertained' so treacherously by Mrs West, Molly and her friends were still expecting Fiona to arrive. As late as Friday night, the plan was still 'on'.

"When Fiona did appear on Friday afternoon, she was more concerned with what had happened to her assistant than what might be happening to Mr Potter.

"She arrived at Inverness to find no waiting car. When she got to the hotel, there was no luggage – and no Jill. She went down to the station and found the luggage – but her assistant had disappeared.

"Molly's guests saw her at dinner that night. For those who did not know about the murder on the train, the signals were still at green. The trap had been laid. The beast had arrived. The plan would now click into action.

"For Miss Stewart, equally unaware – as I was – of what was in store for her, the Saturday edition of *The Scotsman* revealed the sad truth. Jill had been murdered in compartment No. 9 in the early hours of Friday morning and her body cast out of the train in a desolate part of Rannoch Moor.

"It seemed to me that one or more of Molly's guests had launched a pre-emptive strike. They had seen all the luggage being put on board the train at Euston. They had read the labels; seen the suitcases embossed 'FS' in gold; they had attacked Jill, thinking she was Fiona Stewart.

"That was my first thought. But it soon turned out that I was wrong. Over half of Molly's guests knew precisely who Jill was. She had worked for Bernard Potter and Stanley Dixon.

"She had shared a flat with Suzanne. She had been present at the investigation on Dr West. Through her father, she was acquainted with Canon Larkin. The only people who did not appear to know her were Kenny Savage, Lady Emily and Gloria.

"But they had had such gruelling encounters with Fiona that they were unlikely to mistake her for Jill. So, if Jill was not murdered by mistake – by someone thinking she was her employer – then she must have been murdered because she was Jill. By someone who had a grudge against her – not against Miss Stewart."

Raynes smiled a bleak smile.

"The news of Jill's death, coming when it did – when the planned attack on Fiona had already been set in motion, caused consternation here at the hotel. There was no difficulty getting rid of the champagne bottle or the glass. A handkerchief with further vital evidence was quickly washed, ironed and returned.

"But my profile, which was going to feature so prominently at the scene of the proposed murder, was a different kettle of fish. Miss Stewart knew nothing about it. It must be recovered – or else it would give the game away. Consequently, we had the savage attack on Miss Stewart's luggage – every piece slashed open – as one of Molly's guests hunted for the vital document."

"Where was it?" asked Kenny Savage.

"In Miss Stewart's business file. She took it away with her when she left the hotel."

"I could have told you that!" said Lady Emily.

The natives were getting restless.

"You will notice," said the Inspector, "that although the business file was with Jill on the train, it was not stolen then. The murderer was not aware of its importance. But once Jill was dead and the plan had to go into reverse, its recovery became vital. It was proof – damning proof – that a plan had been made. And that Jill was involved in it. She had prepared a document that was to be left at the scene of Miss Stewart's murder. So whose side was she on?"

Raynes paused to let his point sink in.

"Was she working with her employer – her generous employer – to expose Mr Potter? Or was she working with Molly and her friends to undermine and destroy Fiona? If Miss Stewart discovered what Jill had been up to – an act of gross betrayal – then she would know that her trusted assistant was hand in glove with her enemies.

"But wiser counsels began to prevail. Perhaps Miss Stewart would not appreciate the significance of the file? She might attribute it to Jill's renowned thoroughness in approaching any investigation. She had included Molly. Why not also include Inspector Raynes? He too had had a colourful past. It was all par for the course.

"And who was going to tell Miss Stewart? Not Jill. The Inspector had no idea. The rest of them were sworn to secrecy. So perhaps it would be all right? The murder weekend therefore continued on its merry way. 'Chicago '29' and 'Desert Island Deaths' were performed as if nothing whatsoever had happened. Clues were discovered . . . prizes awarded to the winners. Unfortunately, the detective had seen the glass being moved . . . the handkerchief being returned . . . And he had spoken to Fiona."

Mrs West's face was a picture.

Raynes was quietly amused.

She – the perfectionist – was the one who had given the game away. She had been too clever. Too clever by half!

Raynes drew the first part of his exposition to a close.

"So I discovered that Jill Graham was not the quiet, humble little assistant I had supposed. She was undoubtedly a most efficient organizer, but she also enjoyed power. Just like her boss."

Raynes flashed a glance at Fiona.

She looked uncomfortable.

"Twice before, Miss Graham had shown herself disloyal to her employers. Once again, she was betraying a trusted friend."

Raynes looked at the elegant young lady in the front row.

"I think Suzanne will bear me out on this point. Jill asked her lots of questions about Molly which Suzanne answered quite willingly – thinking it was just ordinary conversation. But Jill was actually pumping her for information and what she told Jill was used to create a very nasty profile against Mrs Palmer. It seems to me that Jill was capable of betraying anyone.

"So then . . . who most wanted to kill Jill Graham? An ex-lover? A former employer? Someone who was terrified of being publicly exposed? A friend who had been callously betrayed? A jilted lover? Someone who might have been one of Fiona's victims – and hated both of them? 'Like mistress, like dog!' it has been said. One or two of you have even suggested that I might be a prime suspect . . ."

"You are!" shouted Lady Emily. "It's a big cover-up!"

Raynes ignored her.

"It could be any of these. But I do not think we ought to rule out another delicious possibility. Did Fiona Stewart discover the extent of her employee's betrayal? Did she discover the danger that was awaiting her in Mallaig? Was she tipped off? Did she arrange a pre-emptive strike long before the train left Euston station on Thursday night? Was she herself on that train? Or did she arrange for someone else to strangle the bitch – and make sure her own Judas Iscariot was silenced for ever?"

Raynes smiled.

"That, ladies and gentlemen, is the question we have to answer."

36. *Russian roulette*

Being a dour Presbyterian, Detective-Inspector Cameron found Raynes' approach far too theatrical. Why couldn't the man say who had done it – and why – instead of this long rigmarole?

But Raynes had his reasons. For one thing, he liked to lay out his investigations clearly so that people could see how he reached his conclusions. There was an art to detection – and he liked to conduct things with style.

"So then we come to last Thursday night. The train standing at platform fifteen in Euston station. All the luggage piled on the platform. Nine compartments booked for Molly's guests and one for a fellow-traveller who was about to betray her boss. Who bought the tickets? Jill?

"Once she was on the train with her luggage, she was visited by Mr Potter. It was a private conversation which he wished no one to hear. Stanley Dixon, another old acquaintance, was frozen out. When he re-appeared, the door was shut firmly in his face.

"What was Mr Potter saying to Jill? Was he threatening her?

Warning her? Begging her not to take this step? Did he appeal to her better nature? We do not know. All we do know is that he was in her compartment for quite some time. Canon Larkin saw him go in; but he did not see him leave. Lady Emily heard the sound of voices raised. Did Mr Potter attack Jill then and there? Did he stay with her body till later in the night; and when he felt the coast was clear, did he carry the body down the corridor and thrust it out of the window?"

Mr Potter shook his head.

Raynes continued.

"There is no doubt Bernard had every reason to hate Jill. She had betrayed his confidence, broken into his home, stolen his family photographs and was about to expose him in the gutter press – a step which would destroy his career. People have been kind enough to say that Mr Potter is a wimp – but given enough provocation, even the gentlest of men may lash out. Bernard told me more than once that he preferred to go through the correct channels; but perhaps this time, he was pushed too far?"

Raynes paused.

"Then we come to the case of Stanley Dixon – very similar to that of Mr Potter. He too had employed Jill as his secretary – perhaps also as his mistress – eight years ago. Once again, business matters relating to his firm were made public. But Stanley had not seen Jill for a long time. In fact, he hardly recognized her. She had put on weight. He too wanted to talk to her – but was prevented by Mr Potter.

"Stanley, we are told, still has a blinding hatred for Miss Stewart, whose revelations landed him in jail. He will never forgive her. He had been hoping that it was Fiona who was occupying compartment No. 9 that night. Had she been there, violence would certainly have occurred. Stanley told me that he was 'itching for a fight' that night. He said he was relieved to see it was Jill.

"He also told me – I don't know if it was true or not – that he intended to invite Jill along to his compartment for a drink."

"You double-crossing swine!" exclaimed Lady Emily. "You told me I was your number one choice."

"You were," said Stanley. "Don't listen to him!"

Raynes smiled.

"What shall I say? Stanley spent the night with a most charming young lady. But did he come back later and do something nasty to Jill?"

He left them to think about it.

"Thirdly, we come to the case of Mr Larkin. He has known Jill for well over twenty years and never liked her. Jill's father was a Canon of his Cathedral. He described her as 'always a sneaky little bitch', telling tales and getting people into trouble. She was not working for Miss Stewart at the time Mr Larkin was exposed, but who can doubt that she tipped Fiona a wink and suggested there was a good story to be found in the Cathedral close?

"On Thursday night, Mr Larkin was wandering up and down the corridor of the train – noticing other people's movements. Perhaps he was watching and waiting for his moment of revenge? Because of his illness, Canon Larkin is not too bothered about what happens to him; but he would like to square accounts with his enemies before he dies."

"What about yourself?" said Gloria.

"I'm coming to that," said Raynes.

"About time too!" sneered Lady Emily.

Raynes ignored her.

"Many of you have suggested that because I was a complete stranger, I might have killed Jill thinking that she was Fiona Stewart. But at the time of the train journey, I had no knowledge of either woman. I had no cause to hate them as others did. Only when I saw the profile which had been prepared about me did I feel any sense of anger or bitterness. But by that time, Jill was dead. I plead innocent."

Raynes proceeded to consider the other possible suspects.

"Kenny Savage told me that when he got on the train in London, he had drunk five or six pints of beer. He went into his compartment and slept deeply. No one saw him outside his compartment – so we have to accept his story.

"Now I have concentrated on the men of the party because Gloria said that strangulation suggested a man rather than a woman. Had it been drugs or poison, I might have looked to her or Dorothy West. But I could not imagine either of them carrying a plump body down the corridor of the train. It is just not physically possible.

"Lady Emily was fast asleep. I am told that she was snoring heavily after her night of passion . . ."

"I don't snore!"

"I'm afraid you did that night."

"It must have been the whisky."

"It was brandy."

Raynes smiled.

Lady Emily could never get anything right.

"The one person who might have saved Jill that night was Suzanne. She told me that she got on to the train at the last minute. She was thrown in just as the whistle was blown. According to her, she never knew Jill Graham was on the train. Had she known, she said that she would have gone along and talked to her. As an old flatmate, she might have offered her some protection. But even if they were less friendly than they used to be, it is difficult to imagine the two of them coming to blows.

"Neither Molly nor Miss Stewart were on the train, although it has been suggested that Fiona may have crept on to the train, murdered her assistant, left the train at Glasgow and then flown back to London.

"Such a thing was possible, but Detective-Inspector Cameron has examined the list of passengers and where they were going. Miss Stewart's name does not appear on that list. Besides, if Miss Stewart left the train in Glasgow, how could she have dispatched the body north of Crianlarich? It doesn't make sense.

"But even though Miss Stewart was four hundred miles away, that does not mean that she can escape responsibility for the murder. My investigations have revealed that she was the one person who wanted to punish Jill and the train journey was a very convenient place to do it.

"Let us recall precisely what happened. It was Jill who suggested doing an exposure of Mr Potter. She sold the idea to Fiona as a straightforward piece of investigative journalism. It involved an old friend – but that was nothing new. Jill did all the groundwork for the exposure with her usual efficiency. And she suggested that they might confront Mr Potter at one of Molly's murder weekends.

"Once she got Fiona's approval, she told Suzanne what was planned, knowing full well that Suzanne would speak to Molly, an old family friend. Molly reacted as Jill had expected and took steps to protect her friend and lover."

Mrs Palmer's lips were tense and drawn.

"At this moment, Jill must have contacted Molly to explain the real purpose of her investigation. It was not to destroy Bernard – but Fiona! But it must look as if it was directed against Mr Potter.

"Molly was a party to this conspiracy. She responded as Jill had hoped, by gathering all Fiona's enemies together. Gloria, who had been hoping to go to a murder weekend in Cornwall, was persuaded to come to this one in Mallaig. Gloria contacted Stanley Dixon. Kenny Savage, Dorothy West and Lady Emily were also recruited. Mr Potter was left in ignorance of the real plot and joined the party most reluctantly. It just wasn't his scene – as he made abundantly clear.

"Very soon the opposition gathered together. They were a formidable bunch, most of them determined to murder Miss Stewart when she arrived in Mallaig.

"However, Miss Graham made one mistake. She decided to contact Canon Larkin and ask him to join the group. She reckoned that he had every reason to hate Fiona and would rejoice at her death. But the trouble was, he hated Jill and her father more than he hated Miss Stewart.

"Having agreed to join the murder weekend, he then decided that he might be able to screw some personal advantage out of it for himself. So he contacted Fiona and told her what was being planned for her up in Mallaig."

"You bastard!" said Kenny Savage.

"You creep!" said Stanley.

Molly looked thunderstruck.

"In return for this timely advice, Miss Stewart offered to help him publish his book – a book he was writing about the sins of the clergy. She and Canon Larkin will doubtless make big bucks once the stories are syndicated in the tabloids. He will be happy to get his own back on his former colleagues and the money will help him to make a home abroad for himself and his cats. So, for both him and Fiona, it was an exceedingly good deal.

"Canon Larkin, of course, said nothing about this to Molly or any of her guests. But Fiona now knew what Jill had been up to. She could hardly believe it. But she decided to go along with the planned exposure. She watched her assistant like a hawk. She was determined Jill would never make it to Mallaig. She would die *en route*.

"But who would do Fiona's dirty work? Mr Potter? Mr Savage? What about Canon Larkin himself? He hates Jill. He needs the money. He is ill – perhaps he has not very long to live? Fiona is willing to do everything she can to help him. Will he do her one more favour?

"She offers him a pistol. 'Go and shoot her on the train,' she says. 'Choose your moment but make sure she dies!'

"Canon Larkin is happy to oblige. He has never fired a pistol in his life but it seems quite simple. You just pull the trigger and off it goes."

Nobody laughed.

(Well, it wasn't really a laughing matter.)

"He is nervous about it. He wanders up and down the corridor, waiting till the coast is clear. Although he has given up alcohol, he drinks a glass or two of whisky to give himself Dutch courage – even though it may affect his concentration. He resumes his vigil. But whilst he is going back and forth, someone steals his pistol.

"Now although Canon Larkin would probably have shot Jill quite willingly, the thought of murdering her with his own bare hands is quite a different matter. So he chickens out. He retires sadly to his compartment, finishes off the whisky and puts the empty bottle in the waste bin.

"Jill is safe. Well, she might have been . . . but Fiona is no fool. She knows that Larkin is a weak character. He might change his mind at the last minute. She needs a reserve – just in case. Someone who can be relied upon to finish the job, to get the body off the train and leave a nice little mystery for her to solve when she arrives in Inverness: 'Where, oh, where is my assistant?'"

Raynes looked at Fiona.

She was biting her lip. This was not turning out the way she had hoped. Instead of being a spectator of other people's misfortunes, she was rapidly becoming the villain of the piece. Even though someone else might have done the murder, she was going to get the blame. The murderer would turn Queen's evidence and she would go down.

Detective-Inspector Cameron kept a careful watch on her in case she made a rush for the door. He would make sure she didn't escape.

"So, then," said Raynes, "we come to the reserve player. To a person who said: 'None of us has anything against Jill.'

"Someone who had nothing to gain from killing her. Nothing at all. If he had, he might have killed her long since. But no. He is saving up all his fire for Fiona Stewart when she arrives in Mallaig. He has lots of 'sadistic fantasies' about what he would like to do to her before she dies.

"But unfortunately. Miss Stewart has a hold over him. She has exposed one of his scams; now she knows all about his latest piece of private enterprise. Stanley will go down again unless . . .

"It is a cruel choice. Either he murders Fiona's assistant or he returns to a large, dark prison for many years. Stanley reasons that the best policy is to get rid of both of them. What is Jill to him? If he allows her to survive – even after killing Fiona – the story will still come out. Better to silence the pair of them. So he agrees to do the job."

Gloria looked at Mr Dixon admiringly.

Good old Stanley!

"He hovers round the compartment trying to get an idea of the lay out. To size up his victim. To assure her of his good intentions. 'What about a little nightcap in No. 7?' But Mr Potter is blocking his way. Twenty minutes later, he is still in the way! One can only presume that Mr Dixon concentrated all his passion on Lady Emily for the next two to three hours before he returned to compartment No. 9.

"Miss Graham was strangled. She was dead. Stanley picked up the body and carried it down the corridor, heading for the door beside the toilet. He was wearing his blue silk dressing gown. The body was naked. He was well down the passage when he heard the sound of footsteps coming towards him. Quickly, he flung open the toilet door and pushed the body in ahead of him. Another few seconds and all would have been well.

"But, unfortunately, Mr Stevens, the sleeping car attendant, just caught sight of Mr Dixon going in to the toilet. He remembers the blue dressing gown and he remembers – but cannot quite believe what he thinks he saw – three bare feet!

"It does not really register. Funny things happen on sleeper trains! People get up to all sorts of tricks. He puts it out of his mind. But he recognizes the man."

Raynes allowed the ghost of a smile to play over his lips.

"During breakfast, this morning, Mr Stevens acted as one of the waiters in the dining room. He had a good look at all of you – and he immediately identified Mr Dixon as the man he saw entering the toilet.

"Whilst he was doing this little piece of identification, Detective-Inspector Cameron and I went into each of your rooms in search of the blue silk dressing gown. And, of course, we found it in Stanley's room."

Raynes looked at Molly.

"We found your pass key most useful."

Molly said nothing.

She was devastated. She had never thought that Stanley . . . Why had he never told her that he had killed Jill? Why did he let her go ahead with the real murder plan when he knew that Fiona Stewart was aware of what was planned? The idiot! If he had just told her what he had done, she would have called the whole thing off. Now this wretched inspector would charge her with attempted murder! Fiona Stewart would give him chapter and verse.

Raynes concluded his exposition.

"Mr Dixon waited till the coast was clear, turfed Jill's body out of the train and returned to his charming lady – still snoring in compartment No. 7. Next morning, he got off the train as if nothing had happened. All the guests gathered at the station entrance – except for Mr Potter. Where was he?

"He was looking for Jill. He was worried. He was still hoping to persuade her not to go ahead with the exposure. But she was nowhere to be seen. Her luggage was still there, but the bird had flown. Mr Potter went down the train with Mr Stevens, searching every compartment."

Raynes turned to Gerry Stevens.

"You recognize Mr Potter?"

"The gentleman with the beard."

"Thank you."

Raynes turned to Detective-Inspector Cameron.

"I'm sorry if I've been a little long-winded. But I hope I have made it clear to you – and to everyone – that Stanley Dixon killed Jill Graham on Thursday night on the Mallaig express."

Raynes sat down.

Stanley Dixon stood up.

"I wonder if I might say a few words, Inspector?"

He looked remarkably relaxed.

"As you have said, I was responsible for the death of Jill Graham. I moved the body down the corridor. As Mr Stevens has said, I had nearly reached the door when I heard the sound of approaching footsteps. I went into the toilet as quickly as possible pushing Jill's body in front of me. I kicked the door shut with my heel – but obviously not quickly enough.

"Once Mr Stevens had passed, I waited for nearly twenty minutes before I emerged, I made sure that the coast was clear then I dragged Jill's body to the door, pulled down the window and pushed her out. As I said to you, she had put on weight. She was heavier than I had thought.

"However, you are perfectly correct in the other things you said, Inspector. I did come to an arrangement with Miss Stewart. She had discovered my latest escapade and threatened to expose me once again. However, she very kindly promised to stay her hand if I would do 'the necessary'."

He paused.

"That little job was getting rid of Jill. She told me that if I got rid of her on the journey to Mallaig, she would not only shred the story but also give me £10,000 – the money to be paid into my account three months after Jill's death so that there would be no obvious connection between the death and the payment.

"I agreed to her terms. The murder was committed. The story, I hope, will be shredded. And I look forward – a few years hence – to receiving my £10,000."

He smiled bravely.

"However, even though I was responsible for Jill's death, I would like everyone to know that Fiona Stewart was the person behind the murder. She was the one who pulled the strings. I was only the puppet who obeyed her command."

All eyes turned to Fiona Stewart.

She bit her lip.

She opened her mouth to speak.

Suddenly there was a tremendous explosion in the library. Raynes threw himself on the floor. His hands clawed the carpet. Someone had fired a pistol. But it was not he who had been shot.

Raynes looked up cautiously. There was a fight going on in the middle of the room. Chairs had fallen over. A woman was screaming. Bernard Potter and the young policeman were fighting with Stanley Dixon to get hold of the pistol. Everything was in chaos. Kenny Savage was shouting: "Cheers! Well done!"

Raynes' eyes moved round the room.

Fiona Stewart's body was slumped in her chair. There was blood trickling down her face. She had been shot at close quarters. It looked as if she was dead.

Raynes raced over to her.

There was a bullet hole in her left eye – blackened and horrible.

Detective-Inspector Cameron held her wrist, searching for her pulse.

"Just about gone," he said.

Raynes looked back over his shoulder.

Stanley Dixon was lying face down. The young policeman was fastening handcuffs on his wrists. Molly Palmer slapped Suzanne hard on the face to stop her screaming. Mrs West was picking up the chairs. Gloria was smiling proudly.

Raynes turned back to Cameron.

"Stanley Dixon had a pistol."

"I'm afraid so. He was standing between us and the windows. While he was talking, we had the sun in our eyes. When he referred to Miss Stewart, we all looked at her. We didn't notice that he had taken the pistol out of his pocket. At that distance, he could hardly miss."

"It was her pistol."

"So it was."

Raynes ushered the rest of Molly's guests out of the library.

"Marvellous speech!" whispered Dorothy West. "Really enjoyed it."

Mr Stevens ran a hand through his greasy hair.

"That was bloody terrifying. Do I get danger money?"

"No, lad," said Cameron. "You get the rest of your return ticket back to London."

Mr Dixon was dragged to his feet and pushed over to the door. As he passed Raynes, there was a glint of triumph in his eyes.

"I got both of them, Inspector. The world's a cleaner place."

Raynes said nothing.

He had promised to look after Fiona Stewart. He had failed. So much for police protection.

37. *Winner takes all!*

When all the excitement had died down and Raynes' own nerves were calmer, he descended to the main entrance of the hotel and apologized to the manager for all the damage that had been done.

But the manager did not seem as distressed as Raynes had expected, Instead, he actually reckoned it might make the hotel more of a tourist attraction. You needed something sensational to bring people up to a quiet place like Mallaig. A spectacular murder might be just the thing!

Raynes went back to the library where the police were awaiting a forensic team from Glasgow to be flown in.

Fiona Stewart still lay slumped in the chair where she had died. Raynes looked more closely at the hideous wound.

She must have died very quickly.

Stanley Dixon had been driven off under heavy police escort and Gerry Stevens had gone with them on the first part of his journey back to London. There did not seem much more that Raynes could do.

He had a few words with Detective-Inspector Cameron, who was now very much in charge of the case, and then went downstairs to the cocktail bar where most of Molly's guests were recovering their *sangfroid*.

Molly and Bernard were standing together beside the bar. Raynes went over to them.

"Well," he said, "you got what you wanted."

Molly turned away.

Bernard Potter fingered his glass nervously.

"I imagine the police case will focus on Mr Dixon? No need for us to be involved?"

Raynes raised his eyebrows.

"I expect Mrs Palmer will be called upon to explain the background. How Miss Stewart and Miss Graham came to be involved in all this. I don't think the Court could be expected to overlook the fact that a murder weekend was organized and two murders actually took place. I should think that the Court would hold our hostess very much responsible for all that has happened."

He looked at Bernard.

"But as you say, you will probably be able to wriggle out of it. You have no case to answer."

Raynes turned away.

Mrs West was sitting alone at a nearby table, twirling a glass between her fingers. Her eyes were sparkling.

"Don't you think Stanley was terribly brave?"

"Not at all. He is just a common criminal with homicidal tendencies."

Mrs West lifted her glass.

"I admire him."

Raynes sighed.

"Perhaps you could arrange a nice little evening's entertainment when he comes out. In about fifteen years' time!"

Mrs West shook her head sadly.

"Oh, Inspector. I do believe you're jealous!"

Kenny Savage and Lady Emily were deep in conversation at the far corner of the bar. It seemed that two kindred spirits had finally met.

Canon Larkin was nowhere to be seen.

Raynes went over to Gloria Markham-Jones who was standing beside the window in a pensive mood.

"Another gin and tonic?"

"I should appreciate that."

Raynes went back to the bar and ordered two gins.

He joined Gloria at the window and handed her a glass. She was staring out over the water, looking at the southern point of Skye and the distant isle of Rhum. It was a beautiful summer's day.

"It seems such a shame, doesn't it?"

Raynes looked at her.

"That Stanley should be deprived of all this. He'll be stuck indoors in some dreadful prison for – how long? Ten years?"

"At least. With two murders to his credit, I should think he'll get life."

"But if he behaves, surely they'll let him out earlier?"

"I should think the minimum would be fifteen years."

Gloria downed half her gin and tonic.

It was a gesture of despair.

"I'm sure he'll think it was worth it. He's put an end to two thoroughly evil women. The world should be grateful to him."

Raynes was inclined to agree. In his book, there was nothing more vile than a tabloid journalist, trading in human misery. He had seen them sneaking their way into people's homes trying to get a photograph of a dead child – which they would then syndicate to their fellow vultures for several hundred pounds. They would happily destroy careers, families, reputations just to fill a few columns of some vicious rag. Fiona had been a prime example of that subhuman breed.

"You were fond of Stanley?"

"I've known him for twenty-two years. He's a bit of a scoundrel but he knows how to enjoy life. I once had a holiday with him in Cyprus . . ."

Raynes smiled.

"I'm surprised he didn't propose to you."

"I wouldn't have trusted him, even if he had." Gloria laughed. "I couldn't have competed with that endless series of dolly birds. I might have murdered one or two – but not all of them."

The gong sounded for lunch.

The Inspector and Gloria followed the others into the dining room. They were directed towards a small table for two.

"I don't think I could bear sitting with Molly and Bernard," said Raynes. "They hate me. And I still feel Mrs West is plotting something nasty."

Gloria nodded.

"I wouldn't trust her an inch."

Raynes sniffed.

"What's that lovely smell?"

"The freesias – fresh today, I should think."

The Inspector picked up the menu.

"What are we having today? Cream of Highland Salmon. That sounds delicious. And a Filet de Boeuf Hebridoise. I wonder what makes a piece of French beef Scottish?"

"They probably add whisky to the sauce."
"They have an excellent chef."
"Worth coming just for the food!"
Raynes unrolled his napkin.
"Well," he said, "you always said that it would be a man who did the murder. And you were right."
Gloria smiled.
"Strangulation's a very physical thing. Women are more subtle." She looked across at Dorothy West. "Poison and things." She laughed. "I should know."
"Of course," said Raynes, remembering that he was dining with a very experienced woman, who had probably killed off more people than anyone else in Scotland.
"I think it was very brave of him carrying her body down the corridor of the train."
"A naked body at that."
"He so nearly got away with it. If that sleeping car attendant had been just a couple of minutes later, the body would have been out of the window – and not a finger could have been pointed at him."
"If he'd been thirty seconds later," said Raynes, "he'd have been caught redhanded. I wonder how he'd have explained that."
"It's all a question of timing," said Gloria.
"He was very lucky to be so close to the toilet. If he'd had another few seconds, the attendant wouldn't have noticed the blue silk dressing gown. That rather gave the game away."
"Yes. He was unlucky."
Raynes smiled.
"You were more fortunate."
"Me?"
"You helped Molly arrange the murder weekend. If the planned murder had taken place, you might've been directly responsible."
"But I wouldn't have done the actual murder."
"You would have delegated it?"
"Of course." Gloria smiled broadly. "You know my technique, Inspector."

"I'm beginning to recognize it," said Raynes. "This soup is delicious, isn't it?"

"Absolutely delicious."

"So," continued Raynes, "what would the original plan have involved? Was she going to be stabbed or strangled? Was Fiona going to have an injection or a sip of rat poison?"

"I think it would have had to be a violent death. You were going to be very angry. I think there would have been several bruises to the face. A broken arm. And perhaps a chiffon scarf wrapped tightly round her neck."

"Torn underwear? A bare breast?"

"Something like that." Gloria smiled. "Stanley would have enjoyed it. Perhaps a red hot poker . . . At least he wouldn't have had to carry the body down to the railway station!"

"But you think he would have done it?"

"Don't you?"

"I'm sure that if you'd have told him to do it, he would. But if you weren't there, he might have been less willing."

"Are you suggesting that Stanley lacks . . . moral fibre?"

"No," said Raynes. "He had the guts to kill Fiona in front of four policemen. But I just wonder about the train."

Gloria said nothing.

Raynes finished off his soup and eagerly awaited the fillet of beef.

He looked thoughtfully at the woman across the table.

"You were behind it," he said. "I have no doubt about that, Stanley came and told you Jill was on the train. You told him when to intervene. Told him to make sure of his alibi. To get laid into Lady Emily, get her drunk, on brandy – if not with passion. Perhaps he gave her a knockout pill. And then, when she started snoring, he should whistle down the passage and kill Miss Stewart's assistant. Was that how it was?"

"Just about."

"And where is the chiffon scarf?"

"Burnt."

"No evidence?"

"None." Gloria wiped her mouth with her napkin. She could not resist a triumphant smile.

"But Stanley had second thoughts?"

"I beg your pardon?"

"I think he chickened out. 'A bird shows some style before making a cowardly departure'. Nine and three. Possibly hyphenated."

"Then who did the murder? Canon Larkin?"

Their conversation was interrupted by the arrival of the beef in a dark, rich sauce. Raynes looked at the elegant white china with the thin gold band running near the edge of the plate. Then he looked up at Gloria.

"You were the one who said: 'If she was strangled, it must have been a man'."

"Quite so."

"But what happens if the jockey refuses to mount the horse? Time is slipping away . . ."

"You find another jockey."

"Or you do it yourself?"

Raynes' eyes narrowed perceptibly.

"Stanley has had his moment of glory. He might as well be hung for a sheep as for a lamb. I have no doubt he moved Jill's body. Threw it out of the train. But in my mind, there is no one else who could have done the murder but you."

Gloria laughed.

"Inspector, you flatter me."

"Of course I do. It was beautifully done. Neat . . . tidy . . . not a scrap of evidence . . . not a fingerprint . . . not even the ashes of a chiffon scarf in sight. I have no doubt that Stanley Dixon will happily plead guilty to the murder. But the murderer was you."

Gloria cut into her beef.

"You have no proof," she said.

"None whatsoever," said Raynes. "But I would still like to know how it was done."

There was silence whilst Gloria ate several mouthfuls of the beef and weighed the pros and cons of saying anything to the Inspector.

"We are both experts at crime," said Raynes. "As one professional to another. No witnesses; no written statements. I would just like to know how it was done."

Gloria hesitated for a good while longer but eventually pride overrode caution. As the Inspector said, there were no witnesses. He was tucking heartily into his roast potatoes.

"You are right," she said slowly. "Stanley did chicken out. He came to tell me he couldn't do it. Although he had stolen Canon Larkin's pistol, he just couldn't shoot her in cold blood. Had it been Fiona, he would have been all right. But sentimentality . . . call it what you will, he couldn't do it.

"He came into my compartment to tell me. I didn't really mind one way or the other. I would have preferred to stick to our original plan and attack Fiona at the hotel, but Stanley was worried about his latest scam getting into the Press."

Raynes stopped eating his roast potatoes.

"I waited till the train had been going for two or three hours. Then I went along to compartment No. 9. I tapped on the door. She asked me who it was. I told her it was me. She let me in. She was in her dressing gown – obviously ready for bed. She'd been reading some book. I sat down beside her on the bed and told her that she was in great danger. Fiona had found out about the double-cross and had arranged for Stanley Dixon to kill her.

"She knew about Stanley, of course. She knew he was a ruthless man. He'd already been hovering around her compartment. I told her I'd stay with her and protect her. She believed me.

"I reminded her of the plan we had concocted together. Fiona was to be killed at the hotel in Mallaig. Any false move by Stanley could completely spoil the plan. He must be persuaded to do what had been arranged. Jill was very grateful for my help. We chatted for a long while. Then I suggested that she might like to come along to my compartment for a drink.

"She rose to the bait – quite literally. She stood up. I stood up behind her. In a trice, the chiffon scarf was round her neck. I held it there for about three minutes. It felt about three minutes. And then I lowered her to the ground. Took her pulse. Dead."

Gloria smiled proudly.

"Just like old times!"

She ate a little more of her lunch.

"There isn't much more to be said. I stripped her down to the bare essentials. Left her clothes on the bed. Stuffed her underwear into her handbag. Cleaned every surface I had touched. Made sure I didn't take off my plastic gloves till I was out of the compartment. Then I went along to rouse Stanley." She laughed. "But he was hard at it. No point barging in. I went back to my room and waited till we got past Glasgow. Then I went back and tapped on his door.

"I gave him the plastic gloves. Made sure he put them on. Lady Emily was once again snoring happily. Nothing was going to wake her. 'I've done my bit,' I said. 'You get her out of the window.' Our plan had been to get her out of the compartment window but these things are double-glazed, metal-framed. So it had to be the door at the end of the corridor; and Stanley's more up to carrying corpses down passages than I am.

"So I handed over to him. He collected Jill. He was well on his way down the corridor when he heard that wretched attendant coming the other way. He had the presence of mind to rush into the toilet. He didn't think the man had seen anything; but obviously he did.

"He pushed Jill in – in front of him. Dumped her on the lavatory. Locked the door. But then, I think, his nerve failed him. He was too terrified to come out. He banged on the wall. I was next door in compartment No. 1. He asked me to keep watch whilst he got her to the door. He lowered the window and with a bit of pushing and shoving, he got her out.

"I recovered the plastic gloves and the key to Jill's compartment. I went back and checked things over one last time. Then I returned to Stanley's compartment and had a brandy with him and the Sleeping Beauty."

She breathed heavily.

"Men are such cowards!"

"Well, at least he had the courage to shoot Fiona."

"I didn't think he'd dare." Gloria finished off her last piece of Hebridean beef. "I really didn't. I knew he still had the pistol but I thought he'd go weak at the knees at the last minute."

"But he didn't."

"No. I was proud of him. He'll be proud too. They both deserved to die."

Raynes did not disagree.

"Molly won't forget this weekend."

"None of us will. It's been one of the most exciting moments in my life. I shall make sure Stanley gets a rich reward – when he comes out."

Raynes' eyes twinkled mischievously.

"I don't think it's quite over yet."

Gloria looked at him anxiously.

"What d'you mean?"

"The weekend's not over yet. There's still the dessert. It should be quite mouth-watering. Sticky toffee pudding with rich vanilla sauce."

Gloria relaxed.

For a moment, she had thought . . .

"I love sticky toffee pudding," she said. "Bad for the figure but quite irresistible."

Raynes looked apologetic.

"Well, I'm afraid you won't be getting any. Not for a long time to come."

Gloria looked puzzled.

"What d'you mean?"

Raynes explained.

"I'm afraid you may have underestimated my talents. Many people do. But I am not as harmless as I may look . . . I have learnt at least one thing from Fiona Stewart and her friend. Never go into a confrontation situation without being properly prepared."

He pulled back the flap of his jacket to reveal a small radio microphone.

"Walls have ears – and even suits have their uses. I'm sorry to tell you that there have been more witnesses to our conversation than you realized."

He looked over her right shoulder.

Right on cue, Detective-Inspector Cameron appeared in the dining room and came over to their table.

"Miss Gloria Markham-Jones, I am charging you with the murder of Miss Jill Graham. Anything you say may be taken down and used in evidence against you."

Raynes took her hand.

"As one professional to another . . . It's been a pleasure to meet you." He looked at Cameron. "She's all yours."

Gloria was escorted out of the dining room whilst Raynes tucked into his sticky toffee pudding. It was as delicious as he had hoped. Poor Gloria! Fancy missing such a treat!

The waitress looked uncertain – holding the second plate.

"Will the lady be coming back?"

"No," said Raynes. "Not for a long time."